I0662559

FATHERING SIN

BRIAN STAFF

Brian's Motivation for *Fathering Sin*

The Poet, Phillip Larkin, wrote:

*"They f**k you up, your mum and dad.*
They may not mean to, but they do."

Parents program us with their characteristics and ideas before we have the ability to discern. As we grow we return the compliment by being their gateway to our generation's culture, which they can only observe and not join. Who knows what we absorb from parents, or what they absorb from us? This book is born out of the unconscious influence that generations bestow, or inflict, on one another.

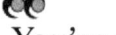
You're not what you think you are, you are what you are.

Brian Staff
2009

Also by Brian Staff:

No Man is an Island - A collection of stories and essays on three dimensions of life.

This collection of stories about life is rather tongue-in-cheek, a bit raw, clearly cynical and, above all, humorous. The open-minded among you will love it. If you are easily offended, then be prepared to be so. All of us need to get through this dysfunctional life somehow. This book is a witty guide to charting your course - you could look upon it as an alternative life-coach. The collection includes a novelette, short stories and essays, which look at life from three angles: the person and their personality, how it can shift and change; the social animal that has to deal with family, friends, co-workers and strangers; and the odd situations that just come out of nowhere and leave us scratching our heads in bewilderment. It is a witty and entertaining look at contemporary life and experiences, and you will either guffaw, groan or cringe as you read.

The Art of Meditation *(to be published late 2010)*

Peter is a middle-aged, second-rate, political cartoonist and, inevitably for one in his profession, an unremitting cynic. His life is a shambles, consisting of failed relationships, ragged finances and rusting status symbols. When desperation overcomes trepidation he subdues his innate fear of the countryside and all things green, and with serious misgivings takes himself off to a retreat center deep in ancient Wales to try and get a new perspective on his life. He doesn't know what to expect, but he doesn't expect what he encounters, which includes love, lust, death and probing questions about life and free-will that blur the lines between caricature and reality. He then uncovers the covert mission of the meditators, which is to act as a recruiting agency for an extra-terrestrial civilization, at which point his cynicism proves fatal.

Fathering Sin by Brian Staff

A WordisWorth book
First published in print in 2010
Printed by CreateSpace

Fathering Sin is also available as an ebook.

Copyright © 2010 Brian Staff
All rights reserved

Library of Congress Control Number: 2010928458

ISBN: 978-0-9802474-2-8

Editor and Designer: Alison J. Macmillan

"... every cop is a criminal, and all the sinners saints"

The Rolling Stones

Sympathy for the Devil

Futile Lives

Flesh cuts easily with a razor-sharp knife. Immediately after death, blood flows only a little less quickly than it does before death. But without the thumping, pumping of the heart, it soon slows down.

Cross-marks are easy to make. Circles are harder because you have to twist the knife around to make the end join up with the start. Sometimes the body will quiver as you carve your message. When it first happens it scares the shit out of you, and you might even spring back from the corpse and yelp, quietly of course. But you realize that it's just a nervous tremor going through the cadaver, not that she's coming back to life; and although it's spooky, it doesn't freak you out any more.

Naughts and crosses, neatly carved along her back - there's method in my madness. Sometimes neck to buttocks, sometimes buttocks to neck - and there's madness in my method.

My knife is of the kind used to cut up balsa wood when making a model airplane. An airplane that one tenderly creates, only to see it crash into the ground at the end of its first flight, the heavy engine in its nose causing it to plummet rather than glide when the fuel runs out.

We all need to have ways of wasting our time, to take our minds off the pointlessness of life. Pointlessness combats pointlessness. The existential irony thrills me as I assiduously go about my carving.

☐ ☐ ☐

I'm telling my story as part of the therapy I'm undergoing. I don't know if it will do any good, but I feel I owe it to someone, maybe myself, or to a God, or to an indifferent Universe. Anyway, what else have I to do?

Now, with hindsight, it would be easy to say I knew what was happening, but I didn't. Before any of this started, before the first revelation (if that's what it was), life was going on as usual, with no hint of anything particularly untoward or even interesting happening to me. I can't point to portentous signs or omens. Nothing. Just life as it is lived by average people everywhere, and I've always assumed myself to be nothing if not average.

I suppose my children wouldn't be classified as average, at least I hope they wouldn't be; not because I'm proud of them and want them to be different, but rather because I'm secretly ashamed of them, scared of them, and I hope there aren't too many other young people like them about.

Of course, as the story unfolds, you, if you're normal - whatever that means - will probably feel an increasing distance building between yourself and me and the acts that are associated with me, and I won't be offended by that; in your position I would react in exactly the same way. But I have one favor to ask, and it is that you periodically remind yourself that I started out as a person the world would consider relatively normal. I've been savagely scarred by events, but I don't consider myself to have changed fundamentally, although I'm aware that in the eyes of many, I and those around me are now a long way from society's acceptance.

I have what you will doubtless think a pathetically modest aspiration, but one which I crave above all else. It is that one day I shall be readmitted to the world of the ordinary. My message to you (if you feel that I'm worthy to deliver one), is Beware. Beware of yourself, and beware of your legacy to the world – it may not be what you think it is.

◻◻◻

Spencer heaved himself out of bed with a reluctance so great he could almost feel a part of his body trying to drag him back.

He'd been dreaming before the phone rang. He was about to do something but he was interrupted before he did it, and he couldn't remember if it was something good or bad, something he would do in real life or wouldn't, something he'd be glad to do or be painfully ashamed of.

He'd had about 3 hours sleep. Last night he'd stopped for a couple of beers on the way home. Then, because his wife already had a bottle of wine open, he'd carried on drinking. By the time he collapsed into bed, he was ready to sleep the sleep of the dead, only to be interrupted by the intrusively arrogant ringing of the telephone and tidings of death itself.

He rolled from the bed and stumbled through to the kitchen, reached for the kettle and turned to the sink before realizing he was on automatic pilot and should get going without his coffee fix, which he needed rather than wanted. He supposed he could survive without it, although he knew his deeply entrenched addiction to caffeine would lead to a headache when his body realized it was up and being asked to function, but didn't have a cup of coffee clutched in its hand.

It was a typical muggy, London summer night. He drove with the window open, hoping the thick air would flush some sense through his still drowsy brain. It crossed his mind that if an enthusiastic traffic cop should stop him he might fail a breath test, which would pose an interesting problem for someone, but he wasn't sure whom.

He found the place easily enough, a few streets from the London Hospital in Whitechapel. It struck him that the reason for his journey was beyond the help of hospitals, but firmly in the domain of chapels, white or otherwise.

He could see the lights from the roadway. Garish as they were, the lights were always a comfort, and he wondered if part of their purpose wasn't to make the police feel less troubled by their task, as if bright light could drive away the evil that had brought them there.

Artificial light is a relatively modern thing, but evil and misfortune are as old as life itself, and although light hasn't had much luck destroying the forces of darkness, it is at least capable of lessening the physical gloom that evil seems to favor.

"Hello sir, sorry to get you out of bed, but I thought you'd want to be involved with this one from the beginning," said Weller.

How, Spencer wondered, did he always manage to look so bloody fresh? Unlike the other Detective Sergeants, no matter what time of the day or night Spencer saw him, Weller looked as though he'd just woken naturally from eight hours of deep, easeful slumber.

He was about ten years younger than Spencer, but he wasn't exactly a teenager and had to be pushing 40. Spencer thought it must have something to do with his wife, who was probably about 30, although she had the body and come-hither look of an 18-year-old nymphomaniac. But no, that couldn't be it. If his wife's acrobatic sexual performances were the powerful, rejuvenating influence in Weller's life, then it ought to be making him look tired and pissed off when he was dragged off her to attend one of these bloody scenes. And anyway, wasn't she religious? A Mormon or something? But maybe that didn't make any difference when it came to sex. In fact, it possibly made it more of an imperative; spreading the influence via propagation and sewing seeds of ... Spencer's mind was doing its own thing, probably thinking it was still in sleep/dream mode rather than awake/reality mode.

He forced himself to stop speculating about Weller, his marital life, his wife's religion and sexuality as he stepped over a piece of discarded pizza stained with blood-red sauce. He approached the huddle gathered at the center of the pool of light, all looking down on the night's spotlighted attraction: a star frozen in her final performance.

"Female, mid-20s, medium build, not entirely Caucasian, mixed race parentage. Violently sexually abused. Looks like a knife was used in the anus. A lot of contusions and cuts to the genitalia and elsewhere. Murdered by strangulation, I should say. Dead no more than three hours - I'll give you the exact time when I've had a look inside and done the calculations, but she was definitely alive until midnight, unless he popped her in the oven for a while to keep her warm for us.

"There's some substantial bruising about her head, possibly made by a hard instrument ... or by a very angry person with a granite fist, although I still think that strangulation was the ultimate cause of death, especially in the light of recent events. But I'll keep an open mind until I've done the complete examination tomorrow."

This authoritative, vaguely flippant, quick-fire summary came from the mouth of Dr. William Best, who had been the forensic pathologist on call for two of the last three similar murders.

"No personal identification," said Weller, adding to the pile of information congealing in Spencer's mind.

"Hooker, most likely. Just career stuff in her handbag - condoms, a large supply of paper tissues and over a hundred pounds in mixed, grubby notes."

A fourth murder in just over a year of similar victim and modus operandi, all within an area of about 20 square miles. There was precious little Spencer could do that wasn't already being done, and the sensible thing would be for him to go home and start fresh the next morning. But accepted practices wouldn't allow him to do anything of the sort. He would have to play by the unwritten rules: stay up until dawn; drink thick, stale coffee; crave - but, he hoped, avoid - endless cigarettes; eat tasteless food that would fill him up but leave him feeling unsatisfied, and give the inside of his mouth the bitter, greasy veneer of rancid lard.

He was gazing vacantly at the corpse as he thought. When he looked up, both Best and Weller were watching him; Best with a quizzical smirk on his face.

"And?" said Best.

"And what?"

"Aren't you going to ask about the condition of the body?"

"Okay, tell me Dr. Best, does it have scratch marks?"

"Funny you should ask," said Best, his smirk forming into a gruesome smile that the bright lights illuminating the victim's death bed accentuated.

"It just so happens it does. I can see the tabloid headlines now, 'The criss-cross fiend strikes again'. Probably in even bolder type than last week and with four exclamation marks this time, just to mark the tally for their arithmetically-challenged readership."

"Would you be finding this so amusing if that woman's mother was standing next to you?" Spencer asked

"But of course not, Inspector Spencer. And what would you reply to said hypothetical mother when she asks why you haven't by now caught the murdering son of a … sorry … the murderer, and saved her angelic daughter from her grisly fate?"

They stared at each other.

"I've never excluded the fact it may be a serial killer. But we should keep our minds open to any number of possibilities until we have firm evidence to push us in a particular direction. You know copycat killings are common, and we shouldn't try to pin every murder in east London on one person, just because the media prefer serial killers for increasing their sales."

Best's grin was now accentuated by the flaring lights of an arriving patrol car. Spencer thought of punching in that face. Of course, he didn't but he wondered just how close he was to doing it. He carried on talking.

"And unless this case provides us with more evidence than the previous three, I shall keep saying the same, but I have to admit that the chances of it being a serial killer are getting to be very strong."

"Ok, I'm betting 100 quid. That should give me and the partner of my choice a decent night out, courtesy of our favorite detective," said Best.

"You give me a solid piece of consistent evidence, Dr. Best - DNA, a fingerprint, a bite mark, anything - and I'll take you on, and what's more I'll likely get the bastard or bastards. But until then we're going to keep our minds open … and, more importantly, infinitely more importantly than our private pissing contest, until we get hard evidence or a good lead, we're not going to nab this killer. Unless, of course, we get lucky, but luck is not a commodity I trust," said Spencer, before turning away and walking into the shadows. He heard a squishing noise, and looked down to see his foot planted firmly in the middle of the pizza he'd sidestepped earlier.

He wandered around, stepping over trash he'd rather not identify. His brain badly needed some blood with caffeine in it, or nicotine, or brandy.

The first body had been discovered by a hysterical teenager, who blurted to a reporter that she'd seen marks gouged into the back of the corpse; lines and circles. After that the press had focused on this at each news conference when a fresh murder was announced. A copycat's perfect haven. Murder someone you don't like, score some lines and circles on their body, and you immediately put up a diversionary smokescreen. The media had stumbled for a while in their attempts to label the killer with a phrase that everyone could agree upon, but eventually they'd settled on the 'Criss-Cross Killer'.

He felt as if he were living in a comic strip. A killer with a silly name, crimes committed in the same part of London that Jack the Ripper had stalked, and a media frenzy that was bounding towards hysteria.

He looked across to the spot where the lights were focused. It was a small grassy area, with a couple of rickety wooden benches that looked as though they were held together only by the gang slogans sprayed over them and the chewing gum squashed into their slats. Four spots that would have been flower-beds in their heyday were now open-air dumps for spent needles, broken bottles and crushed cans. It was one of those places created with the best of intentions; to offer a bit of rustic relaxation amidst unremittingly squalid urban surroundings. It was now the domain of tramps, druggies and winos by day, and hookers and perverts by night.

He was walking towards his car when a thought occurred to him and he returned to the group under the lights.

"She had money on her?" he said to Weller.

"Yes."

"The others didn't, did they?"

"No, but I ..."

"These women always want payment up front, so some of that money could be the killer's. He was always sensible enough to take it with him in the past, so maybe he's getting careless. Make sure you get the lab to examine the notes carefully."

"There you are," said Best. "Now you see why Mr. Spencer is a much esteemed detective. He's a regular Inspecteur Maigret," he said, pronouncing the name with an exaggerated French accent.

And we all know why you're a pathologist, thought Spencer; because you like fiddling about with dead women on cold mortuary slabs.

"I'm going back to the station," he told Weller, ignoring Best. "I'll call Devons, but I doubt she'll put in an appearance."

"What a pity," said Best, interrupting again, "I could do with a bit of erotic titillation."

"If you're looking to Chief Super Devons for your titillation, you must be spending even more than your usual amount of time sniffing formaldehyde," Spencer said, setting off for his car.

Devons sounded confused and sleepy when she first answered the phone, but true to character, she was soon firing on all cylinders, spitting questions at Spencer.

"Anything different?"

"Not much as far as we can see." He told her about the money. "He must be leaving signs somewhere. Any hooker would smell a rat if a bloke wanted to have sex with gloves on in June."

"No body fluids?"

"We won't know until they open her up, but he didn't leave any in the past. No hair, no skin under the finger nails, nothing. This could be different, and if he slipped up over the money he may have made other mistakes."

"It's nearly four now. I'll be there in a couple of hours for your report. We'll be even more under the microscope now."

"I know," said Spencer, but the phone was already humming the dial tone in his ear, a tone which he interpreted as being accusatory, or even blatantly reprimanding. An image of her, hair tousled and naked shoulders, swept across his mind, causing him to take too big a gulp of his much needed coffee and scalding his mouth.

Hidden Mind

When does irritating behavior become aberrant? I've always been curious. As a child I drove my patient, poorly-educated mother to distraction with my constant questions. My father took to calling me 'Y'. He would say "Y this, Y that. You've always got a Y for us." And although he made a joke of it, I know that my questioning was an embarrassment and a worry to them - an embarrassment because they could give me so few answers, and a worry because this unremitting inquisitiveness struck them as being unusual, unwelcome, and even potentially unhealthy behavior within a family that had previously been without intellectual aspirations.

Even at school I annoyed my teachers by my never-ending quest to discover what lay beneath the facts they taught us. It wasn't enough for me to know that something happened, I always needed to know why it happened, and my dogmatic pursuit of understanding was often at variance with my teachers' equally dogmatic wish to complete the syllabus with the minimum number of disruptions and deviations.

In particular, I remember the lesson in which we were first introduced to a formula that quantifies the extent to which metals expand when heated. I liked and respected our physics teacher, so I delayed my questioning until the class was finished. As I approached his desk, I thought I detected a barely-suppressed look of exasperation clouding his face as he noticed me skulking towards him.

"Yes, Henderson." he said, "What is it, now?"

"Sir, you've explained to us how to predict the amount of expansion in metals, but you didn't explain why they expand when heated."

He shook his head and turned up the corners of his mouth into something that could pass for a smile - if you didn't look at his eyes.

"Everything expands when it's heated, Henderson. Gas, solid, liquid. Everything, even small boys. Well, that's not strictly true, they have a tendency to ignite, burn, shrivel up and collapse into a pile of ashes, or so I've found in my many experiments on the wretched creatures."

"But why, sir?"

Again he shook his head, but I saw a strange look in his eyes. It may have been sheer annoyance, but I felt then, and I'm almost convinced now, that it was anxiety. When he spoke it was with an uncharacteristic assertiveness and none of his usual deflective humor.

"You'll have to wait until you get to university before you find that out. It's very complex. It's due to changes at the molecular level."

And I suspected as he said it that he didn't really know the answer, and I believe he knew I'd seen through his bravado. I quashed the feeling of superiority welling within me, feeling unentitled to it.

I was being completely unrealistic wanting to know everything. But having begun to ask questions, there didn't seem to be any logical reason to stop being inquisitive just because the examination boards had drawn an arbitrary line in some rarefied academic ether, defining what we need not know.

Ironically, my single-minded pursuit of answers did me no favors academically. The lower levels of the education system reward perfect regurgitation of what is taught, and discount any knowledge acquired outside that limited framework. Luckily, I was adept enough at playing the system to get into university, where those with a limited focus were still more likely to succeed by playing the game strictly according to the rules defined by generations of pedants.

It was at university that I discovered the pleasures and rewards that come from living my own life, having my own opinions, being able to control my universe rather than have others control it for me; it was as powerful a need as an illicit drug, and it was a fix that I fixated on.

Four Lost Souls

Spencer's phone buzzed. Instinctively he sat upright. Merely to have Devons summon him provoked a soldierly reaction. He straightened his tie and brushed off the shoulders of his jacket as he walked towards her office - he had to remind himself he wasn't a nervous boy scout about to go on parade.

Devons, like Weller, never looked tired. She might appear harassed, or annoyed, or downright angry, but he'd never seen her looking vulnerable. When he'd phoned her early that morning and she had appeared befuddled at first, it was the first time he'd ever caught her with her guard even partly down.

Sally Devons had appeared from nowhere just over a year ago, at a time when the division was the subject of fervent criticism. It was mostly justified, based on the fact that three detectives and two men from the uniformed branch had been found to be not only taking money from drug dealers, but also engaging in drug trading themselves. Devons was empowered to sort the mess out; and it was made plain by the Home Office and the Home Secretary himself that she could trample on any bodies she cared to in doing it. In fact, for the sake of the overt ritual cleansing the powers needed to demonstrate draconian action and the more bodies she trampled on, the harder she trampled on them, and the more obviously purgative she made her crusade, the better.

At one of her first group meetings, she said: "I'm going to stamp on any dodgy practice that I come across, hard. There are no holy cows."

"Except you," a voice behind Spencer mumbled, and although Devons showed no sign of hearing the remark, the detective sergeant who made it was, a few months later, back on the beat as a uniformed constable, earning an unexciting salary and with no prospects of doing anything else for as long as he stayed on the force.

Devons sniffed out the wrongdoers and slippery practices like a tenacious hound. She was focused, incisive, intelligent, and politically sharp. She was good in front of her inferiors, superiors and politicians. Only the most stubborn or ignorant of her subordinates would deny her strengths. But none of the people who worked with her daily did anything other than dislike or fear her, and nobody seemed inclined to revoke that dislike, no matter how laudable her achievements. To Devons, this lack of rapport with her underlings seemed to matter not one iota, and she spent all of her skills and charms managing up and out, not down and within.

"Well?" she asked, as Spencer eased his tired body into a chair. He had learned not to expect greetings, even cursory ones, and she seemed to look upon small-talk as an unprincipled violation of the taxpayers' money invested in the constabulary.

"Here's the report." Spencer said, handing her the document. "It says it all, which is not much so far: body found, money, strangulation, and noughts and crosses."

She seemed to take far too long to read it, as if she were analyzing every line and what was unwritten between them. Spencer wished he'd checked it more thoroughly before allowing it to be subjected to her sharp and inevitably hypercritical scrutiny. Not for the first time, he felt like a schoolboy in the presence of his least favorite teacher. A senior schoolboy perhaps, but a relative child nonetheless.

"Tell me you have at least identified the victim?"

"Not yet. We're checking on the streetwalkers who use that area regularly. There's about a dozen of them that we know of. There are no missing person reports that link to her, but it's early yet, she'll barely have been missed, being a lady of the night."

"Do we know that for sure? Just because she was carrying condoms and a bulk supply of tissues doesn't mean she was doing business. She might have been a raver."

"No, we don't know for sure, but it's a good ...," he paused before saying 'guess' - Devons didn't appreciate words like that - "... probability."

Devons dumped the report on her desk, leaned forward, her eyes piercing Spencer's. "I'm combining all four investigations into one dedicated team that I'll head personally. We're going to re-examine all the evidence from the previous three cases and look specifically for links. We've done it before, and we're going to do it again, and we're going to make the Home Office run every test they're capable of, and then some."

There was some sense in recycling existing information to see if it could yield up any secrets under a new and more intensive analysis, but Spencer didn't expect anything to come of it. If evidence wasn't there, it wasn't there, and no amount of impassioned hunting would uncover any. He could imagine just how the lab would react when told of the new priority. They would remind him, as if he needed it, that doing the same thing repeatedly and expecting a different outcome was the definition of lunacy.

"You've put me in a spot over this," said Devons.

"How?"

"I went along with your line last time about this not necessarily being a serial killer, but now it looks like you were wrong, dead wrong, literally."

Spencer tried to look unconcerned as her eyes continued boring into his.

"I didn't say it wasn't a serial; I said we had no evidence either way, and we still don't."

"I'm not going to lynch you. When I take advice I take the responsibility that goes along with it."

She studied the report again. Spencer yawned. He realized he was gazing at his boss, but he was too tired to care. She was plain and did nothing whatsoever to make herself look more attractive. He tried to imagine her with lipstick and blushing cheeks, dressed like a model on a catwalk, flaunting her body. He was trying to see in her the latent sexuality that some of his colleagues said they felt when in her presence, but he couldn't.

Perhaps it was her smell. He had noted a definite smell about her now and again. It wasn't an artificial scent; it was something more intimate than that. He thought back to his childhood and the strange smells that surrounded his sisters as they entered puberty. He came to associate it with physical changes that would both fascinate and intimidate him. It was neither pleasant nor unpleasant. He sniffed to see if it was detectable now, but the deep intake of breath triggered another yawn.

"You'd better go and get some sleep," she said, without looking up. "I assume Weller's handling things at the moment."

"He needs sleep before me. He's been up longer," said Spencer.

"Work it out between the two of you, but I'm calling a meeting for 9 this morning. and I want everyone to be there. I'll be expecting them to be ready to work until they drop. If I see anyone who's not in a state of chronic and terminal exhaustion between now and when this case is put to bed, I'll have their guts.

"We'll call a press conference for 11. We won't have much to tell the bastards, but at least I want them to see we're up and running and they'll only accuse us of trying to keep it quiet if we don't go public right away. We can't win with our delightful friends in the media."

§

The press conference was not a success. Spencer was sitting one side of her, and Jim McRae, a Public Relations specialist from the Home Office, on the other. Jim was a 60-year-old, overweight Scotsman with a deeply lined face and a solid mass of white hair that looked as if it was glued in place. He spoke with a drawled and frequently incomprehensible Glaswegian accent, his mouth barely moving as the words burbled out. But he was a shrewd individual and, thanks to the vast amount of time he spent entertaining reporters in bars and restaurants, he was generally popular with the media.

The three were facing 20 or so journalists and the usual jungle of news-gathering technology, which has supplanted the notebook and still camera from the days when Spencer first started briefing the press.

Devons made her statement, gathered her papers and made to leave, as if she had far more important things to do than satisfy Fleet Street's thirst for blood.

"Er, are they any, er … are there any questions … er …"

Jim McRae was hardly the most fluent public speaker at the best of times, and the fact that Devons was obviously in a rush had made him even more bumbling. "Er … if there are any questions … er … then we'll …"

"Yes," said Devons briskly, her clear enunciation seeming particularly sharp in comparison to Jim's rambling. "I'll gladly take questions, but I have to remind you that there's very little that we can discuss at this point."

"Chief Superintendent," called Toby Renton, a minor reporter from one of the major tabloids. "Have you identified the victim?"

"No, I've already said that," replied Devons, letting the room fall silent after her terse statement.

She could have done that differently, thought Spencer. She could have made it sound as if she wanted to appear open and keen to keep the media in the picture. But she was bitter about the criticism of her department over the handling of the previous murders.

"Is there a picture of the victim?" another reporter called out. "We could run it to help make the identification."

"Well … er … that sounds … er …" mumbled Jim.

"We're not in the habit of releasing mortuary photographs so that you can titillate your readership," said Devons.

Spencer winced. Jim McRae had a short coughing fit and reddened appreciably. Given his age, weight and habits, Spencer realized that Jim was a prime candidate for a heart attack, particularly in a setting like this.

"Any unusual marks on the body?" called one of the agency reporters.

Devons said nothing. Jim looked at her, saw that she didn't seem inclined to answer, and took a stab at replying himself.

"The … er … forensic evidence … is … er … under review … we … er … the autopsy will … er …"

"Surely it doesn't take a pathologist to see if she's got naughts and crosses etched into her skin," a reporter from the local press bellowed. "Come on, give us some facts."

"You've wasted our time bringing us here if you don't intend telling us anything," someone else yelled.

"Are you feeling under pressure, Chief Superintendent? Do you think your career is on the line if you don't show some progress soon?" Toby Renton shouted over a number of voices being raised as the pack began to sniff a cover-up.

"I've told you all I can tell you at this stage. We will contact you again when we have more to disclose. For now, bandying around speculation could harm the investigation, and I now need to get back to running that investigation and find the killer, or killers, who are responsible."

Spencer twitched when she said "or killers." Publicly she was still allowing room for doubt as to whether there was one perpetrator or more, but he knew she was deferring to him in holding this point of view as nobody else thought it likely. He didn't know whether to feel flattered or even more stressed.

The room fell silent as Devons spoke, but when she stopped, the fusillade of questions resumed, and when Devons stood to signal the end of the meeting, the noise level doubled. Devons strode from the room without a sideways glance.

Spencer followed her out, leaving Jim McRae standing alone at the front of the room, flapping his hands and saying "Okay boys, okay now, come on lads, just calm down a bit, come on now."

It was a full 20 minutes after Devons stalked out before McRae managed to extricate himself from the scrum of reporters and join Spencer and Devons in her office.

"Why did you let that fucking idiot Toby Renton into the briefing?" Devons' tone was controlled and almost singsong, which made it all the more ominous.

"Asking me about my career prospects. Jesus Christ! Who the hell does he think he is?"

"Sally, we can't limit who comes to press conferences," Jim said.

He didn't work in Devons' organization so he could call her what he liked, but Spencer noticed her eyes widen at being called by her first name and not as "Chief Superintendent" or as the quaint 'Ma'm' that British police officers continued to use as an acceptable honorific for superior female officers.

"Why not?"

"Because ... because ... because we can't. That would amount to censorship."

"So if Playboy sent a reporter, or The Beano, or the Anarchist Weekly, or we got a thousand journalists from Bumfuck who-knows-where, we'd have to rent the bloody Albert Hall and brief them, pander to them, sit back and have them insult us? Jim, get a grip!"

"Sally ..."

"In future we'll vet who comes to press conferences, and we won't allow junior, sicko, bottom-feeding, hack creeps like Toby Renton to come in. Is that clear?"

"Sally ..."

"And if that isn't clear, I suggest you raise it with your boss and I'll raise it with my boss and we'll let them mud-wrestle it to a conclusion."

"Sally ..."

"Thank you, Mr. McRae. Can you please excuse us now? I have some urgent matters to discuss with Inspector Spencer."

As Jim left the room, Spencer turned to his boss, whose face was as expressionless as a rock.

"Remember Spencer, if my head is on the line, so is yours, and if you or your team as much as take too long a pee break I'll ... Slackers have no place on my watch and no career opportunities in this force."

□□□

Know and Control

I studied physics, but before long my attention was diverted towards the mysterious beast to which we paid regular, ritualized obeisance, the departmental computer.

In the late 1960s when I began my time at university, computers were only just emerging. They were huge, science-fiction-like devices, and it was common for some of we acolytes of the fabulous animal to forego cheap booze at the student union for the chance to tinker with the electronic marvel. As a result, we often knew more about the computer than the lecturers – who seemed to be just as much in awe of it as the students - and we wallowed in our feelings of omnipotence.

What so attracted me to the computer was the fact that if I studied it assiduously enough, I would be able to know everything there was to know about it. As a logical, man-made but completely rational beast, it could do no more than its manuals prescribed, so by studying these materials I could thoroughly master the subject and leave no room for uncertainty, or further questioning, or doubt.

Within a particular frame of reference - albeit a particularly constrained and a singularly logical one - nothing could be hidden from my enquiring eyes. I saw, for the first time - and it should have troubled me to see it, perhaps - that my lust for knowledge was nothing of the sort; it was rather a fear of the unknown and a terror of the unknowable. In the modern vernacular, I would be termed a 'control freak'.

I transferred to the newly-formed Computer Science faculty at the end of my first year. One or two friends and my personal tutor questioned this decision to change course, but I was completely oblivious to any advice that came between me and what I saw as my 'true calling', and I use the phrase advisedly - my attraction to computer science had all the conviction of a spiritual conversion and a religious mania.

I met a girl at this time, Cynthia. Looking back, it's astonishing to me that we managed to build a relationship out of so desultory and unpromising a beginning. We would sit in my room in the student halls of residence, listening to Pink Floyd and Jimi Hendrix records played at an excruciating volume, drinking Newcastle Brown Ale and smoking French cigarettes. Or we would sit in her room in the flat she shared with two other girls, listening to Leonard Cohen and Fairport Convention, drinking unspeakably bad wine and smoking joints under posters of a charismatic Che Guevara and inscrutable Chairman Mao.

At some point in the evening, we would drag our jeans off and engage in perfunctory sex that I don't think either of us particularly enjoyed. I remember wondering more than once if the outcome was worth the effort of struggling with my Levis, and it wouldn't surprise me to learn Cynthia was thinking the same, if not more strongly.

We could go for days without seeing each other and, in my case I know, without thinking about the other. In the student union bar one evening, I got talking to a stranger who told me at length about the girlfriend back in his home town that he doted on, pined for and lusted over. "Have you got a woman?" he asked, when the subject of his dream lover temporarily slipped from his mind.

"No," I said, and it was some hours later before I realized I'd completely forgotten about Cynthia, with whom I'd been paired for about six months by then.

Strange then, that over 20 years later I find myself married to her, with three children. I think we got married primarily because we couldn't think of any good reason not to, and I suppose we both thought - I know I did - that few opportunities would present themselves in the future. I reasoned in my more private and introspective moments that if I couldn't find a willing partner in the liberal atmosphere of a 1960s university, I stood little chance of ever finding one in any other setting.

I think we both accepted the cosmic inevitability of our misfit alliance from the outset, and with such low mutual expectations, how could we possibly be disappointed?

We graduated at the same time, Cynthia in psychology, and me in the subject of my slavish addiction. We moved into a flat in the seediest part of unremittingly seedy Kennington, not far from the Elephant and Castle, an area dominated by a massive, concrete, fort-like, multi-story car-park, which derisively overshadowed ethnic markets on one side, and abutted a tangle of roads, overpasses and underpasses on the other, which seemed to spew out from it like ruptured intestines. Our neighbors and other people I encountered in the nearby streets always struck me as looking just as depressed as this most hopelessly depressing part of the city. But it suited the nihilistic existential pretensions we had at the time.

Our lives seemed to be taking place in black and white, like scenes from a melancholy film of the sixties, played out against an accompaniment of soulful saxophone improvisation, dripping taps and shuddering, lead pipework.

I managed to get a job with the government as a computer scientist, and Cynthia got into the social services department of Camden, one of the inner London boroughs known for its liberal attitude towards drugs and prostitution. On two salaries we enjoyed a reasonable lifestyle, until 18 months into her career Cynthia got pregnant, and she has never worked for money since.

Our first child, Leo, was an accident; our second, Morag, was a surprise; and our third, Charlotte, an unmitigated disaster as far as our finances were concerned. It seemed as if we only needed to have sex once in order to set another fetus growing in Cynthia's productive womb. We took our spontaneously created family in our stride, and accepted that our standard of living was going to be depressingly low for as long as we could imagine. In fact, things didn't turn out too badly, but solely due to an ironic Act of God, deadly ironic given we were and are both atheists.

Cynthia's father was a businessman and religious fanatic with whom she'd never had a particularly good relationship. When she and I set up home together before we married, he made it plain he thought it was a bad idea, a sinful act, and not one he would condone, to the extent that we hardly ever heard from him or his wife (who was Cynthia's stepmother - her natural mother having died years before). But when both were killed in a car crash on the way home from a prayer meeting, only a few days after our third child saw the grey light of a South London day, we were surprised to learn that Cynthia and her brother were the sole and equal beneficiaries of their parents' unexpectedly wealthy estate.

We bought a house in Islington - then a relatively down-market but up-and-coming area that attracted the likes of us - escaping the poverty and privations to which we had resigned ourselves. I wonder now whether our fates would have been different had a divine intervention not made it so easy for us, and whether all that has happened has resulted from God making us pay for the fortune bestowed upon us and our disbelief in his existence.

My career has never really gone anywhere. I've always done my job well, but my bosses have frequently pointed out that although my technical knowledge is second to none, I lack the ability to differentiate the logistically important from the intellectually stimulating - a criticism to which I happily admit but never respond, much to the frustration of my superiors. In fact, I've become something of a legend in the close-knit world of government computing officers.

"If," I've heard it said, "you want to know the role of a particular file or subroutine in a particular version of a particular release of the XYX series operating system, don't bother contacting the manufacturer, call Phil Henderson." This can be said with derision, grudging respect or, occasionally, awe - it doesn't really matter to me, I'm not like I am for any other reason than that is how I live my life, the geeky master of a tightly controlled and neatly circumscribed universe.

Several years ago, when our children had passed the stage when they needed supervision from us and had reached the stage at which they resented any parental involvement in their lives, Cynthia decided it was time for her to return to the world at large. Since then she has been running a shelter for battered wives in the East End of London. Her increasing involvement with this cause means I see less and less of her, and given my children also seem to prefer to be out of the house, particularly when their parents are in it, I now live more of a bachelor life than I did when I was a bachelor.

We've managed to stick together - although my son, Leo, has appeared to be keen on provoking a schism since he entered his anarchic adolescence. "So?" was his habitual response when we questioned him about his poor school results, and he would grunt a desultory "shit might fly" if we tried to gather the family for some activity such as a trip to the coast. Not that he had outgrown seaside trips, as we discovered when the police called one night to say they had locked him up for drunkenness and engaging in lewd behavior on Brighton beach.

I can't really believe that most families are quite as lacking in cohesion as mine, especially outside the liberal environment of Islington. A saving grace in helping me believe we are comparatively well-adjusted has been the occasional story of family disaster that Cynthia has imparted to me, based on her experiences at the battered wives' shelter.

Unfortunately, it is not only stories that greet me when I return from work, sometimes it is the battered wives themselves, whom Cynthia invites to stay in our home when the shelter is either full to capacity, or when the victim has been tracked down by the delinquent partner intent on continuing his ardent battery where he left off.

Even more unfortunately, on one memorable occasion one of these highly undesirable partners managed to trace his inadequately sheltered prey to our house. If Leo hadn't laid into the man with a vigor I was unaware he possessed, and a baseball bat - which, likewise, I was unaware he possessed - then the poor woman would have certainly suffered even more.

This incident had a further disturbing consequence when Leo began to take a distinctly physical interest in the woman he had protected, an interest that she seemed happy to encourage. But the burgeoning relationship between the then 15-year-old Leo and the 35-year-old female was cut short when she began inviting another man to visit her at our home and, to judge from the noises we heard during these visits, to "fuck their brains out," as Leo put it. At this point, the normally tolerant Cynthia decided matters had gone too far, and suggested that the lady's need for shelter from her pursuer had been surpassed by our family's need for shelter from her.

At this time, my teenage daughters, Morag and Charlotte, had not outwardly demonstrated any of Leo's sporadically hostile characteristics and highly demonstrative truculence towards his parents, but I have to admit we haven't imposed very much authority on either of them, so it would be hard to see exactly what they could rebel against, even if they were so inclined.

Morag keeps herself to herself, and, in a remarkable parallel to my relationship with her mother, I sometimes almost forget she exists. Charlotte, on the other hand, is rather hard to ignore, and Cynthia has had quite a struggle upholding her liberal values when a more stringent Victorian approach may have been more suitable. This was most clearly illustrated when we discovered 13-year-old Charlotte, wearing what looked to me like no more than a wide belt, entertaining a much older man in her room.

"OK then, is that it?" was all Charlotte said when we reproached her. No objection. She merely smiled and picked up her music player, the act of putting on her earphones indicating we were dismissed from her room and intimating the rebuke would have no modifying affect on her future behavior.

This lack of control in my family unsettled me and I took even greater solace in my work, where I am a king of a sort.

□□□

Pecking Order

Spencer entered Devons' office just in time to hear the pathologist summarizing the results of the biopsy over the speaker phone. Weller was already there.

"... in reasonably good health. I would put the time of death at a half past midnight, give or take 30 minutes, caused by strangulation with a piece of cord or something similar about an eighth of an inch thick. I can't be precise at the moment, but it wasn't wire and it wasn't rope, so think of something in between. The killer was probably behind her when he did it, possibly penetrating her at the same time."

"Wait a minute," said Devons. "Is that speculation warranted?"

"What do you mean?"

"Can you be sure he was screwing her while he killed her?"

"No, but ..."

"Then leave it out. Just tell me what you know or can reasonably infer. We can rely on the papers to add the smutty conjecture."

"Chief Superintendent, I can assure you that ..."

"What else?" said Devons, cutting Best short as his righteous indignation gathered momentum. He sighed loudly and continued.

"Multiple lacerations to the genital area, around the anus and on the buttocks, thighs, stomach and breasts. Inflicted with a sharp knife - a Stanley knife or something of the sort - administered after death. A more patterned form of scarring on her back, the zeroes and crosses sort that we've seen on a number of bodies recently. The victim had smoked marijuana in the 24 hours before she died, but not within the previous six hours. There was a moderate level of alcohol in her blood, but she wasn't seriously drunk."

"What about the perpetrator?"

"Sorry, not allowed to speculate."

"You are when I say you are," Devons growled. Her ability to express anger suddenly was, Spencer thought, one of her most powerful and frequently exercised attributes, and he guessed it might be more tactical than emotional.

"The cord was pulled upwards and backwards, so the attacker was probably taller than the victim. The victim was five six, so he, or she, must have been at least five ten. Or, there again, the victim could have been on her knees, in which case the perpetrator could be a dwarf."

Devons rolled her eyes. Best paused, possibly waiting for laughter or censure, but charged silence was the only sound in the room.

"The burn marks from the cord were deep enough to imply considerable strength or anger, or both. From the slash marks I should say that he, or she, was right handed, and that he, or she, meant to cut deep and not just to mark the body, but not so deep as to expose organs."

"This 'he or she' business. Do you have any reason to believe it could have been a woman?"

"No," said Best. "Do you have any reason to believe that it wasn't, Chief Superintendent?"

Spencer saw Devons' jaw tighten.

"Anything else?"

"Not on the body. Nothing but seemingly unremarkable East End dirt under the fingernails, no sperm in the vagina or the mouth or the stomach or anywhere else, no fresh bite marks."

"Was she a whore? You can speculate again, but don't get carried away."

"She was no virgin. Plenty of evidence of activity around the vagina and some around the anus, but the killer did so much damage with his knife that it's hard to say how well used those areas had been."

"I'll expect your written report by 6 p.m."

"Chief Superintendent, I've been working here since ..." but his words were lost as Devons jabbed at the button that terminated the call.

She turned to Spencer.

"Any news on her identity?"

"Not yet," he said, "We're banging on doors in the neighborhood and talking to the local hookers and pimps to see if anyone has gone missing, but a lot of them aren't up and about yet."

"What about the money?"

"The lab isn't hopeful," said Weller. "They may be able to get something, but at the moment it looks like a lot of partial prints that are going to be very hard to lift."

"So," said Devons, "as we stand right now, you're telling me that we have absolutely nothing, apart from a slowly decaying, anonymous cadaver. Is that right?"

"Yes, but I'd be surprised if we don't have her identity by this time tomorrow. Whores tend to keep an eye out for each other, especially ..."

"Especially since the police force don't seem to be able to protect them," interrupted Devons irritably, again spontaneously igniting.

"What else?" she asked.

"We're pulling out the records on the usual suspects, but don't plan to approach any of them until we at least know who she was."

"And what if we don't find out who she was?"

Spencer was becoming so stressed at this fusillade of questions that he found himself answering without thinking.

"Then we'll approach them anyway."

"So why don't we do it now?"

"Because we won't have the resources until the house-to-house is finished."

"And what are you two doing?"

"I was going to suggest that Weller and I went on a pub crawl."

Devons stared at Spencer without speaking, her expression blank.

"Dr. Best said she'd been drinking. Pubs are possibly where she did her picking up as well, so we might get an idea of who she was and who she'd been with if we do the pubs in the area. Then, if that doesn't work, tonight we'll need to put the squeeze on the local dope pushers, try and see if any of them recognize a recently departed customer."

"We'll next meet at 6 p.m." Devons said, giving no sign as to whether she agreed with his plans. "I'm dragging in all the resources I can get my hands on. I'm in overall charge of the investigation, but you're responsible for the day-to-day operations," she said, looking and nodding at Spencer. "I want you to make sure every officer is being used to the best possible effect, and as overused as you can make them without provoking too many fatal nervous breakdowns.

"If I suspect that you're under-performing, I'll be down on you before you know what's hit you. If I find out about any problems before you do, you're for the high jump. I want a comprehensive status report on the other three previous murders on my desk by 8 o'clock tomorrow morning, and I want to see the lead officers in each of those cases at 10 o'clock tomorrow morning."

Uncharacteristically quaint, thought Spencer, that she should use the "o'clock" notation. He saw her more as a "oh eight hundred" sort of a person. Why, he went on to wonder, was he trying to find something likeable about her, when she was laying the law down so unpleasantly?

A few years ago, he would have bridled at being spoken to like this by an officer who, compared to him, knew so little about running a murder investigation. Looking back ten years, the idea of a 35-year-old policewoman lecturing a 50-year-old, hard-bitten detective would have been completely unthinkable. But times had changed, and Spencer knew that this boat was definitely not one worth rocking.

As he walked back to his office, the thought occurred to him that he should just quit. There and then, on the spot. The idea was so powerful that he stopped and stood stock still. The thrill of being rid of all the crap that had suffused his job over the years and now seemed to constitute the major part of it was intoxicating.

As he realized he was doing a reasonable impression of Lot's wife and needed to start walking again, he felt as if his next step could be the metaphor for a change of life. If he was brave enough to take it.

□□□

Close Encounters

I heard the news of the fourth killing on the radio at breakfast. Leo seemed to find the whole thing extremely amusing.

"Another scrubber bites the dust, hee ha!" he announced through a mouthful of toast spread so thick with margarine, peanut butter and strawberry jam that I wondered how he could get it into his mouth and whether his arteries would be able to survive the onslaught. In light of his increasingly offensive behavior, I had a sudden, shameful, wish they wouldn't.

"One less candidate for the shelter," he said, looking at Cynthia and grinning in a way that was certainly unpleasant, and possibly lascivious.

She ignored him, which seemed to be all one could do to Leo these days. We could hardly agree with his bizarre and often malicious comments, and to argue with him invariably led to scenes, which varied only in their degree of hostility.

"Tell me, mother," he persisted, "how is the deep-fried-wives' shop these days?"

"What do you mean?" she said, as she continued to grind oranges into the juicer, aware that any reaction or show of anger would make him even more objectionable.

"Well, you deep-fry battered fish, don't you, so it's obvious you'd deep-fry battered wives as well, and then serve them in tabloid newspaper with greasy chips, salt, vinegar and long, fat, slithery, slippery gherkins. I'm not totally stupid, mother."

Cynthia, like me, was getting more and more concerned about Leo and where he was headed in life, but less and less able to do anything about it.

He had finished school and was working on a building site for the summer before starting university in the autumn. Leo has always been well built, and the heavy work he was doing was adding some impressive muscles to the bare torso he frequently displayed around the house; bare, that is, apart from an ever-increasing array of tattoos I scrupulously avoided trying to read or interpret.

The threat of physical violence, which never seemed to be far below the surface with our son, now was all the more intimidating, and we had no reason to believe that we, his parents, were more immune to it than anyone else, in fact, just the opposite.

"I think it's horrible," said Cynthia when Leo had gone and was no longer able to interrupt and ridicule our conversation.

"What?" I asked, thinking she could be talking either about Leo or the murders.

"Those killings. I always get the impression when they say the victims were prostitutes, it's as though we shouldn't care so much as if they'd been housewives or pensioners or nurses or nuns or something. Lots of the women at the shelter have been on the game, some probably still are, but that's not to say they're worth any less. A life's a life."

I knew what she meant. I knew it because the reaction she'd been criticizing had been my reaction too, and although I tried to get it out of my system, I wasn't having much success.

"But they're taking a hell of a risk when they do that work," I said. "AIDS, VD, getting beaten up. It's like when a mountaineer dies, or a bungee jumper, or something like that. It's still a tragedy, but they know what they're getting into."

"These women don't do it for fun!"

"No," I said, wishing I hadn't said anything, which was increasingly becoming the way I felt about interactions with my family.

As if Leo's erratic lifestyle and disturbing behavior weren't bad enough, and Charlotte's accommodating nature towards older males wasn't also considerable cause for concern, Cynthia accidently stumbled upon the dubious values being espoused by Morag, our otherwise placid and self-contained elder daughter.

Purely by chance, when trying to locate the source of a damp patch that had appeared on the kitchen ceiling and was spreading rapidly across it, apparently beneath Morag's room, she inadvertently discovered an eclectic assortment of printed materials hidden under Morag's bed. I say eclectic, but the materials were focused around four major themes - pornography, violent anarchy, illicit drugs (production and consumption thereof) and bomb-making. Rather than describe the contents of these documents to me, Cynthia suggested I should take the opportunity to review them first hand when I next found myself alone in the house, which turned out to be the next day.

The pornography was beyond anything I thought humanly or zoologically possible, certainly if pleasure was the objective of its participants.

The drug literature was not of itself that disturbing, but was made so by the 'tasting notes' (spiffer, moonriding, multiorg, whoa) scribbled in the margins in Morag's handwriting, intimating she had tried most of the variety of substances described.

The documents exhorting the reader to anarchy were, likewise, annotated by Morag with lots of big bold strokes and ticks implying she was at one with the extreme sentiments being expressed. The bomb construction guidelines were marked with a highlighting pen to designate the key techniques, ingredients and recommended sources of supply.

I huddled on the floor of Morag's room feeling - amidst the wreckage of my daughter's supposed innocence - quite dumbstruck, not only because our daughter was involved in the subjects laid at my feet, but also by the fact such documents even existed. I'd seen pornography before, but nothing like this, which was, for the most part, too depraved to be arousing; and as for the anarchic ravings, they would have made the Trotskyites from my university days tremble and run to their mothers.

Cynthia and I discussed it that night in bed, whispering as though we were the ones doing wrong.

"Where on earth do you think she got it from?"

"Perhaps one of her friends gets it for her."

"Could it be Leo?" Cynthia asked.

"Could be, but they would have to have a pretty chummy

relationship for that to be the case, and I don't think they do."

"Do you think she really practices that stuff?" she asked.

I thought for a moment as to which part of the 'stuff' constituted the greatest cause for concern, but was unable to rank the subjects in order of odiousness.

"How do we raise it with her?" Cynthia continued.

I knew Cynthia would never admit to having been through Morag's personal effects, even if she had discovered a dead baby seeping its bodily fluids through the floorboards and staining our kitchen ceiling.

"We'll just have to watch her closely in the future, and hope something comes to light we can bring up with her," I said.

"But there's been no sign of anything like this in the past."

This wasn't altogether true. Some months previously, my wife had let slip her normal conciliatory role and had castigated Leo for one of his more tasteless outbursts.

"If you think I'm bad, you should see what your darling little mousy Morag gets up to when the cat's away." As he spoke, he jabbed his middle finger at Morag. I thought nothing of it, assuming it was just an attempt by Leo to add more disharmony to what he was already manufacturing. But, looking back, I remember the unusually vehement and intense expression on Morag's face as Leo spoke, and which I initially interpreted as understandable loathing, but which could just as easily have been a mixture of rage and fear of discovery.

"Kids get interested in that sort of thing," I said, knowing full well most adults didn't, let alone children, and some of what we'd discovered could have possibly made even Leo shudder.

"The chances are that she'll just grow out of it." I didn't believe a word of what I was saying, and I'm sure Cynthia didn't either.

"But what if she tries some of it out before she grows out of it?"

"Well, the pornography, I ...."

"What?"

"Nothing," I said. I was going to say getting involved in pornography wasn't likely to be life threatening, but given some of the photographs in Morag's collection, I was probably going to have to change that point of view. "It's the bomb making part that's most worrying."

"Doesn't that just go along with anarchy?"

"Not necessarily, it could be criminal. You may grow out of being an anarchist, but I'm not sure you grow out of being a criminal."

"But how do you grow *into* being a criminal?" she said, close to tears. "How did we end up with children like this? A hooligan, a teenage nymphomaniac and a ... a ... a whatever Morag turns out to be? Do you think she's committed any crimes already?"

I had no idea, and given it was too late to do anything about the past, I didn't really see much point in dwelling on it either - it was out of my control. But thinking of the bombs described in Morag's stash, I couldn't shake off the idea that some sort of metaphorical explosion was inevitable, given the forces that were building up in our family.

§

It was only later that I thought back to the first time. It was too insignificant to remember on its own account, and it wasn't until events unfolded that I saw its potential solemnity.

I was sitting in front of a computer screen at home. I think my daughters were in the house, but Cynthia was at the shelter and Leo must have been out because there was no cacophony of noise thumping out from his bedroom, which he had designated "off limits" to the rest of us, unless invited, and we never were.

I was running some diagnostic tests on a component board that had been playing up, and I was staring blankly at the monitor whilst it flashed and flickered its way through the video tests. Then, completely out of nowhere, a scene manifested before me. I knew at once I wasn't actually seeing it through my eyes. It was as though my mind had presented me with an image as it would in a dream - completely real within the context of the dream state, but completely imaginary outside of it.

There was a room, it was a bedroom. The walls were decorated in purple and red, there was a leopard skin throw over the bed, and a chandelier dripping with baubles. It had probably been put together with the intention of conveying regal opulence, but instead appeared embarrassingly tacky.

The lights were dim and I had no real appreciation of the detail of the room, which was completely unfamiliar to me, but at the same time I got the impression I had a strong connection with the place, and it was somehow important to me. Then the image disappeared just as suddenly as it had sprung up, and although I could remember very little of what I had actually seen, I felt powerfully influenced by it.

I put it down to something to do with the frequency of the flickering images on the monitor in front of me - knowing that flashing lights can induce fits, hallucinations and other unwelcome reactions in some people - and although nothing like it had ever happened to me before, I didn't really give it a lot more thought at the time. It was curious, but compared to the behavior of our children, for example, it didn't seem to be worth worrying about unduly.

Now, I'm amazed that I shut it out of my conscious for so long.

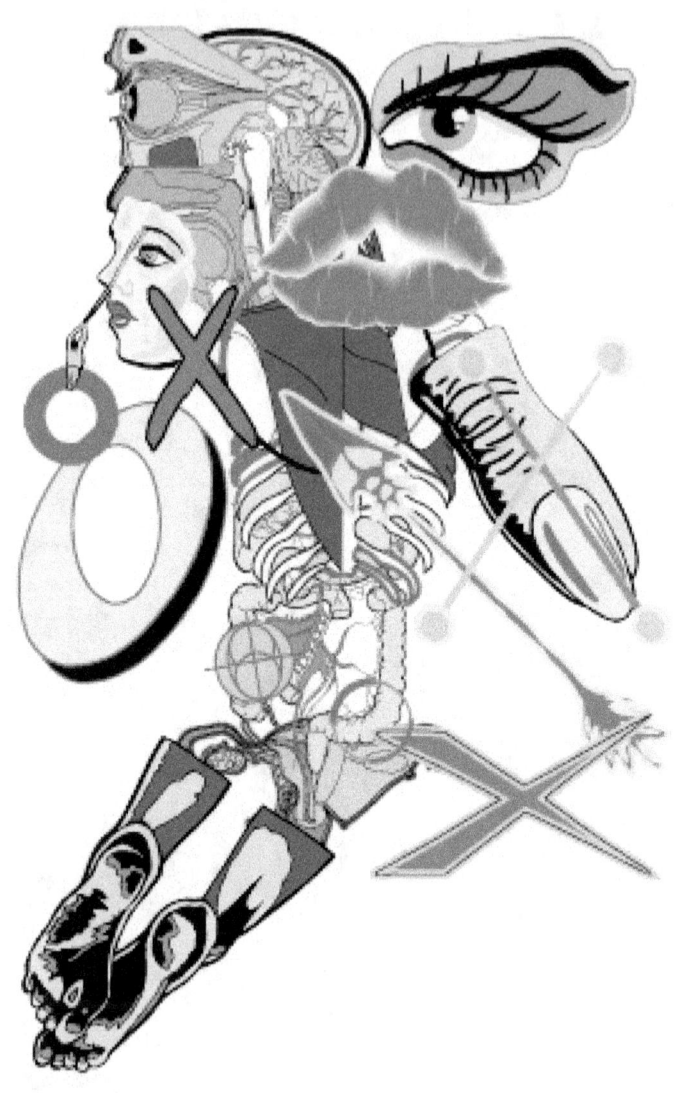

Under the Skin

As Spencer stepped out the police building, the sun managed to squeeze its way between the clouds and the rain stuttered to a stop. He raised his face toward the sun, as if to inhale every bit of warmth and energy he could. Forgetting he didn't have any, he reached inside his jacket for his pack of cigarettes. He pulled out the eerie picture of the dead woman's face taken at the mortuary, and brooded, hoping the image would yield a clue.

Even though it was broad daylight, the murder area seemed to be no less foreboding than the night of the killing. Gloomy buildings surrounded the sad garden where they had found the body. Despite being secluded, the garden was only a hundred yards or so from a busy road, where there were pubs and places a hooker might tout for business before coming to this blight on the neighborhood to relieve her customer of his money and his sperm.

The nearest two pubs yielded nothing relating to the case, but the Scotches he drank there perked up his spirits. In the third, the George and Horn, the young barman, who Spencer immediately labeled homosexual because of his bleached hair and exaggerated, coy lisp, confirmed he had been working the previous night. When Spencer showed him the picture, he whimpered at the sight of the dead woman's pallid face, then scrutinized it while clasping his hand over his mouth, his eyes like saucers.

"Oh my God. I know her, I know her!" he said, his face now as white as his hair. Spencer thought the man was going to throw up.

"Is this … is this … was this picture taken after … was this …" He gulped and slapped his palm to his forehead.

"Sorry about this. I know it's not very pleasant, but we have to find out who she is," said Spencer, realizing his policeman's blood must be chilled, but not altogether ice. "Do you know her name?"

The young man started to hyperventilate. He leaned forward and clutched the edge of the bar, his arms locked in front of him, and his posterior jutting out behind him. Spencer didn't know if he was collecting his thoughts or struggling to control his stomach, but he knew he had to give him time. He didn't allow himself to be optimistic. The barman could be mistaken, and he was proving himself excitable enough to be unreliable.

"I think … yes … maybe it's Mary, or something like that. But I know her friend, she's Samantha." He pronounced the name 'SaMANtha', with an emphasis on the middle syllable and the last syllable spoken with extravagant use of his tongue. Spencer winced.

"Samantha used to go out with Seb, who worked here, in our kitchens. He'll de-fi-nite-lay tell you where to find Mary, I mean, not find her because, you know, well …."

And that was it. Two phone calls and a visit to a shabby flat - which looked less habitable than Saddam Hussein's hole in the ground; a conversation with Samantha, who, upon seeing Spencer's ID barred the door and sneered "I know nothing and even if I did I wouldn't tell you lot," but then spent a full five minutes sobbing wetly into his jacket; a ride to the mortuary in the presence of a WPC who was able to take over the role of consoler and sponge; a hysterical but positive identification; and it was done.

He called Devons from his car, but failed to detect from her tone that she was even slightly impressed by his ability to turn words into actions so quickly.

§

Almost a week passed and they were no closer to catching the murderer or murderers than they were when Spencer first stood over the body haloed under fluorescent lights in the Whitechapel night.

It was around 9.00 at night and Spencer was in his office, going through the files on the previous three cases to see if he could find any common threads buried deep in the reams of information. He'd tried it before, both on his own and in brainstorming sessions with colleagues, but he was trying one more time because his intuition told him there may be something there somewhere that would reveal itself eventually, like a scene from a half-forgotten dream.

Four murders. A stabbing then three strangulations. In the first there had been no additional mutilation apart from the fatal stab wound and the strange scratchings on the victim's back; in the second there had been some additional cuts - delivered posthumously - to the breasts; and in the third, extensive slashing damage had been inflicted all over the corpse, even behind the ears. Apart from the etched crosses and circles, the individual murders were hardly more similar to each other than they were to hundreds of others he could pull from the files.

For this reason Spencer still clung to the suspicion there may be more than one killer involved. Discounting the criss-cross marks that anyone who heard the early news of the murders could copy, there was no material evidence linking the four. There was no hard evidence at all he kept telling himself as he scanned the files, and that was the phrase haunting him when he looked up to see Sally Devons standing in the doorway with an expression on her face that could have been one of mild amusement, or disdain. He had no idea how long she had been standing there, watching him.

"I've had it for today," she said, "do you want a drink?"

He didn't. He wanted to go home and catch up on some sleep. But this was too momentous an opportunity to pass up. C.S. Devons had never been known to socialize over drinks with a subordinate since her arrival, so he was breaking new ground.

Rather than going to the nearest pub, and the one in which there were bound to be some familiar faces, they walked to a wine bar where Devons ordered a bottle of Burgundy and two glasses without bothering to ask Spencer what he'd like.

She started off asking for an update on the investigation, and then asked him what he was doing personally, so he thought it was just an extension of work in a different setting, but then she leant back, kicked off her shoes and sighed.

"So, we've got nothing, have we?" she said, but conversationally, and not like a sergeant major addressing an unfriendly audience, which was her normal mode of delivery, even when talking to one person in private.

"No."

"Okay, tell me what you think."

"What do you mean?"

"I know you reckon I'm an upstart. A text-book copper, a neophyte with no investigative flair, and that's okay, because it's partly true. But you've been around a while, we all know that, so tell me what your guts are telling you. I'll give you five minutes to say what you like, about the case, about the investigation, about the way I'm running it, about anything. No interruptions and no criticism from me. Five minutes of the world according to Spencer."

He collected his thoughts, which didn't take long, because he already knew what his opinions were, although he didn't much think Devons would like hearing them.

"One or possibly two killers working independently. One killed the last two and probably the last three, but someone else may have killed the first one. Male. Intelligent and scrupulously careful. Probably has no criminal record. He's been storing this up for some time, and now he's decided to act and has realized how much he likes it. He'll do it again unless he gets caught, kills himself, or has such a fright he reckons it's not worth the risk anymore."

"I thought you didn't have much time for profilers. Sounds like you want to be one yourself."

"That's not profiling, that's pontificating, and there's not a reasonable copper couldn't tell you the same thing, given the chance to speculate over a glass of wine. But it doesn't mean anything without physical evidence or some leads."

"How do we catch him?"

"We don't, until he does it again and only then if he makes a mistake or he's caught in the act."

"Or unless someone tells us. Someone must know who he is."

"Why must they? He works on his own. Look at the records. Serial killers are invariably loners. A profiler would tell you he's either irrevocably single, divorced, or living in a loveless marriage to someone he doesn't communicate with. These blokes get off on the secrecy, the furtiveness. Why tell anyone? That would take most of the pleasure out of it and expose him to a risk that might bring a premature end to his fun."

Devons knocked back her wine and refueled both glasses. She sank back into the chair, tipped her face towards the ceiling and rubbed her neck. "Tell me, Spencer, why do they do it?"

"Are you asking me as male or a copper?"

"Either, both. Why are there so few female serial killers?"

"Perhaps if we knew why women don't do it, we'd know why men do. We'd know what restraints men lack that women don't," said Spencer

"Only some men, thank God."

"I'd bet there are a thousand men in London who'd like to be doing what he's doing, maybe ten thousand, and some of those would be doing it if they thought they could get away with it."

"And if we don't catch him soon they'll be thinking they *can* get away with it," said Devons after downing another large gulp of wine.

"Probably, which is why I'm guarded about yelling 'serial killer' before we have some proof. Serial killers are very rare, they just sell more newspapers. There could be a copycat on the loose, maybe even more than one."

"Christ, I hope not. Catching one is obviously beyond us. If there's more than one we stand no chance."

"Well, if there's anything going to encourage others to have a go, it's our inability to catch the first guy, or even get close to fingering him."

"Thank you for those words of consolation. Now you're telling me our incompetence is putting the whole female population of the city at risk." She smiled, which was something she didn't do very often. Spencer smiled back and their eyes met in a way Spencer hadn't experienced with her before. It was a friendly exchange, but it made him feel unsettled and exposed in way he couldn't fathom.

"Do men hate whores? Does having contempt for the woman make it easier to use her?" she said, inclining her head slightly, but still gazing at him. It was almost a coy gesture, almost, but not quite, because her eyes were now piercing and coolly appraising.

"I don't know that it's got anything to do with hate. The psychologists say it's all about domination, don't they? Kids dominated by their mothers, adolescents rejected by their girlfriends, men scorned by their wives. Then they decide to get their own back."

"But you, Spencer, can you understand it? Do you get as outraged by killings like this as you do by child abductions?"

"No, but nor would a woman, I shouldn't think."

"But do you have any idea where this man is coming from? Can you see what earthly pleasure he can be getting out of it? Cutting up the bodies, taking time to score his weird little symbols on their backs after he's killed them?"

"No, but I don't see what pleasure people get out of watching ice skating. You need to ask another homicidal maniac about what it's like to be a homicidal maniac, not Mr. Average."

There was a pause. Devons looked at the ceiling again and Spencer watched her, reverting to his occasional activity of trying to work out what was attractive about her, if anything. He sniffed the air to see if the smell was there. Yes, there was definitely something. He'd heard of chemicals that some animals create to attract mates by smell. Perhaps that was the secret of Devons' magnetism, a magnetism that a few days ago even the cool-headed Weller had admitted to feeling. He went to sniff again, but Devons spoke.

"Maybe it's time to get proactive."

"Like how? Bait?"

"Yes. Get some WPCs out on the street in fishnet stockings and see what they can do for us."

"It may help them supplement their pay, if they take to it," said Spencer, but Devons gave no appearance of listening, or even hearing. He felt hollow.

VIBRANT DREAMS

The second time was more memorable. It was several days after the discovery of Morag's alter ego, and I hadn't been sleeping well. I was concerned of course, but I have to admit the greater cause of my restlessness was the fact that Cynthia was tossing and turning for most of the night, out of the same concerns over Morag.

When I did fall into a deep stupor one night, it was to have a bizarre dream I would have gladly exchanged for another night of light, fractured sleep. The dream itself wasn't that odd, though I can't remember having had one quite like it before.

The content wasn't particularly outrageous, given the latitude the dreaming state has to create weird and troubling images. In my dream I seemed to be going about my life on a normal day, at home and at work. But everywhere I went it was as though people were viewing me with great suspicion, trying to avoid me, staring at me from a distance but avoiding my gaze when they were close, and if they spoke to me it was with extreme reticence. It was as though I had been ostracized for some reason, but I had no idea why this should be the case.

Then I found myself in my work-cube, which had become a kaleidoscope of changing snake-like shapes and murky colors melding, parting, and then exploding. My computer monitor loomed over me, staring down derisively as I cowered on the floor. It spat out 3-D numbers and letters, which streaked towards me, swooped round when I tried to get under the table and bombarded me with what first felt like bricks then changed to snow-flakes.

When I managed to raise my head above the desk and caught a colleague's eye, I called out. But as soon as I did so, the colleague's facial features disappeared, leaving me staring into an abyss from which zeros and ones, spewed like vomit. My faceless colleagues, dressed in robes of magenta, crimson and violet, grouped and marched towards me. Just when I thought they would stampede over me, they turned away, the faces of my family appearing in the backs of their heads. They were smiling, and I saw myself floating towards them, arms wide open. A tiny red glow pulsated from Cynthia' stomach, becoming larger and brighter, opening out and framing her, while the expression on her face turned to one of outright disgust. The dream was so disturbing because every image was sharply delineated, and every scene was played out in bright colors, giving the events a prominence and a clarity that made them seem bolder and, as a consequence, hard to dismiss as the mind's meaningless ramblings.

As the dream progressed, I started shaking and sweating. I hurtled through a vortex and found myself in the same over-decorated bedroom that had appeared to me when sitting in front of my computer monitor a few weeks previously. Nothing happened in the room to offer a dramatic finale, I was just there. When I awoke, I got out of bed and staggered through to the kitchen. My heart was thumping and my mouth was dry. I looked around and saw evidence of Leo from the remains of a Chinese takeaway that had been thrown on the floor, and the spicy pepper sauce that had congealed into a bloody mass where he had dropped it.

For some time I felt deeply disturbed, and it was the fact I felt so disturbed that was more troubling than the dream had been in the first place. I was convinced I had done something wrong, something to be ashamed of, and something that the characters in my dream obviously disdained with the full strength of their razor-sharp, brilliant, technicolor representations. The fact that it was an overcast day and reality was dull and flat compared to the vibrancy of the dream images, further contributed to the prominence of unreality over reality, and emotion over fact.

I tried to think why I should be feeling this way, and it wasn't very difficult to come up with an acceptable interpretation. The world, as represented to me by my subconscious mind, was shaming me for the way in which I had raised my children. I was about to unleash upon an unsuspecting society one violent sociopath, one drug-crazed anarchist, and one teenage sex-maniac. Cynthia's appearance in the dream as one of the people treating me with the greatest amount of contempt and suspicion didn't quite square with this explanation, given they are her children too. But whereas Cynthia's loose-handed parenting was based on her belief that children should be raised in an environment free of excessive parental control, my deficiencies as a parent were simply due to laziness and the abrogation of the responsibilities that society has a right to expect of any conscientious father.

Cynthia's failings as a mother were due to her liberal 1970s education - she almost certainly put more effort into being a parent than most conventional mothers, it was just misdirected effort. My failings came about because I didn't care, or rather I cared more about my own intellectual well-being than I did about that of my family, and now my conscience was going to make me painfully aware of the fact.

This reasoning felt sound, and in the same way that one can feel relief when a mysterious illness isn't cured, but at least is identified and given a name, I began to calm down. I had found a plausible explanation for the basis of my dream.

Later in the day I remembered the room that appeared at the end of the dream and in my previous hallucination. I realized this component, upon which most of my anxiety seemed to be focused, remained completely without interpretation in my conscious mind, but was obviously a major disturbance to my subconscious. It was as if a life was taking place in a parallel universe of which I only had the occasional glimpse, and over the next few days my major preoccupation was that at any moment I might slip out of this universe and into the other one, where I have no control and where I am frightened, confused and unloved to the extent of being loathed by everyone in it.

FUGUE ALLEY

The evening started out well enough. Claudine and Lisa were in the Black Dog on Windle Street by about 9:00 p.m. They'd had a few drinks at Lisa's bed-sit before setting off – heavy on the Bacardi, light on the Diet Coke - and were starting to enjoy themselves in the pub when Harry turned up. They knew a couple of blokes standing by the bar had been eyeing them up, and they were expecting them to make a move at any moment - a move they would find a way to encourage if it didn't come soon - but when Harry appeared it put the damper on any overtures from the promising talent at the bar.

Claudine swore under her breath, not only at the missed opportunity but also at the presence of Harry who, although amiable enough at first, was guaranteed to make her flesh creep within five minutes of his arrival. As usual he was all over Lisa, first joking with her, then nudging her, then whispering in her ear, then touching her in increasingly intimate places. And, as usual, Lisa responded by first pushing him off, then brushing him off, then not doing anything at all to stop him, and finally touching him in much the same way he was touching her.

Claudine knew exactly how it would work out. Lisa and Harry would go off together, and then tomorrow she would get a phone call at about lunchtime from Lisa, who would be either angry or tearful, telling her what a bastard that Harry was and that she was never going to have anything to do with him again, ever. Claudine would say "Oh yeah" and Lisa would get annoyed at not being believed and would hang up in a huff, but their friendship would be repaired within a day or two and Harry's good standing would be repaired within a week or two, then the whole sorry rigmarole would be ready to replay.

Despite her contempt for Harry and her equal disdain for Lisa's handling of him, she could see why her friend always fell for it. Harry was tall, well-built, not one hair was misplaced. He had sculpted cheekbones, thick eyelashes, a sensuous mouth, was a satisfying lover - according to Lisa - and drove a sleek BMW with tinted windows and a personalized number plate. He was also dripping with cash and quite funny, if you could accept he wasn't as funny as he thought he was, nor as free with his money as he might have been.

What Claudine couldn't understand was why her friend, who was attractive enough to find another man with most of these attributes, kept falling for a bloke who lied to her, humiliated her, cheated on her, abused her verbally and, on at least one occasion, abused her physically. The person Harry really loved was Harry, and no mere woman was going to displace that rival. But by now she was bored by the whole Lisa/Harry business, and she settled into drinking and looking around the bar for a potential escape route.

Lisa and Harry left, but not before Harry had suggested a threesome, which Lisa took to be a joke but Claudine knew bloody well wasn't.

"I've got enough for two," he said, when Lisa was out of earshot.

"Then fuck yourself with what's left over, or give it to the dog to chew on," Claudine told him.

She decided to stay on and see what happened. She wasn't intimidated by sitting in a pub on her own, even a pub with a reputation like that of the Black Dog. She knew how her presence could be interpreted - a single woman, drinking steadily and unashamedly assessing every man in the place - but she was open to any advances, even if they were business propositions. She wasn't a whore, not a professional at any rate, but she had done it for money, and she would do it again without any moral compunction, provided the financial inducements were great enough. She felt due some compensation for her ruined night out.

Her career as a part-time hooker had started off innocently. She'd been out on a pub crawl with some friends when a foreign-looking stranger started talking to her. She had no clear recollection of how the conversation had gone - he didn't speak very good English, the pub was noisy and she was as high as a kite, what with the booze and speed she'd taken earlier - but they ended up going back to his place and screwing the night away. He gave her a hundred pounds.

"It's a bit more than we agreed, but it was worth it," he said, which was a complete surprise to Claudine because she wasn't aware they had agreed that she was doing it for money, let alone how much. As she walked home, she thought how easy it had been, how straightforward, just like selling potatoes, and she wondered why she'd let herself be screwed by so many men in the past - usually with no pleasure on her part - without asking them for money too.

She'd never thought of taking it up full time. Even though it would pay a damn sight more than she earned as a receptionist, she would then have to admit to herself that she was a prostitute and she was bound to get a police record eventually, which made her feel uneasy. Although not of particularly angelic stock, nobody in her family had a police record, and she didn't want to be the first if she could avoid it. She was also frightened by the pimps who latched onto any girl they knew was working the streets, took their money, and made their lives a misery.

She was about to give up and go home when a man came and sat beside her without her noticing. When she turned round to see him there, she jumped.

"Christ! Where did you come from?"

"Islington", he said.

"No. I mean, Jesus. You just appeared."

"Sorry. Did I give you a fright? Do you mind if I sit here?"

"Please yourself."

He was middle-aged, 40 or 50. She wasn't that good with ages. Normal. Didn't look like a nutter. She could tell from the way he was looking at her they were on the same wavelength, so as long as they could get the terms right, she would at least make some money out of what had turned into a disappointing evening.

"Are you here with anyone?" he said.

"No, I'm here on business."

"And what business is that?"

"Guess."

"I may be in the same line of business."

"Well, I hope you don't expect me to pay you," she said.

He laughed. "What do you charge in your line of business?"

"Depends what I'm selling."

"Well, what would you charge for an oral examination, say?"

"Hundred."

"That's a lot."

"I'm worth a lot."

"One mouth is pretty much like another."

"Then go find another mouth."

"How about 40?"

"Wanker."

"Yes, but not tonight, I hope. How about 50?"

"Sixty."

"Done."

She sipped her drink, watching him out of the corner of her eye. The man was looking around the bar, his eyes avoiding Claudine's.

"Isn't that your wife just come in?" she said.

"What?" he said, spinning around to face the door, and then emitting a peel of laughter. "Very funny. Shall we go then?"

"Nah, let's do it here. Get your cock out and lay it on the table. But I don't suppose it'll lay down now, will it, it's probably staring at the ceiling with its mouth watering by now"

He laughed again, but his eyes were troubled, or expectant, or guilty. Men, thought Claudine, what pathetic bastards they are. She got up, knowing he would follow like a drooling dog following a juicy bone. Outside he caught her up. He was bigger than he'd seemed at first. She hoped he was clean.

"Where are we going?" he asked. "I know somewhere we can ..."

"It's alright," she said "There's a place round the corner we won't be disturbed." And anyway, she thought, to judge by the state of you, this isn't going to take long. She made for a dark lane. She'd used it and been used in it before, and it would serve the purpose again. Claudine stopped.

"Okay darlin', let's get on with it," she said. "Give us the money first."

He counted three 20-pound notes into her hand. She stuffed them into her handbag then dropped to her knees.

"Wait a minute," the man said.

"What for?"

He stepped behind her.

"Do you think I'm going to kneel down here waiting ...?"

"Oh, my God!" he said.

Claudine assumed her services were no longer necessary, and the man had beaten his personal best for premature ejaculation. But when she turned round, she saw he was no longer interested in her, or sex, but was rummaging through a pile of rubbish.

"What the fuck are you up to?" she said, getting to her feet.

"Look!" he said, pointing into the pile.

"I don't know what you're bleeding well playing at, but ..." She stopped, looked, and a few seconds later was spewing the results of her evening's drinking onto her shoes.

MURDER MAYHEM

It was five weeks since the last killing, almost midnight, a Saturday. Weller was there before him.

"Have you called Devons?" Spencer asked. "She said she wanted to be at the scene next time."

"No, should I?"

"No, leave it to me; she'll bloody well go into orbit, no need for you to get the bollocking."

"Don't tell me," she said, answering Spencer's call on the second ring.

"Afraid so. An alley off Windle Street, near a pub. We haven't had a good look because the team isn't here yet, nor's the pathologist. But it's definitely a young woman, definitely mutilated, and to judge from the surroundings she was probably working."

"Damn it!" said Devons. "Who found the body?"

"A couple with similar intent. By the state of the body it looks like she's been here for some time."

He wished he could tell her some good news in the shape of a tangible lead. He wondered why he needed to impress her. She reminded him of one female teacher when he was an infant, and towards whom he bore strange and unsettling feelings. How little has changed in over 40 years, he thought.

Devons swore, which in the past would have been relatively unusual for her, but it was becoming habitual as the string of murders grew and the number of leads didn't.

After she'd hung up, Spencer stood staring at the silent phone as if it was his fault and he was about to be punished. Guilt by association, he thought. She knows I didn't do it, but I'm a man, so I'm that much closer to the almost certainly male creature who did do it than she is. He found it curious and unsettling that Devons made him think in this guilty way, but then he'd never worked for a woman before, let alone on a murder case with a strong sexual component. He wandered around for a while, chatted about football and other trivia to some of the other officers, and eventually returned to the body.

"Where are the two young lovers who found her?" asked Weller.

"Roscoe's taken them to the shop to get statements. But we won't get anything useful out of them."

Spencer noticed the vomit on the ground. "What's all this? Has Roscoe been up to his tricks again?"

At the first post mortem he had attended, just as Best was removing the stomach from the deceased, Detective Constable Roscoe had famously spewed up the vibrantly tomato-colored contents of his intestines over Dr. Best, his assistant, the corpse, and everything else within a six foot radius of his gushing mouth. Dr. Best, far from sanguine at the time, later recovered his bizarre sense of humor to say he was considering submitting a paper to The Lancet because he thought Roscoe's exploding guts were worthy of note, given the scattering power they had achieved, and which, Best thought, might qualify for a new world record.

"His and hers," said Weller, pointing to what were two noticeably distinct piles of sick; one of them, strangely, flecked with black streaks. "The girl threw up when she saw the corpse, and the bloke threw up when he saw the girl throw up. Chain reaction."

"More like domino effect, given the color. I've never seen black vomit before."

"She must have had squid for dinner."

"Or maybe she'd just given a Jamaican a blow job." They both laughed.

"And sucked a bit too hard." They laughed again.

"I'm glad you're managing to amuse yourselves," said Devons, who had arrived unnoticed.

"Gallows humor," said Spencer.

"You need a killer before you can build a gallows, and it would be bloody unrealistic to expect to see one of those anytime soon," she said, looking from one man to the other, with no trace of humor in her face or in her voice. "Do we know who she is?"

"She's carrying a donor card in the name of Sarah Benning; we're checking it now," said Weller.

"A donor card? Would a prostitute carry a donor card?" she said.

"She could carry one," said Spencer, "but the organ recipient might be a bit nervous if they found out about her profession."

"Where's the pathologist?"

"He's right behind you, Ma'am," said Weller, as Dr. Mortensen walked towards them. Mortensen was the opposite in manner to Best. Whereas the former was usually too forthcoming with his opinions, Mortensen was so cautious as to be practically obstructive. Weller and Spencer wandered towards the road as Devons stayed with the pathologist beside the body.

"He'll take an hour fiddling about and then tell us it's a dead female and we're to wait for his report if we want to know more," said Weller.

"He won't get away with that tonight, not with Devons breathing down his neck. She'll have him slicing up the body here and now if he doesn't give her something to be getting on with. Either that or she'll start on the autopsy herself with her nail scissors."

Two uniformed constables were standing at the point where the lane met Windle Street, keeping a growing band of gawkers at bay. Spencer's heart sank when he saw a TV news van arrive.

"Bugger! Devons will love this!" said Spencer, thinking back to a week after the last murder, when local residents had demonstrated in the street outside the police headquarters to draw attention to the lack of progress in the investigation. As Devons pushed her way through the crowd, she was caught by a camera team and a journalist who wanted to know if she would care to enlarge upon the "no comments" she was scattering amongst the protesters. She paused, recognizing that she had to say something unless she wanted to come across as the cold, heartless career cop the media were starting to label her. Most of what she said was sensible and controlled, but she lost her cool at the end of the interview and, as a friend of one of the deceased pushed her in the back and the reporter shoved his microphone further up her nose, she snapped "I can assure you we are going to catch this killer before he can strike again."

For Devons, normally so politically savvy and unflappable, it had been a serious blunder to promise the unpromisable. Rumor had it she'd offered her resignation as a consequence, which was unlikely, but it was a story that offered solace and comfort to her enemies and detractors.

Now her claim had proved as baseless as it had appeared when she made it, and the journalist heading her way would soon be in a position to inform London of the fact.

Spencer recognized the reporter from the last time. Devla O'Caroll was an attractive, Irish woman, mid-20s, with red hair, grey eyes, and a compact body, whose manner would usually begin pleasantly enough, but would soon turn nasty if she thought she was getting nowhere. And she tended to think she wasn't getting anywhere  if she wasn't getting the answers she wanted, regardless of whether her idea of the truth had any relation to the real thing. Spencer had dealt with her before and had no doubt her attitude was generally anti-police. It would be interesting to see how Devons handled her this time.

"Good evening. Detective Sergeant Spender isn't it?"

"Detective Inspector Spencer and you're Deirdra O'Coral, if my memory serves me right," he replied, matching the slight.

"Something like that. The London News. I understand there's been another killing."

"We've found a body."

"What can you tell me about it?"

"Very little at the moment."

"A young woman?"

"Yes." Spencer knew these people scanned the police frequencies all the time, and he imagined them jumping for journalistic joy when they heard the report of the body's discovery humming into their headsets.

"Have you identified the victim?"

"We're looking into that now."

"Is that a 'no'?"

"We found identification but we have to check it, we wouldn't want to jump to conclusions, would we?"

"Quite. I take it you don't have the perpetrator in custody." Not a question, and stated in staccato, or perhaps Spencer was just being over-sensitive. The woman actually had a pleasant, mellifluous way of talking, with her warm Irish brogue pushing its way to the surface every now and again, but he wasn't going to be fooled into dropping his guard by a charming accent.

"No, we don't have anyone in custody."

"Nor suspects." Again, not a question.

"No, but we've just got here."

"When did it happen?"

"The pathologist only arrived a few minutes ago - we don't know yet."

"You must have some idea."

"Yes, we do, but we don't broadcast ideas."

"Unlike the press?" she said, raising her eyebrows.

"That's for you to say."

"Can you tell me anything at all about the victim - color, age, features, state of the body, scratch marks?"

"Not yet."

"Can I ask you to speculate on whether this is another one down to the person responsible for the recent killings?"

"You can ask, but I won't. Come on Devla, be reasonable. We'll know more in an hour. You don't need this until the breakfast news, and we'll give you as much as you want by then."

"I doubt that."

So do I, thought Spencer.

"Is that Chief Superintendent Devons by the body?"

"Yes."

The reporter had been looking over Spencer's shoulder while she fired questions at him, and he knew she saw him as nothing more than a barrier to the person she really wanted to be interviewing.

"Will she give me a statement?"

"I don't know if she'll give you a statement, but she may talk to you. Wait here, please."

Spencer walked down the lane to Devons, musing that there had been no move to record anything of what he'd said. Devons looked extremely pissed off when Spencer told her about the journalist. She sighed and her shoulders sank, then she pulled herself up to her 5' 10" height as she took a deep breath and set her jaw in a firm line.

"How do I look?" she asked.

"Intimidating," he said, without thinking, surprised she should have asked his opinion on a relatively personal matter, and also surprised he'd given it.

"Good," she said, and strode off to meet the reporter.

The lights came on as she approached the camera crew. Spencer moved closer to hear what was being said.

"Chief Superintendent, shortly after the last murder you committed to finding the killer before he would have the opportunity to strike again. It now seems likely he has struck again. What would you like to say to the people of East London regarding the failure of the police force to resolve this case as you promised you would?"

Devons didn't miss a beat. She was in with her response straight away, almost too quickly, as if she'd been prepared for this and was giving a contrived answer.

"My statement shortly after the death of Maria DeCinzo was

an expression of the strongest possible desire to catch the killer, and a reasonable expectation based on the tremendous work and dedication my team is putting into the case. We shall be continuing our strenuous efforts to rid the streets of this menace."

"What do you have to say to the local prostitutes, who claim the police aren't taking the investigation seriously because of who the victims are?"

"It's completely untrue. There is no distinction being made between this case and any other murder case."

"And what about the allegations the killer may be a serving member of the police force?"

"I've heard that rumor and I don't believe it's worth commenting on."

"But I'm sure the public would like you to comment on it, regardless of what you believe, Chief Superintendent."

"I think the claim is without foundation, that it is malicious, and that it has the potential to hinder the investigation."

"But you can't rule it out?"

"We're ruling nothing out, but that particular line of enquiry seems to have no merit. Now, if you'll excuse me, I have to get back to work."

When Devons rejoined Spencer, he could almost see smoke coming out of her ears.

"That bitch! Trust her to focus on that bloody silly story. She's not happy with making us look incompetent, now she wants us to appear corrupt as well."

By the next afternoon, the identity of the victim had been confirmed as the person registered on the donor card, Sarah Benning. But none of her organs would have been of any use even if the police had been able to release them because she had been dead for between 24 and 26 hours by the time the body was discovered.

Like the first killing, the victim had been stabbed to death and the carved circles and crosses were similar to those inflicted on all the bodies, so nobody mentioned the possibility of it not being the work of the same person, even though there was still no physical evidence linking the killings.

The self-styled 'boyfriend' of the deceased, who reported her disappearance several hours before the body was discovered, denied she was working as a prostitute or that he was involved in her business.

"She's got a degree," he had yelled into Weller's impassive face. "Her father's a fucking church warden. I'm a member of the bloody Conservative Party!"

However, the facts that she had prior convictions for soliciting, that the local Streetwalkers Support Group sprang immediately into action, and that her boyfriend was a convicted drug dealer and pimp, detracted from his fiercely articulated indignation.

§

The story alleging the murderer may have been a serving policeman had been started by a local paper after a friend of the first victim reported the deceased had been seen talking to a uniformed officer outside a nightclub shortly before her death. It gathered pace when witnesses came forward - to the paper initially, not the police - saying the third victim had been seen drinking with a man dressed like an off-duty police officer - that is, wearing a blue shirt, black trousers and boots - just hours before her body was discovered. At that point the national press took it up, and television and radio immediately jumped on it.

Devons' interview with the fire-breathing Devla O'Caroll fanned the flames again, not by what she'd said, but by the look on her face as she'd said it. Spencer, who'd been standing off to one side of her when she gave the interview, didn't get a chance to see the full-frontal version until he caught the breakfast news on the police station's cafeteria TV a few hours later.

"Hillary Clinton on steroids finds Saddam Hussein sodomizing her daughter while being cheered on by Sara Palin and Osama Bin Laden," was how Roscoe described Devons' expression. The disgust and outrage was plain to see, and subverted the reasonable and evenly delivered words that accompanied her manic gaze.

"Now," she was telling Spencer over a snack meal in her office late in the evening, "we've got to waste valuable resources proving there's nothing in this cock and bull story." She stood up halfway through her sandwich and stalked around the office.

"I've a good mind to get those so called "witnesses" in here and have them study mug shots of every officer in the Met. Let's see how they feel about spreading malicious dirt after they've been through a few thousand photographs of well-scrubbed, fresh-faced constables. This is London, for Christ's sake, not New Orleans!"

"If they look at enough photographs they're bound to convince themselves somebody's face fits, then we'll be putting some poor sod under unwarranted suspicion," said Spencer, trying to offer the voice of reason.

"But how else are we going to kill this inane story? And if you say 'by catching the killer', don't expect to get recommended for promotion any time soon."

"It shouldn't be hard to come up with a list of men on patrol in the vicinity of the club the night of the killing. Once we've eliminated them we'll be able to say we've looked into it, but until then we'll just be accused of doing nothing."

"And what if they pick out a face?" she said.

"Then we mix that face with a few dozen other random faces, and show them to the people who say they saw the off-duty copper in the pub."

"And what if they pick the same face?"

"Then we've either got a problem ... or a killer."

Devons eyes flashed and she made as if to say something, but then seemed to steady herself and went on calmly, but with barely concealed derision in her voice.

"Spencer, are you telling me you think there's something in this load of crap?"

"No, not really, but I've been around long enough to rule nothing out. Remember what this division was like two years ago. Remember why you were sent in here in the first place. Her Majesty's Metropolitan Police Force has had uniform men and detectives involved in bribery, blackmail, grievous bodily harm, perjury, assault with a deadly weapon, theft, intimidation, sexual assault and sexual harassment. To me that means worse is possible, and it also means the public will think worse is going on unless we comprehensively prove otherwise. Before you cleaned things up, we almost had to begin by *excluding* officers from some investigations before we started *including* known felons on the suspect list."

"I didn't expect to hear that from you," said Devons.

"I would never have had the right to say it when I joined the force, but you've got to face the fact that not only do some people find being a cop gives them some tasty opportunities, but it actually attracts criminals to join in the first place, knowing their sole intention is to get their feet under the table so they can start nicking the family silver."

"I know some of our PCs aren't exactly going to give Albert Einstein a run for his money, but I can't imagine any of them would be so stupid to chat up his victim wearing an anorak over his uniform," said Devons.

"Nor can I, and this killer is nothing if not careful, which means it should be easy to rule out police involvement and get back to finding who's really doing it."

"On which subject," she said, making fists of her hands and shaking them in unison, "how exactly are we going to find out who is really doing it?"

"Like I keep saying, unless he makes a mistake or we get lucky or somebody shops him, we're not going to find out. There have been serial killers around the world who kill dozens before they get caught, and some never get caught. There's no such thing as a stupid serial killer. The one-off killers, the emotional killers, they're the stupid ones, the impetuous ones. Serial killers spend their whole lives planning what they're going to do and fantasizing about what they've done. Fooling the police is part of the stimulation. We're as much a target of this as the hookers once the initial thrill has started to wear off."

Devons stood looking at him, nodding her head slowly. She sat down and picked up her sandwich, but put it down again without taking a bite.

"Why do you do this job, Spence?"

Spencer put down his own sandwich and took a deep swig of coffee. At this precise moment he would have given a week's pay to have a cigarette clamped between his fingers that he could draw upon, before blowing out wisps of the smoke towards the ceiling as he ruminated on the question.

"To start with I loved it. Then I needed it, like a drug or an intravenous drip. Then it needed me, like some animals need parasites. Then it just became part of my life, like background music you only notice when it's not playing. I don't need it anymore, and I'm not sure I'll miss it that much when I retire, but it's always going to be a part of me, whether I'm doing it or just remembering it. What about you?"

Unlike Spencer, Devons didn't need to collect her thoughts – it was as if they were always on the tip of her tongue.

"Because I like being in control, because I'm a perfectionist, because I like getting filth off the streets, and because I like proving that my sex is as good, if not better, than the other."

And that, thought Spencer, would also perfectly describe the mentality of the killer.

Ire Unleashed

Although he seemed to be intent on turning into some sort of parent-hating monster and societal misfit, I was most upset by the distance that had grown between myself and Leo. When he was a young child we got on well together and I was convinced he was possessed of the same love for knowledge and understanding as I.

My response to his inquisitiveness - so different to that of my own parents - was to nurture his curiosity and encourage him in it. We used to spend hours leafing through books and working on the computer and I felt not only that he and I were establishing a firm bond, but that we actually had some sort of ability to communicate without words. He was intelligent and particularly adept with the computer, so adept I sometimes wondered how long I would be able to stay his teacher and not turn into his student.

I supposed that our genetic material being so similar, our brains must have a similar structure, and given I was doing much to teach him how to think, it seemed perfectly feasible that we would develop the art of being able to read one another's minds, albeit to a limited extent. To the amusement of the rest of the family, by the time he was 10 we were often able to finish each other's sentences, and when the family played a silly game based on extrasensory perception we invented one Christmas, the only two people able to achieve any significant degree of "thought transference" were Leo and I.

But by the time he was 13 things were very different. I clearly and painfully remember the first time Leo told me he didn't want me to help him with a problem he was having with his homework. Soon after this, one evening after I pointed out something he was doing incorrectly, he asked me to leave him alone when he was working on the computer. When, at the age of 14, he told me to "Fuck off!" with a vehemence that left me completely speechless for minutes afterwards, I saw the ties that had once existed between us unravel before my eyes.

I have no idea what caused this change of attitude. It wasn't merely as if a bond had been broken, leaving a cold but otherwise unexceptional relationship in its place, but also as if an intractable barrier had been erected between us that I would never be allowed to cross. It was done in such a way as to imply that the fault was all mine and that I was stupid for not seeing where I had been in error.

When I once timidly asked Leo why he didn't want me to work with him anymore, he simply looked at me, sneering, as if it wasn't worth explaining a reason I should already be aware of, then he shook his head and walked away.

Cynthia was unable to cast any light on the matter, and I even resorted to asking Morag, thinking Leo might share his innermost thoughts and concerns with his siblings.

"You don't think he'd tell me anything, do you?" she'd said.

"He'll get over it," Cynthia suggested. "Boys need to distance themselves from their fathers in order to establish their own personalities. He'll come around when he knows who he is."

But if this were correct, finding out who he is has turned out to be a tempestuous and never-ending search. By the time he was 15 and his behavior had gone beyond the merely tiresome and was increasingly repugnant, I'd given up expecting him to ameliorate his attitude, and I was looking forward to when he would leave the rest of us in peace.

"I just wonder if I've done something," I said to Cynthia once, when I was still thinking that I would like to repair the rift.

"Of course not," she said, but then added, troublingly, "have you?"

I couldn't think of anything that would explain what was happening, but I was bothered and a little irritated by the fact that Cynthia needed to ask.

But when my own problems became so much worse, concerns about my interactions with Leo moved into the background.

§

I was at work, studying a printout and trying to track down a bug that for months had been plaguing the department's System

Resource Accounting software, and to which the people responsible for that software had been unable to find a fix. I knew they didn't like handing these bugs over to me, as they saw it as an admission of defeat, and to them it was humiliating that someone with no specific expertise on a subject that they lived and breathed every day might be able to repair it.

I stared at pages and pages of hexadecimal characters for over an hour. The "post mortem dump", which the computer spews out showing what led to its unwelcome and premature decease that I was inspecting was over one hundred pages long, and would probably be, to most people, a useless and thoroughly intimidating document. But whenever I see a stack of paper that records the demise of a computer program, I react in the manner of the true techno-nerd, and I begin to experience a pleasure that is often elevated to a tangible excitement.

Like an Egyptologist deciphering hieroglyphics which most people would find meaningless, hoping to gain insight into another world, I am seeking insight into the world of the computer, and given it is an environment predicated on pure and inviolable logic, I, unlike the Egyptologist, who has humanity to deal with, can be sure I will come up with a perfect and rational explanation to an event in the world I am investigating.

I was homing in on the problem, filling the pages with my own explanatory jottings, when I felt a slight dizzying sensation, which I first put down to my rapid scanning of column after column of densely printed memory locations. But when a clear and recognizable image filled my vision, I knew it was more than just an optical illusion, and not just a passing thought that would quickly move out of the way and let me get on with my job. What I didn't know was how it would fill and dominate my life, in one way or another, for the foreseeable future.

Like the dream I had experienced recently, the vision was extremely vivid - the colors were unnaturally bright, and the edges of everything much more clearly defined than in life itself.

I was being led through a sea of people, all of whom were looking in one direction, and although I craned my head, I was unable to see what they were looking at. They were all dressed like peasants from the Middle Ages, but their clothes weren't dirty or shabby, simply primitive. It was as though they were extras in a film - a Robin Hood film from the forties perhaps - because what they were wearing was neat and clean and not as you would expect of real clothes worn by real people from that era.

They were standing on their toes to get a better view of something, and some had lifted children onto their shoulders. We didn't seem to be in the open, but rather in some sort of enormous building, possibly an aircraft hangar, the walls and roof of which were so far away that I couldn't see them but somehow sensed they were there.

Then one of the spectators turned and spotted me. He looked frightened at first, but then shouted angrily, pointing in my direction, and as faces turned towards me, I saw in all of them a mixture of repugnance, hostility and fear. They began yelling at me, and it was then I realized I couldn't move my hands, which seemed to be bound behind me, and that two burly escorts, one to each arm, were pushing me through the crowd, which was now exclusively looking in my direction.

My heart was racing, my mouth was as dry as sandpaper, and there was more and more noise from the crowd. The spectators were engulfing me and my two escorts, and although nobody else touched me, I could feel their anger and was frightened by the certain knowledge that for some reason these people hated me.

Then the crowd, which was growing ever denser, suddenly parted and I found myself standing in an open area. There wasn't anything I could see holding them back, but the spectators pushed no further forward, seeming to be restrained by an invisible but impenetrable barrier.

My escorts stopped and hauled me round to face the crowd. Everyone seemed to be shouting and shaking their fists at me, their hatred completely without constraint. One of my escorts laughed, and I turned to see his face - it was Leo, wearing the familiar contemptuous expression he saved for his mother and me. He and his colleague yanked me back round, almost knocking me off my feet, and I was confronted by a large wooden structure.

It took me a few moments to understand what I was looking at. The wood was new; I could smell it and discern the beautiful pattern of the grain. It had that pleasing odor of freshly worked wood, a smell I've always found comforting, but didn't in these circumstances. There were wood shavings on the ground, and screws, nails, tools and pots of glue scattered about, as though the construction was still under way or just recently finished. I was about to speak, to ask Leo or the other man what it was, when I looked up and saw the gallows, with an empty noose hanging in the air.

I felt my knees buckle, but my escorts were dragging me towards a stairway leading up to the platform. I tried to kick out and pull back, but like a nightmare in which fear can't be translated into a physical reaction and escape, it didn't achieve anything and I was soon being held upright by my captors at the top of the structure. The noise from the crowd was deafening and seemed to penetrate my whole body and make it shake even more than it was already shaking from fear alone. They were shouting "Go on! Do it! Do it!"

The noose was in front of me, the rope neatly coiled round and round on itself above the dangling loop. I desperately searched for the word to describe the tidy knot, as if defining it would put me in control.

"It's called the collar," said Leo, laughing, interpreting my thoughts and ridiculing me. Then, not having noticed them before, I saw my wife and two daughters standing a few yards away. They were dressed in long black cloaks trailing to the ground behind them. Their heads were hooded and bowed, and I thought they were crying, but then they looked up and I saw that my daughters were laughing, laughing so much that tears were rolling down their cheeks. Charlotte's cloak fell open to reveal large breasts, barely concealed by a low cut blouse, and Morag opened her mouth wide to expose sharp and bloody teeth.

Cynthia was just looking at me blankly, as though her eyes weren't really focused on me, and she was shaking her head. She seemed to look in Leo's direction and open her eyes wide, as if expecting him to say something, but then I was shoved firmly in the back and made to move forwards.

I was dragged towards the noose. My face was a few inches away from it, and the roar of the crowd crescendoed. The rope reminded me of when I'd learned to tie knots as a boy scout – if only I could have been back there again. I looked around, and everywhere there were faces, all of them hostile, all of them egging me on to put my head through the loop.

I opened my mouth to yell, to say there was a mistake, there was no reason for me to be here, but my words were trapped at the back of my throat, and no matter how I strained I couldn't get them out. I felt the veins pumping in my neck as I struggled to be heard. But when Leo spoke I heard him so clearly it could have been me speaking.

"They don't want to hear you," he said, "they just want you ..." but he left the final word unspoken, and laughed. I mouthed the word for him, "Dead?" which made him laugh even more.

I felt the noose on my shoulders, then tightening around my neck, then digging into my flesh. An indescribable, giddying fear enveloped me. I looked down at the trap door beneath my feet, which I noticed were encased in shiny black boots. There was a crash, a whooshing noise, and I felt myself falling, but instead of seeing space pass before me, I saw numbers, and I realized I was scanning down a column of memory locations on the printout of post mortem dump.

I blinked. I couldn't believe I was in my office, half way through hunting for a software bug. The vision had been so vivid that reality was more bewildering than what I had just imagined. I was bathed in sweat. I had no idea what time it was or even what day it was. I had never, ever, been more terrified, not even on the occasion when Leo had told us he'd put a lethal dose of cyanide in the food we'd just eaten. I stumbled to the toilet. I thought I wanted to be sick, but when I got there I didn't know what to do, so I just slumped on the wash basin, my dilated pupils staring at my sweat-beaded face in the mirror, a face that looked so ashen it was barely recognizable to me.

I went back to my office, but I couldn't stay there. Just the sight of the printout on my desk made me feel nauseous. I made an excuse about feeling ill - not that it was an excuse, I'd seldom felt more unwell - and went home.

I don't know what happened during the next few hours. I think I was aware of people talking to me and of figures coming and going, but the first clear memory I have is of Cynthia's face gazing into mine from only inches away, close enough for her features to appear distorted. When I first saw her, I was immediately and terrifyingly reminded of her as she had appeared on the scaffold.

I don't remember seeing anything of Leo, which was just as well, because I assume the lack of sympathy he showed towards me in the vision was much the same as he would exhibit in person.

I felt that my programming had broken down, just as the computer's had. Both me and the computer program were doing something crazy and running wild. But where the computer had shut the errant program and left a trail to diagnose the fault, my mind was out of control, with no greater power to correct it and no clue as to what was wrong.

□□□

Mind of a Killer

"What, you mean Chingford as in Chingford, Essex?"

"Yeah. He phoned about 20 minutes ago. He asked for you, but they put him through to me," said Roscoe. "It was a D.I. Cheeseman. He wondered if he should speak to Devons, but I managed to talk him out of that."

"Good, we don't want to get her all steamed up for no reason. I'm coming in. I should be there in an hour, probably less. Call Best. See if he's free this afternoon, or Mortensen if Best can't make it. I'd like one of them to attend the post mortem, preferably Best. I'll call Devons, when I'm sure she needs to know about it."

He hung up and allowed himself the bitter-sweet luxury of a few moments of sitting staring into space, knowing it was all the relaxation he was likely to get for a while.

The day had looked so attractive in prospect. His plan to spend time in the garden was ruined, and he'd also have to disappoint his wife by telling her their planned and overdue night out wasn't going to happen. If what Roscoe had told him was accurate, then the madness was about to begin all over again. Late nights, early mornings, snatched food, too much rancid coffee, poor sleep, a stranger to his own home, and more pressure, a lot more pressure.

The body found in Chingford at first sight seemed to bear a marked resemblance to the corpses found in East London. Strangled, mutilated with a knife, no obvious clues and no suspects, obvious or otherwise. There was no solid reason to link the cases, but Chingford wasn't very far away, and even if logic didn't tie the crimes together, the media would.

§

"They say they've got nothing at all?" Devons asked as Best was driving them to Chingford in his elderly but immaculately maintained Daimler.

"Not a thing," said Spencer. "The woman was a known prostitute, but they thought she'd either given up or was doing business somewhere else. They used to run across her all the time, but nobody had seen her on the streets for over a year. It sounds similar to our third and fourth girls - strangled from behind and comprehensively mutilated."

"Noughts and crosses?"

"Probably. There's a lot of mutilation, but they say they can still make out the more organized wounds."

"Shit! Chingford. Why bloody Chingford."

It wasn't a question, and if it had been, there was no answer to it. Devons was just finding another way to express her frustration, as if the town of Chingford could be blamed for adding to her problems.

When they arrived at Chingford police station, Chief Constable Bennet - a self-proclaimed 'old friend' who seemed to have a soft spot for Devons, to judge from an expression that fitted somewhere between fatherly pride and adolescent lust - was there to greet them, and with an arm draped over her shoulders he took her off to talk about the handling of the case and the media.

Spencer turned to face D.I. Cheeseman.

"So, you're dumping one of your problems on us, are you?" said Cheeseman.

"Well, we've not managed to catch him, so maybe he thinks you'll be more of a challenge."

"What are Bennet and your C.S. talking about, assuming you know?"

"I don't know, specifically, but I would assume it's about how we can back you up, and how you can keep us in the picture so we can tie this one together with the other five, if they deserve to be tied together."

"Will you be giving us people?"

"I expect so, if you need them, and you'll probably be given them even if you don't," said Spencer, wondering why Cheeseman was asking questions he must know were too early to answer.

"But you won't be running the case?"

"That depends on what our bosses decide, but I wouldn't have thought so unless we get a definite connection.

"They tell me she's quite a ball-breaker."

"She knows where she's going, and she doesn't usually see people as obstacles she won't be able to get around."

"So she tramples all over them, bollocks first?"

"If she needs to."

"We get our share of sex crime. Man on woman is decreasing, male on male is increasing, adult on child is holding steady. We're as fucked up as the rest of the world. No more, no less. Do you think it's your criss-cross man?"

"Depends on what the pathologist says, and whether the mutilations are similar. Even then it could still be copycat," said Spencer.

"Well just stay out of my hair and let me do the job you lot can't seem to," said Cheeseman, turning and stalking away.

§

Devons filled them in on the way back to London later that afternoon. Weller would be seconded to Chingford starting the following day, and would be able to draft in other resources as needed, but for the time being Bennet had insisted his force run the investigation.

"I'm not staking my reputation on it," said Best, "but I bet almost anything you want, including this Daimler, that it was the same killer, even down to the pattern of the mutilations."

"We can't wait for him to make a mistake," said Devons, "God knows how many more he'll kill before we catch him, or where he'll pop up next."

"Perhaps the good constables of Essex will catch him for you, Chief Superintendent," said Best.

In the rear view mirror, Spencer could see a supercilious smile on the face of the pathologist.

"That would solve all your problems, wouldn't it now?" Best continued.

"Yes, solve my problems and end my career. They'd love to solve a case based on one killing when we couldn't catch the bastard after five. We need to get women officers out on the streets as decoy hookers."

"Can I volunteer to be involved in the auditions?" said Best.

"No thank you, even though I'm sure you've a lot of experience in that particular area of human abasement."

"Will you be training the young ladies personally, Chief Superintendent?" he went on. Devons ignored him.

"Even if they don't catch him, at least they can look out for the other hookers. It's just damage control, but it'll keep the Streetwalkers Preservation Society, or whatever the hell they call themselves, off my back."

"Who's talking to the media?" Spencer asked.

Devons looked out of the window as she replied. "Bennet is going on local television tonight. We'll feed the press the line that we've met and talked, but we're keeping an open mind for the time being. There'll be complete information sharing and we'll be providing various resources to back them up, blah-de-blah-de-blah."

She turned back to face Spencer. "They haven't had time to check out the boyfriend and so forth yet. Who knows, maybe it'll be open and shut."

"Never," said Best, "unless the boyfriend killed all the others as well."

Devons muttered something under her breath, and the rest of the journey passed in silence, apart from Best humming what sounded like an operatic aria. When they got back to the station Devons asked Spencer to come to her office.

"What did you make of Cheeseman?" she asked.

"Very antagonistic and wanting nothing to do with us."

"Bennet was very guarded about him, as though there was something he had to tell me, but wouldn't, or couldn't."

"He probably guesses Cheeseman doesn't want to work with us.

It's hardly surprising that he distrusts another force, most coppers do."

"Exactly, so why should Bennet seem particularly uneasy about it? Just keep an eye on him. I don't want anyone pulling tricks on us from the inside."

§

Driving home, glad he and his wife would be able to go on their date after all, Spencer nevertheless started to brood. He couldn't remember ever being quite so frustrated with his work as he was by this case. Nothing they did led anywhere. Each time they thought they might be onto something, they always ended up marching down a blind alley to come face to face with a brick wall with "No evidence!" scrawled upon it.

Spencer had taken a long time reviewing the first murder, in the belief it may be the key to all the others. It took place indoors, at the prostitute's home and place of business, a garishly decorated bedroom, whereas all the others had been outdoors. At first Spencer thought this might point to a different killer, but he now thought it likely the culprit went into this first crime not knowing what he was going to do next.

Perhaps he didn't intended killing at all; but he must at least have harbored some violent fantasies he wanted to play out, and he ended up going too far. Then, having killed, he decided he liked it, that it was the turn-on he'd been looking for in his disappointing life and his failed, humiliating relationships. Now he wanted to repeat the thrill, to kill again, but going to someone's place of business to do it was too risky.

Killing gave him his perverse pleasure and made him feel comfortable. His method of killing and mutilation had become his calling card, and knowing he was playing with the police and stoking the media frenzy added to his excitement. And why should he ever stop? The police weren't even close to catching him, and even if they were, had he got to and gone past the point where he could stop, even if he wanted to?

Spencer tried working through the complete drama in his imagination all the while trying to imagine the killer's thoughts and motivations: from picking up a whore; to feeling the excitement of pending sex and violence; through the supposed thrill of seeing the fear in the woman's eyes as she realized he was a maniac and she was about to be attacked; through tightening the cord around her neck, pulling on it even harder, hearing screams stifled into frantic gasps; looking at the freshly murdered body; morphing into an even grosser beast to savage it; and then methodically scratching meaningless symbols on its back.

After doing it he felt altered, as though he may have absorbed something of the other man. He wondered if it was wise for him to play these mind games, worrying about where they would lead. Some police don't start bad, but they end up that way through the company they keep, and the devious thoughts they need to have to enable them to understand and then catch their prey.

§

He thought he was making a reasonable job of relaxing, but towards the end of their meal, when his wife said "You can talk to me about the case if you like," he realized he'd fallen silent for some time.

Is it a Criss-Cross Cop?

"I wasn't really thinking about it. It's just it's on my mind such a lot that my brain seems to slip out of gear every now and again, and I find myself not so much thinking about it as feeling it."

He paused and took a sip of the claret they shared a taste for, remembering that Devons favored Burgundy. "Why do you think people do these things? Why do most of us handle our problems in ordinary ways, but others resort to extremes?" he asked.

"Perhaps he doesn't see it as a problem. I often wonder if the idea of 'criminal as victim' isn't overdone. Perhaps he's not suffered bad relationships at all, he just prefers to live out his weird fantasies."

"Do you think he could be an ordinary sort of person, with just this one peculiarity? The man on the Clapham omnibus with a dirty secret?" he asked, glad of her fresh perspective.

"I'm not a psychiatrist. I wouldn't know."

"But you see a lot of patients who go on to need psychiatric help. They come to their GP first because they don't know where else to go, or their family doesn't know where else to send them. Can people have one part of their life that goes off the rails whilst everything else stays completely normal?"

"I suppose so. It's just like any illness. One piece could go wrong while the rest stays the same, doing its job as normal. But I can't imagine one section of the brain going haywire while the moral, judgmental part of the personality just sits back happily, washes its hands of the deviant part and doesn't get involved."

"These people are like an illness, a cancer in society, and policemen treat the symptoms, not the disease," Spencer said, looking around the room as if expecting to see signs of the diseased criminal world everywhere, even in an up-market restaurant.

"A cancer cell doesn't see itself as evil, it just does what it has to do to propagate and survive. Unfortunately, the effect of what it has to do is harmful for the rest of the body."

"But the cancer cell's a parasite. This killer probably sees himself in a virtuous light."

"Possibly. But it could also be that prostitutes turn him on, or even that he thinks they're not real people, just sexual fantasy figures he can play around with as he likes."

"Which is what they are for a lot of men, hence the success of the profession through the ages," said Spencer.

"Exactly. They promote themselves as something unreal, idyllic, sex without strings, without obligations, without consequences. The killer extrapolates beyond that to believe they're make-believe, just a figment of his imagination that he can dispose of as he wishes, and that murdering them has no moral consequences either. Still no evidence?" His wife asked.

"Not a thing. I pity the first suspect we pick up."

"Why?"

"Because there's no evidence. Whoever we arrest will have no way of proving they didn't do it, unless they have a cast-iron alibi. We could take any individual off the street – a priest, a copper, a eunuch - and tell him to prove it wasn't him, and he wouldn't be able to do it, because there's no evidence to show it was anybody else. As things stand, it could be our waiter over there, it could be me, you, anyone. The whole world is suspect. You know, I've even thought of confessing to it myself."

His wife raised her eyebrows, but said nothing through the amused but slightly artificial smile that was starting to spread over her face.

"I'm slightly serious. If I confessed, nobody could prove it wasn't me, and I sometimes think society is just looking for a fall-guy it can pillory and then move on to the next bit of titillation. And wouldn't it be wonderful for the scandal sheets and the late night talk shows to have a senior policeman, boringly respectable in every regard, admit to something so squalid? I'm sure half the nation would feel it had confirmed rather than shaken their beliefs. Cop as criminal, criminal as cop. This could be my only chance to be famous, albeit fraudulently."

"What happened to those claims the killer might be a policeman?"

"We checked them out, and we made a big show of doing it. None of the people who said they'd seen an officer talking to a victim were reliable. When we gave them the opportunity to come and look at photographs they mostly cried off, except for two, and the best we got from them was 'It wasn't him but he looked a bit like that, maybe'. Complete waste of time, but politically adroit."

"What do you do now?"

"Fritter some resources away on more pointless searches, try to look busy, and wait, and wait, and hurry up and wait some more."

"Until he kills again."

"Yes, and he will. I'm sure of it. There's no reason for him to stop. He's just getting into his stride. He's got his technique refined, and if this Chingford thing tallies it means now he's started to move about, so we can't even focus on one area. The next one will probably be somewhere different again. He's full of himself. He knows what he's doing, he knows he likes doing it, and he knows we haven't got any idea who he is. He feels as though he's in control, of his victims and of us; and that probably turns him on as much as the killing."

Spencer stopped. He'd said enough. He might just as well have been in Devons' office eating a sandwich and drinking a cup of coffee, rather than relaxing over an expensive meal and a fine wine.

"I'm sorry," he said. "We get so little time together, and when we do I'm pre-occupied. I've never looked forward to retirement as much as I have over the past few months. The hopelessness of this case is like the hopelessness of police work in general - lock one up and wait for another one to commit a crime. Then let the first one out and wait for him to offend again. No healing, just more bloody problems to bandage up and push out of sight, hoping the blood doesn't seep through the dressing and drip on the floor."

"Not unlike being a doctor, in some cases."

"But at least you get some complete cures. I can't say we get a lot."

"Life is a terminal disease. Every doctor fails in the end."

"And every policeman fails from the beginning."

"Let's have some brandy," she said

"Let's have lots," he replied, anticipating the peace he would feel when the alcohol knocked his mind into oblivion. Until tomorrow.

Behind the Facade

When Cynthia's features sharpened, I was jolted out of my shock. As I described to her the scene which had drilled into my being - the gallows, the family's presence, Leo's malice, and the force of the world's hatred, I began to see it in a different light. It was just a dream. I told her I'd be fine after a good night's sleep, so I took two of her sleeping pills with a large glass of brandy and was rendered comatose until the next morning.

When I awoke I felt completely recovered and intended going to work. But as soon as I imagined being in my office I began to feel adrift, unable to separate what had happened from what I had imagined when I was last there. I shut my eyes, but rather than shut out the world, I felt myself being pulled into a dark and dank alleyway.

Seeing me sweating and shaking, Cynthia urged me to go to the doctor, but I didn't know what on earth medical science could do for me. Until then, my only dealings with doctors had been in relation to physical ailments, and the thought of trying to explain what I'd been through yesterday and why it had terrified me so dramatically just seemed like too big a task to handle. But then I looked across at Charlotte, and as I saw her staring at me, shrinking back into her chair, I was convinced I had to do something, if only to demonstrate to my daughter that her father had regained his sanity by having his illness categorized and a treatment dispensed. It was ironic to sense I was arousing fear in one of my children, when in recent times they had held the monopoly on frightening me.

I went to open the door to begin my journey to the surgery, but as soon as my hand touched the handle, the vision of Leo pushing me towards the gallows re-appeared.

"I can't go", I said, releasing the handle and retreating while watching the door and willing it to keep the horrors at bay. I turned to see Cynthia coming towards me, her arms spread out. I thought she was barring me from making any further move back into the house.

"Will you come with me? Just to the end of the road," I said. "I'm sure I'll be alright after a while. Sorry." But by the end of the road I was shaking so badly I could barely place one foot in front of the other, and she had to practically drag me all the way to the surgery.

When we had been waiting for over half an hour I felt embarrassed about taking up Cynthia's time. I told her to go, convinced I could handle things on my own from then on. But Cynthia wasn't so sure, and something about my behavior must have told her I couldn't be left alone. She was right, because a few minutes after this I burst spontaneously into tears and she had to take me outside so we could walk around for a while and spare the other patients the embarrassing spectacle I was making of myself.

§

Dr. Spencer was patient and sympathetic as I told her everything I could remember. When she asked me if anything similar to yesterday's experience had happened before, I told her about the dream in which everyone had seemed to distrust me. At first I was lucid and spoke easily, but the more I went on the less I was able to say, and before long I was stumbling over words and eventually I couldn't speak coherently at all.

She gave me a glass of water to wet my dry mouth, but I still couldn't coax myself into talking with any fluency. I started weeping again, silently, out of frustration of not being able to make myself understood, and out of fear of what was happening to me. For one who likes to be the master of himself and his surroundings, this feeling was completely abhorrent as well as terrifying and humiliating. I welcomed the comforting hand with which Cynthia patted my back.

"This isn't my specialty," I heard the doctor say, "so I really want your husband to see someone who has more experience in this area, and I would like to arrange that as soon as possible."

"Do you have any idea what it is, doctor?" Cynthia asked.

"I'd rather not speculate," she said, glancing towards me before returning her gaze to Cynthia. I sensed she didn't want to talk about it in my presence.

"It could be anything from a case of nervous exhaustion, which will go as soon as it came, or possibly something a little more complex than that. I'd like to call the hospital now and arrange for your husband to be seen right away."

After an interminable hour or so the receptionist came to tell us we should go to the London Hospital in Whitechapel to see a Dr. Jennings in the Psychiatric Unit. I may have been wary of mental illness before suffering from it, but now it seemed only sensible to own up to my condition and get help before it got any worse.

□□□

Trapped and Exposed

"We're putting officers on the streets posing as prostitutes," said Devons. "I'm asking for volunteers, then we'll make the selection based on suitability. They need to be able to act the part - don't say a word Roscoe - and be able to look after themselves. The local ladies have either pissed off to the West End or are surrounded by pimps for security, so our man is probably scared off. We can fix that by putting some solo women back in his field of play."

"What, exactly, are they supposed to do?" asked Weller, making his question sound reasonable, and not as full of the doubt and derision he had expressed to Spencer when talking about it earlier. "I mean, if they look convincing, they're going to attract a lot of attention."

"That's the idea."

"But most of that intention is going to be ordinary punters. How will they know the bloke is the killer? They won't be able to do that until, well, until ..."

"Until they've got his cock in their mouth?" she said. They all laughed, but Spencer wondered if any of the others also felt slightly aroused by what she said.

"Well, I'm just ..." Weller began, but Devons interrupted him brusquely. She gave no impression of wanting to hear anyone's opinion.

"The decoys will be under continuous surveillance. If they have any suspicion whatsoever that the man has violent intent, they'll give a signal and the backup team will haul him in and search him. If he's clean they'll give him a two minute lecture on safe sex and the importance of family values and let him go. Our killer must be carrying a knife and probably a cord, so if we find those we could hit the jackpot."

"This may sound like a stupid question, ma'am," said Roscoe, "but why do we need to use officers at all? Why don't we just tell the streetwalkers what we're up to and let them tip us the signal?"

"Absolutely correct Roscoe. It is a bloody stupid question. How do you think the average prostitute would react to being spied on while she's doing business? And what makes you think they'd have the presence of mind to signal us when some punter is counting fivers into her palm."

"Even some of our WPCs may be tempted to take the money and shut up," Weller muttered to Spencer out of the side of his mouth.

"Bloody lunacy," said Weller when the meeting was over. "Think of the amount of time it's going to eat up? And what makes her so sure he's going to strike here again? It's just as likely to be Chingford or somewhere else."

"How are things over there?" asked Spencer. It was the first time he'd seen him face to face in the two weeks since the last murder.

"I'm finished. They've got nothing. That bastard Cheeseman thought he was going to wrap it up in no time, cocky sod, but he got absolutely nowhere, just like us. Devons called me last night and told me to be here this morning. From cock-sucker Cheeseman to cock-sucking WPCs. From one bloody waste of time to another."

§

The first week was a fiasco. To begin with, the police decoys were terribly self-conscious, and two of the volunteers - brazen and full of confidence at the early evening briefing sessions - were back in the unmarked surveillance cars shedding tears barely half-an-hour into their stints.

"I knew this wouldn't work," said Roscoe, when he, Weller and Spencer were having a pint together one evening.

"Well, I wouldn't gloat about her being wrong, if I were you," Spencer said. "She told me she would be dressing you and Weller up in drag if this didn't work."

"Yeah, right," said Weller, "and why not. May as well be fucked by a hairy pervert as fucked by Devons, which is what we'll all be if she doesn't get a result soon."

As the exercise wore on, the decoys were being solicited with an infrequency that indicated they weren't fooling anybody, and if they couldn't dupe a horny, desperate punter with a bloodstream full of alcohol, they were unlikely to fool a smart, cool-headed killer with ice in his veins.

Sanderford, a great bear of a man, the uniformed cop in charge of the investigation, an avuncular character who would make the women feel secure, turned out to be less avuncular and more lecherous than anticipated. He said the officers stuck out like "sore pricks in a convent bath house", and it was only by arranging some afternoon coaching sessions by an allegedly retired and reliably discreet streetwalker that their technique improved enough to be credible.

Eventually they started to achieve results, and a stream of men was reeled in for admonition or further questioning. The clean-up rate for the Whitechapel force was breaking all records. They'd made a number of arrests of drunks, drug pushers, petty criminals and a miscellaneous selection of low life. A few had been cornered who were carrying offensive weapons - "Yeah, stuffed down their trousers and ready to come out and poke somebody in the back of the throat", said Roscoe.

§

"OK, everyone, give me reasons why we should continue or abandon this," said Devons at a review meeting.

Only Sanderford seemed keen to promote it.

"You know," he said, "we're catching people we didn't know existed, and these WPCs are getting invaluable experience. We're getting results and we may yet unearth the killer."

"Are you sure you're not just saying that because you enjoy playing pimp to all those impressionable WPCs in their tight little black skirts?" said Devons.

Spencer was beginning to wonder if she wasn't finding the exercise a turn-on herself, as he knew a few of the men in the surveillance teams were.

It was understandable. They all met for the briefing before going out on the streets, the women, some of whom were decidedly attractive, wearing micro short skirts, showing their suspenders, and blouses so tight the buttons popped.

They spent the nights on duty together, letting themselves become absorbed in the sex industry and the squalid pursuits of East London after dark. There was the common bond of the work, and the humor that was an inseparable part of it, which bordered on the hysterical at times. And to pull the units even closer together, there was the element of danger the girls were confronting and the reliance they placed on their backup teams. All in all, the shared experience of risk, excitement and long periods of tedium had the makings of an explosive emotional cocktail, and even if it resulted in nothing dramatic from the point of view of the case, Spencer suspected it might have unforeseen and torrid repercussions for some of the police officers involved, male and female. He often wondered if prostitution had the power to attract and disarm police officers in the same way that other criminal behavior sometimes did, and after this exercise he had no doubt about it.

"We're tying up 50 officers a night," said Spencer. "It's possible we're frightening him off, in which case we can't win, because as soon as we pack it in, he'll strike again."

"And we'll look stupid," said Roscoe.

"We can't keep it up forever, just because we're afraid of him killing when we jack it in," said Devons. "Policing is like any medicine; sometimes you have to make compromises and let sick patients die just so you can use your limited resources to help healthier ones live. I'm going to give it one more week and then abandon it unless I have a very good reason not to."

§

Two days later Spencer was out with one of the surveillance teams watching over Detective Constable Gayle Waterman, who was one of the best decoys in that she looked the part and had easily adopted the hooker's way of strutting her stuff. The team included a beefy constable, Bob Attinger, who was bursting with enough hard-packed muscle power to make even Spencer feel secure, so the girls must have been delighted to know he was looking out for them.

Spencer had noticed Gayle looking Attinger up and down when he was changing his shirt. As Spencer watched the girl, dressed in her tart's garb, appreciatively surveying Attinger's steely musculature, it was hard to believe it was two police constables preparing to go to work.

A man approached Gayle. She started to talk to him, and she moved about slightly to ensure she was able to signal to the team if she needed to. She played with her hair.

"That's it," said Attinger.

"That's what," said Spencer.

"Gayle told me she'd like to try something different, and if she thought she was on to something but didn't want us to intervene yet, she'd make that sign."

"So what does she do now?"

"She makes for that alley over there, we can see into it from here. Then she'll either deal with it herself or signal us to go in." Gayle was still talking to the man as they spoke.

"Does Devons know about this variation?"

"Well, no ... we only decided to do it earlier. Gayle thinks we may be frightening them off too quickly."

As they watched, the girl and her punter made for the alley. They could see into it to a depth of about 10 feet.

"If she gets out of sight we go in after her, signal or not," said Spencer.

They could see her, but not very clearly. The two seemed still to be talking, negotiating terms perhaps, but Spencer realized he had no clear idea what they would be talking about. How could she be maintaining the punter's interest at this stage without getting down to business?

"We're going in if she's not out of there in ten seconds," he said.

"No, she's alright. He's probably harmless and she's giving him the naughty boy lecture."

"Then why doesn't she come back out into the street to do it and involve us?"

"She's okay, she ..."

But Spencer was already out of the van and running. By the time he got to Gayle, Attinger was alongside him. They had been yelling as they ran, but the attacker was so intent on his purpose it had no effect. Even as they pulled him away he tried to shrug them off and get back to the groaning body of the policewoman. It took both of them to subdue him, and Spencer didn't interrupt Attinger as he delivered several thumping kicks to the man's solar plexus even though he was no longer a threat.

It couldn't have taken more than 15 or 20 seconds for the two of them to come to her aid, but in that time the attacker had beaten her face to a pulp, ripped most of her clothes off in the areas that interested him, and sunk a savage bite into her breast. The key to his success was ammonia, which he had squirted in Gayle's face, rendering her defenseless as he got his sudden and vicious attack under way.

What made it worse was that Spencer knew from the outset this wasn't their man, and although they had succeeded in capturing a violent lunatic who needed to be locked up, they had only managed to do it at a considerable physical cost and - he didn't doubt - subsequent psychological damage to a police officer. The man's methods had nothing in common with those of the killer, and he wasn't carrying anything that implied he had a murderous intent. Devons was understandably livid.

"Whose bloody idea was it to let the girl get out of sight?"

"It was something she'd hatched up with the team. She thought they were scaring off potential attackers too quickly. But she was never out of sight."

"Why didn't you nip it in the bud?"

"It was the first I'd heard of it, and I told them we were going in if she didn't come out of the alley pronto, but by that time he was already laying into her."

"Is she alright?"

"Well, she'll heal physically, but she's very shaken up. She thought it was the killer and we hadn't noticed she was in trouble and wouldn't get to her in time."

"And you're sure this bloke isn't the killer?"

"Completely, unless he's totally changed his way of working."

Devons said nothing for a while, just sat staring at the surface of the desk in front of her.

"Chingford haven't got anywhere, so at least they can't humiliate us, not that I take a lot of satisfaction from that at the moment," she said, leaning back with her hands clasped behind her head. Her breasts became outlined against her blouse, and Spencer found himself taking interest in her femininity again. Over the months, his feelings for her had gone from grudging respect and formal politeness, to genuine respect and a depth of friendliness that surprised him, even though he still felt intimidated by her at times.

He had stopped asking his colleagues why they found her attractive, because he now found her attractive himself, although he was still unsure why. He felt mostly comfortable with her, and believed she liked his company. He didn't flatter her, condescend to her, nor was he secretly critical of her. He supposed he was one of the few people who could act normally towards her, and she sometimes spoke to him with a bantering familiarity he had never heard her use outside of their conversations.

Their working closely together had also forged a stronger bond between them - albeit one borne out of frustration and a feeling of failure - and the hooker exercise had added a tinge of eroticism to their work and now, it seemed, to their relationship, from Spencer's perspective at least.

□□□

Agent of Evolution

Dr. Jennings was a fat man with a pasty complexion. But his flabby face was crowned by a head of curling silver locks of such magnificence that his unattractive features were more subdued than they would otherwise have been. I told him about the vision and the dream that preceded it, and he asked me endless questions about my life, family and job, which, when I laid out the details of my existence in front of him, all sounded relatively ordinary and unlikely to provoke a bizarre reaction.

"Have you been under particular pressure at work lately?" he asked.

"No, not at all. I love my work."

"You can love something and still be intimidated by it."

"Not me," I said, wondering if we were still talking about work, not that I love anything else that I'm aware of.

"What about at home?"

"Oh, well, the usual things. Teenage children, you know, difficult." I thought about Leo's hostile cynicism, Charlotte's precocious sexuality, and Morag's anarchic tendencies, although I didn't mention them. But he wasn't so easily put off, and he asked me to describe life in our house in great detail, which, as I did it, made us sound like a frightening bunch of certifiable misfits, with the exception of Cynthia.

"And you don't think any of this is getting to you?" he said, and I wondered if he was thinking I had described an environment that would drive anyone to distraction, or worse.

"No, not really," I said, although I now sensed it was probably more abnormal to take our children's behavior in my stride than to get worked up about it. Dr. Jennings' unchanging expression made it impossible for me to tell what he was thinking about my domestic situation and how I reacted, or failed to react, to it.

"Good relationship with your wife?" he asked.

"Yes, very, we've only really had one bad row, and that was soon over."

"Tell me about it."

"Well, it was silly. She found a copy of a pornographic magazine in my briefcase. Someone at work had planted it there."

"Really?" asked Jennings, raising his eyebrows.

"Yes, really," I said. "I don't need that sort of thing. I'm known as something of a nerd at work, and I suppose some of the younger people thought it would shock me."

Jennings still had his eyebrows raised.

"Look," I went on, "I don't care if you believe me or not. It wasn't mine. It was as big a shock to me as it was to Cynthia."

"Did she believe you?"

"Well, no, not at first."

"Did you care if she believed you?"

"Yes, of course I did. Cynthia's very sensitive to anything that degrades women. She was upset, but I couldn't do anything to convince her it was a joke that someone was playing on me."

"How did it work out?" he asked after a long silence.

"She was really incensed, threw something at me, a banana I think it was ... anyway, she calmed down, a bit, although she barely spoke to me for a week."

I didn't bother to tell him that Leo, who was 10 or so at the time, witnessed the argument, and said nothing but also cooled to me considerably after it happened. I probably should have taken time to explain it to him, but I was more concerned about convincing Cynthia than Leo, assuming he was too young to appreciate fully what the row was about.

Jennings and I chatted on and I thought I came across quite well in general, and given I was starting to feel much better, I was surprised when he suggested I spend a few days in hospital.

I sat alone with Cynthia in a waiting room while he made the arrangements.

"I feel okay now. Why do I need to be admitted to hospital?"

"I don't think you're quite alright yet. I think it's best to get you sorted out. It'll only take a few days."

"But I feel fine, really. I don't think there's any need."

"Look at your hands."

My hands were trembling. I hadn't known there was anything wrong until she pointed it out.

"And do you know you're making noises?"

"What noises?"

She looked away and didn't answer.

"What did he say to you?" I asked. Cynthia had seen the doctor on her own, and although it must have been to discuss something he didn't think I should hear, I still wanted to know what it was.

"He just told me what he thought the problem might be. He can't be sure, that's why he wants you to go into hospital, but he's got an idea."

"Well?"

"He didn't think you should be told. He thought it might upset you."

"That's a bit out of date isn't it, patient's rights and all that?"

"He thinks it may be some form of paranoid psychosis, probably just something brought on by pressure, something they can cure very easily if they get the diagnosis right, which is why he wants you to go somewhere they can observe you for a day or two."

"But why did it happen?"

"He thinks you may be worrying about the family, but you're suppressing it, and it's just burst out in this way."

"I'm not aware of being upset."

"That's his point. If you were outwardly upset you wouldn't be brooding on it subconsciously."

"But what about you? You're handling things okay."

"The shelter keeps me sane. If it wasn't for that I think our children would have driven me mad long ago." She paused, and then grabbed my hand. "Sorry."

"What for?"

"I didn't mean to say you were mad."

Her apology affected me more than her comment, which I hadn't really registered, and I certainly hadn't taken it as an insult.

"But I still think it's unnecessary to lock me up."

"They're not locking you up," she said elbowing my arm in a cajoling gesture. "It's a hospital, for observation, just that."

"But couldn't they just try me on some drugs first?"

She gave no appearance of wanting to say what she said next, but she said it anyway, probably to stop me arguing like a child trying to talk his mother out of taking him to the dentist.

"People with your condition, well ... people with the condition he thinks you may have, can do strange things, and, well ... we can't keep an eye on you all the time, can we?"

I didn't ask her to explain what constituted "strange things", because I really didn't want to know, and the thought I might go on to live out some of the scenes that had, thus far, been limited to my hallucinations, convinced me I should do as Jennings suggested.

Although I knew what I'd imagined had been solely a function of my wayward brain, I still kept seeing parts of the vision I'd had the day before, and they were almost as disturbing as they had been at the time. It wasn't the moment of execution that bothered me so much, nor even the thought of dying. What really troubled me was the knowledge that so many people - in fact everyone involved in the vision and the dream that preceded it - thought I was worthy of such a fate.

Looking back, it's easy to see how my subconscious might have been constructing a multicolored guilt complex out of my perceived crime of unleashing three maladjusted and potentially destructive forces – our progeny - on society, and if that's what Dr. Jennings saw as a possible cause, I suppose it looked like a reasonable conclusion. But it wasn't an explanation I could be happy with, because I had an overpowering feeling I had done something more likely to attract opprobrium than simply failing in the upbringing of my children, although I still had no idea what it was.

□□□

Sex and Violence Savored

It was obvious what had happened from the expression on Weller's face and the half of the conversation Spencer could hear him having on the telephone the next day.

"Walthamstow," he said, hanging up the phone. "That was Cheeseman. A woman was murdered last night, only about a mile from where the last one was found in Chingford. Stabbed, not strangled, but he says the mutilation is the same. They only found the body two hours ago."

Devons was away at a conference in Manchester, but they left messages for her and then drove to Walthamstow, where Cheeseman was stalking about like a caged animal.

"It's your fucking killer again," he said, as angrily as if it were Spencer and Weller who were committing the murders, just to upset his crime figures.

"Convicted whore. Same sort of knife work. Why the fuck has he come to my patch? I've had Bennet crawling all over me since the last one, now I'll not have a moment's peace."

Strange, thought Spencer, that he should expect a moment's peace in this job. Nobody could realistically sign up to be a copper and be looking for peace. It was his job to create peace from disorder, futile a goal as that might be.

"I think he wants to beat your Devons to the killer, that's why he's so steamed up about it."

Yes, that figured. Despite the matey show when Devons and Bennet had last met, Spencer didn't doubt Bennet would be delighted to embarrass Devons by getting the killer before she did.

§

It was a pub car park. The whole area had been cordoned off, but it was approaching opening time and the landlord was starting to ask how much longer they were going to be discouraging his customers with crime scene tape and flashing blue lights.

"I know this is serious and all that, and you've got a job to do, but

I always get a load of trade on a Friday lunchtime, and they won't come in when they see all this going on, will they?"

"Believe me, mate," said Cheeseman "your trade will go through the bleedin' roof when we're out the way. There's nothing attracts business like a good murder."

No, thought Spencer, nothing has changed since Dickens' day and long before that. Despite being outwardly repulsed by it, most people find somebody else's murder to be just about the most interesting thing under the sun, and the more gruesome and perverse, the more intense and persistent the interest.

"Who found the body?" asked Weller. "I did," said the landlord. "Well, not me exactly, but my dog Samson here. He was out here going bloody crazy, barking and running around like a mad thing, so I came out and saw a leg sticking out from behind the dumpster. I didn't look no more, I just run inside and called you lot."

"Really? You didn't look closer."

"No, well, it's happened to me before. When I run the pub in Catford. There was a bloke stabbed in the toilet one night. I went in there after closing and one of the cubicle doors was shut, so I looked under and saw this pair of feet. I thought it was a drunk passed out, or else some clever sod hiding so he could sneak out and rob me or drink himself silly later on. So I bashed the door down and there was this body in there. He was sat on the seat and had a knife in his chest. All the blood went down the toilet. There weren't a drop on the floor hardly. I still have nightmares about it. There's no way I want another body to be dreaming about."

His face was blank as he spoke, his eyes unblinking and unfocussed. When he'd finished speaking he wandered off, possibly reliving the event he wanted to forget.

Spencer had often considered it strange he never dreamt about the ugly sights he'd seen over the years, neither the living nor the dead ones.

"Know who she is?" Spencer asked Cheeseman.

"Jane Vernon, well known whore of this parish. Record as long as your arm, mainly soliciting, but a bit of petty theft and drug possession thrown in, and a couple of drunk and disorderlies. Cream of society. No loss, really," said Cheeseman, betraying his feelings for the people he was employed to protect from being randomly and savagely murdered.

"Bag full of condoms – wouldn't be surprised if she was recycling them by the look of the bloody things. Pills. No cash. I wanted to get the landlord to take a look at her, see if she's a customer of his, but he says he's not up to it. He'll come to the morgue later when we've got her cleaned up and out of his car park. This place is a well known pickup joint, always has been."

They looked at the body. A white woman, youngish, multiple stab wounds and additional lacerations of a more superficial nature of the familiar cross and zero variety. It was what the press would describe as a 'frenzied attack', in a parlance intended to convey outrage but, at the same time, to thrill. Spencer could imagine the headlines. "Criss Cross Killer Carnage Continues – Woman Slashed to Death by Demonic Sex-Obsessed Murderer in Pub Car Park – Landlord's Dog Sniffs Out Mutilated Corpse."

Sex, violence and a nice furry animal, all packaged into one attention-grabbing story for the breakfast time reading of a nation who, despite what they say, love to be outraged and would probably care more if the dog had been murdered than the prostitute whose limp body was lying before him.

"Might not be our man," said Weller. "We went to a similar killing in Stevenage last week. Stabbing, some mutilation. But it was an ex-boyfriend they arrested the next day. Not every murder in London's the same bloke."

Cheeseman muttered something under his breath that was almost certainly insulting. Weller and Spencer exchanged glances but said nothing. There were too many unknowns. It was possible the Chingford and Walthamstow murders were down to a new killer altogether, or two separate killers, or that one of them was the East London killer and one wasn't, or that both the latest crimes were attributable to the East London killer. If they found no physical evidence apart from the corpse, they would still be floundering in a sea of uncertainty, and rancorous uncertainty as far as Cheeseman was concerned.

Weller and Spencer were about to leave when one of the detectives who was hunting around the body called them back.

"We've found this. A part of her blouse is ripped off and thrown here, and this was lying on top of it. We've only just noticed it; it was about two yards from the body."

It was a bit of material, unmistakable even at a glance; a wavy-edged piece of cloth of the type opticians supply with glasses for cleaning the lenses.

"Lying on top of the piece of blouse, you said?" Spencer asked.

"Yes, definitely."

"No doubt about that?"

"None sir. We've got photographs of the scene that'll show where we found it." He was holding the cloth in a gloved hand, but Spencer guessed it would be practically impossible to get prints from it.

"Read me the name on it."

The detective flicked the cloth over and read "Robert Chang, Optician, 225 Commercial Street, E1 and a load of Chinese looking stuff as well."

"Be careful with it. Bag it up straight away and make sure the lab check it for everything. There could be DNA evidence on it if he's the sort of person to spit on his glasses to clean them, I know I do."

"Jesus Christ!" said Weller. "Have we got lucky at last?"

Spencer said nothing, but he could feel his hands tingling and butterflies in his stomach. Driving back into town, Weller kept talking about the potential lead as if it was going to close the case. But although Spencer was tempted to share some of his enthusiasm, he forced himself to face facts. In the best possible scenario, the cloth belonged to the killer, who had somehow dropped it after murdering the girl. That was plausible. In the exertion of the attack his spectacles could have easily got steamed up, and if he was the obsessively neat sort of person these types often were, he could have paused to wipe his glasses meticulously rather than just wipe them on his sleeve. Then the cloth slipped from his fingers and he walked away, unaware that his usually scrupulous care had let him down.

But there were other, less attractive possibilities. It could have been planted to mislead them, another thrill for the killer to know he was sending them in all sorts of wrong directions. Or it could have been someone else, someone who discovered the body before the landlord and his dog, but for whatever reason decided not to report it. Or it could have been lying there before the murder took place, and somehow contrived to be blown on top of the fragment of blouse, or possibly have been lifted out of the open-topped dumpster by a mischievous breeze. But even so - and this underlined their desperation to find clues - it was a promising lead, and although it might reduce the number of possible suspects to the several thousand who were customers of Robert Chang, Optician, it was still a huge narrowing down compared to what they'd had.

§

He was back at the station when Devons called. She went silent for a few moments when Spencer told her about the cloth, and then she started methodically working through the doubts he had already used to water down his own expectations.

"And even if it is connected with our man, it may be another killer altogether. I'm leaving this bloody waste of time conference. I'll be back at the office late today or first thing tomorrow."

"Isn't the Home Secretary speaking tonight?"

"No, he's cancelled, and I'll gladly forego the prospect of watching my fellow senior police officers waving their dicks around for another day."

"What about Cheeseman? He'll assume it's his case until he's told otherwise, and he won't want us around."

"Leave that to me. His boss is here, looking as though he's

thoroughly pissed off with life. I'll square it with him before I leave. The fact the cloth's from East London ties the murder back to our man. I think Bennet will be glad to get Cheeseman off the case, he doesn't rate him very highly and likes him even less. Has anyone contacted the optician?"

"Weller is on his way over there now. I've told him to get samples of the cloths they use or have used in the past, and to get some idea of the numbers we're talking about. It'll be thousands, I would think, but that's a manageable number."

"Okay, is that all?"

"Yes, I think so."

"Spencer?"

"Yes?"

"I enjoy working with you."

He couldn't think of anything to say, but he didn't have to, because she just went on to say "see you tomorrow" and hung up. He sat staring at the phone he was still clutching, and when he put it back in the cradle his hand was trembling slightly.

□□□

Spectacular Lead

"You're joking, aren't you? Eleven thousand men? There must be more money in being an optician than I thought. Shortsighted of me not to have noticed that." It was as close as Spencer ever heard Devons come to making a pun, and her expression was so bland he wondered if she knew she had.

"The Chinese community flocks to him. The place is like something you'd find in a Hong Kong back street. You're more likely to be understood if you speak Cantonese than if you speak English. Cockneys must have a hard time in there," Spencer told her. "We're lucky. He only started keeping most of his records in English when he moved from Walworth."

"Thank God for that. This case is already costing us enough without having to pay for someone to translate the evidence before we can understand it. The Chinese don't go in for serial murders like this, do they? We should start off with all the non-Chinese on the list. It might be an unwarranted assumption. But I think a shortcut is justified to begin with, and with Mr. Chang's customer list, ignoring the Chinese on it to start with is going to represent a hell of a time saving."

"There's some bad news too. Chang was evasive, but I wouldn't be surprised if his records were full of holes. I pressed him on the subject but he turned orientally inscrutable on me. I suggest we get a Chinese policeman to go over there and double check."

"You think he might be holding something back? Why?"

"He could be thinking this is really some plot by the Inland Revenue to see if he's declaring all his sales, but I think it's more likely his record keeping just isn't that accurate and he's embarrassed to admit it. It would be a loss of face. They didn't use a computer at the cash desk until recently - they used to use an abacus."

"Jesus. Well, even then, it's a bloody sight better than anything else we've got to work on. Did they come up with any more from the crime scene?"

"They're giving the cloth the full treatment, but they're doubtful they'll be able to lift anything from it."

The phone rang. As she spoke, Spencer watched her face and, for the hundredth time, tried to work out what was making her attractive to him, and even, most puzzling of all, what was causing her to show signs of returning the attraction. She was 15 years his junior. She had short, raven-black hair and even, unexceptional features. She wore little make-up and clothes that did nothing to flatter a physique that appeared to have larger than average breasts and hips, but also thicker than desirable waist and thighs. She wasn't pretty or handsome, but neither was she ugly. It should have been safe to call her plain, but that somehow ignored a quality about her he was still unable to define, and which he attributed to her powerful position in a world traditionally ruled by men, a position she continually justified by her strict control of herself and those around her.

He wondered why she seemed to like him more than any of his colleagues, and whether the stirrings of sexual attraction he was beginning to feel towards her were reciprocated. Not that he intended doing anything about them even if they were. His marriage was sound and gave him everything he needed, and yet he was aware he was starting to obsess about Devons in a way that was as disturbing as it was arousing, and he suspected the disturbance and the arousal were inseparably linked and fuelling one another.

"That was Bennet," she said, hanging up. "That asshole Cheeseman says he's onto a lead. Reckons he's got witnesses to the fact the victim had some customer who was stalking her. A bloke who'd fucked her once and decided he was in love with her and that she would fall in love with him, given the chance and enough rum and coke. He wanted her to give up the game and move in with him."

She paused and gazed unblinking at Spencer. He had no idea why, nor how he should react to it. Then she went on as though the pause had never happened, as though time had just stood still for a few seconds, loaded with some incipient meaning she had been unwilling or unable to put into words and he was still trying to untangle.

"Our superstar detective on the streets of Chingford infers this stalker couldn't get his way with the love of his life, so he decided to make her his forever by killing her. They're looking for him now, but his home appears to be deserted. Cheeseman concludes he's probably gone and topped himself in Epping Forest so he can meet his darling in heaven, or wherever it is that whores and perverts meet up when they're not in Walthamstow."

"I would never have expected Cheeseman to have such powers of imagination, let alone deduction, said Spencer."

"Nor would Bennet, that's why he phoned. But it's not that unreasonable, in theory, so they're chasing it for all they're worth, especially Cheeseman, trying to prove that his one, suburban brain can outshine the collective mental firepower we city slickers have used to no avail."

"What's his name, this Essex Romeo? We can check it against the Chang list."

"Henry Losely, but it sounds like a waste of time to me. If he loved her he might have killed her out of frustration, but he wouldn't have mutilated her, would he?"

"Probably not, but stranger things have happened."

"Sad waste of a body really," Devons muttered, staring wistfully into space.

"What?" Spencer asked, assuming she was uncharacteristically philosophizing on the wastefulness of murder.

"God went to all the trouble of making that amazingly complex machine, only to fuck up at the last minute and put Cheeseman's head on it."

§

They checked the optician's data for the name Losely, but it didn't appear.

Spencer couldn't concentrate. All the time he was working, the image of Devons was sitting in his head, bothering him and stimulating him in equal measure.

☐☐☐

Visiting Scraps of Memory

Bill Eckert could have been a doctor, or at least some sort of employee of the hospital. It was hard to accept he was just another patient, and his intelligence and ordinariness provided me with considerable comfort at first - if all my fellow patients had been patently crazy, I would have been forced to consider myself to be in the same lamentable shape.

Bill liked to extemporize. Subjects came up at random and although generally lucid, he seemed to have a somewhat singular viewpoint.

"The basic difference between men and women is the orgasm. For women, relationships start at the orgasm, but with men they end at the orgasm. Men see sex as the objective, but women see it as one part of the big picture. How can the sexes get along when they're always looking at life down opposite ends of the same telescope?"

He was in his 50s, with wavy black hair flecked with silvery grey. His face was craggy and deeply lined, as though he'd been through a lot and his face had borne the brunt of his experiences, few of them pleasant. He moved slowly and seemed to be relaxed, but I noticed he very seldom blinked, and when it came to the time to take medication he had to work his way through a formidable handful of pills.

"My first wife, with her it was sex. We'd come together through sex, so that was what we did in our marriage. It was like glue holding it together. The more she knew that sex for me and her was completely different, the more the glue dripped off, and the more the marriage came unstuck. For her, sex was a demonstration of the fact we loved each other, but for me it was just a shag. I appreciated her more when she brought me a cup of tea in bed. Sex was just bodies going at it for their own selfish pleasure, but when she brought me a cup of tea, she was doing the work and I was getting the pleasure.

"We men do romantic things because we want sex. Women are romantic because they've had sex. It proves something for women, but for men it's just something we need to do. For women it says something about the man, but for the man it says something about himself. It proves he's still a man. Women don't need sex to prove they're women – they prove that by how they decorate their bedrooms and how much they like chocolate."

I didn't really think about what he said, and I knew much of it was arrant twaddle, but he talked cheerfully and with animation. The hospital setting was so unsettled and gloomy that I soaked up his pronouncements like warm sunshine.

"With my second wife, sex didn't come into it. We were friends for ages, then when we started going out together, we just went out together, we didn't even kiss. Then one day, after about a year, we had sex, and I swear it wasn't until afterwards I realized we'd really done it, and I think it was the same for her. It was just no big deal, it was a natural part of our relationship that just came about, and even now we find ourselves having sex by chance rather than getting obsessed about it."

He stared into space for a while before speaking again. These pauses could go on for minutes, although he would often go to speak several times but then stop himself, as though he needed precisely the right words to break the almost sacred silence that seemed to pervade the hospital.

"Course, it was better with my first wife, more satisfying, I mean. But it fucked up all the rest of our marriage."

We never discussed why we were there. In fact, unlike patients suffering physical illnesses, nobody ever discussed their condition, except those who contended there was nothing wrong with them, and it was only those who most blatantly had something wrong with them who made these loud denials.

My treatment was managed by Dr. Mary MacAndrews, a middle-aged Scot with a brusque manner but a warm smile. She didn't wear a white coat, and after two long conversations with her I almost forgot she was treating me at all. We just talked freely, which, from her point of view, was probably the objective. Of course, unlike a normal conversation, there was no equal exchange of views. The focus was very plainly on me and what I thought, and whenever I asked her something about herself or for some opinion, she quickly steered the conversation back in my direction.

Sooner or later, every session would get around to discussion of my family life, which she, like Dr. Jennings before her, must have suspected was the key to my problem and the explanation of my unsettling reaction to it.

"Your son, Leo, tell me about him."

I started from the child with whom I'd had a remarkable rapport and mental empathy, and ended with the young man who despised, victimized and scared me.

"Do you think you have much in common with him?"

"I used to. I thought we were practically clones. It was so easy for me to tell what he was thinking, it was almost scary. But he was friendly then, so everything we shared was pleasant, but when he came to dislike me, the fact our minds might be connected in some way was disturbing."

"What, you mean you were afraid he might be able to see what you were thinking?"

"Yes."

"Why did that make you afraid?"

"I don't know. I've never had any thoughts I should be afraid of. It just struck me as intrusive that we could see into each other's minds, even if it was for party tricks mostly."

"Did you ever try to get into his mind for any other reason?"

"When he first started going off the rails I suppose I may have tried to understand what had gone wrong, but by that time he was as much a mystery to me as anyone else."

"And you tell me you're afraid of him now?"

"Yes, a little, well, quite a lot actually. He seems to dislike us – his family - more than anyone else. He's hostile in general, but it's me and his mother he's particularly antagonistic towards, as though we're to blame for something."

Sometimes when talking to her I felt I was wallowing around in a thick mental goo. A viscous mud attached itself to all my thoughts and made them stick together and lose mobility and any sense of direction. I kept catching glimpses of where she might be leading, and I presumed she thought I was hiding something - unconsciously suppressed memories of being abused as a child perhaps, or even consciously suppressed memories of me abusing my own children.

Every now and again our discussion became so hopeless I wanted to tell her something outrageous, as though I could make some random, fictitious admission and she and all my confusion would go away. But I couldn't tell if I wanted this breakthrough to happen for her sake or mine. I wanted to be talking to Bill Eckert instead, listening to his unchallenging, asinine statements on male-female relationships and other inconsequential subjects.

§

"Try imagining you're on Death Row," Bill said to me out of the blue one day. "You've run out of appeals and you're sure to die the next day and you're lying in bed thinking about it. You could imagine you've got some terminal disease if you'd rather, but that can be vaguer. You don't really know how long you're going to live in that case, and your thinking would probably be affected by your illness anyway. But if you're on Death Row, you can be in perfect health and able to think clearly."

He looked at me waiting for acknowledgment. I nodded, assuming I had to transport myself mentally to some claustrophobic, fetid and steamy prison in Texas in order for him to continue his monologue with the assurance I was on his wavelength.

"There's nothing in the world to worry about, is there? Nothing you can do that will influence anything or anybody. You've got no worries, no responsibilities, nothing."

I waited for the insightful punch line, but there wasn't one.

"I put myself in that state of mind at night when I'm in bed. Makes me sleep better."

I started to see why he was here and why he needed so many pills, but that night I actually did as he suggested, and I fell into a deep, dreamless sleep as the imaginary prison doors slammed shut.

§

Cynthia visited me as often as she could, although the journey from Islington took a couple of hours. I told her she shouldn't sacrifice her work at the shelter, and I was happy if she came every couple of days or so.

On her first visit she had brought Morag, who sat huddled into the fur rimmed hood of her anorak, peeking out every so often to stare around then retreated back under her disguise. She said almost nothing, and looked at me with glazed, unknowing eyes on the rare instances when she paid me any attention at all.

She brought Charlotte on her second visit, who, we thought, paid far too much attention to one of the muscular male nurses. To judge from his expression, it seemed he wouldn't be averse to taking advantage of her interest - despite their 20 year age difference - if Cynthia hadn't hauled Charlotte away at the earliest opportunity. Since then, Cynthia has come alone, so I was daunted when I was called to the visiting area, 10 days into my stay, to find an unaccompanied Leo awaiting me.

"Hello, farrrthaaar," he said, exaggerating the word to make it sound insulting and ridiculous, which had become his usual way of addressing his mother and me.

"Don't think this is a social visit. I'm just here at the request of your wife, my occasional mother, to bring you some extra clothes. I suppose you've messed the old ones or something, as part of your condition." He leered at me, as though he was taking delight in my illness but disgusted by it or me at the same time.

"Thank you, Leo."

"No need to thank me. I had nothing else to do. Mater paid my fare, and she gave me an extra tenner to buy my cooperation, not that you can buy anything useful with a tenner these days, but she's not to know that, she doesn't get out very much, doesn't know what it costs to make a young person happy any more, probably never did, poor old cow."

He stopped and looked at me, over his glasses. Leo and I both wore thick lensed spectacles, and he had taken to wearing his perched on the end of his nose. With his shaved head, ear-ring and a strange symbol tattooed on his forehead, he looked every bit the thug he was, and the perched glasses, which often give people an air of intelligence instead only seemed to add to the menace that he exuded.

"Tell me, Daddy, what do they do to you here? Electric shocks, lobotomy, chemical castration perhaps?"

"Talk, mainly. I take medication, just some sort of anti-depressant."

"Can I have some, please, I'm feeling a bit depressed myself, particularly since I got here and saw you. What do you talk about?"

"Anything and everything."

"Well," he said, as though I was a small child he was laboring to extract information from, "give me some examples then."

"About my work, about the family, everything."

"Oh, I see. They think the family's to blame, do they? Quite right. You lot drive me up the bloody wall, so it's only fair we've done the same to you, we being your creation, as it were, out of your loins, so to speak, Frankenstein's monster, Rosemary's baby and all that."

He didn't know how literally I agreed with him. I harbored no doubt we had spawned at least one monster, and possibly three. Cynthia and I continued to be occasional drug users for some years after our college days, and in my greatest moments of self-criticism I wondered if our addled egg and sperm hadn't somehow contrived to create misfits in the womb, although my reasoning brain told me our level and frequency of consumption made this hypothesis unlikely.

"Do they let you out?"

"Of course. It's not a prison."

"Oh, *of course*," he said. "Well I don't know, *of course*, what you can do in a place like this, never having been in a loony bin myself, personally, *of course*. So where do you go? Anywhere special, or do you just hang around the nearest public lavatory with all the other perverts and nutters, *of course*."

I was happy that my medication was having a powerful sedating effect on my emotions, because I didn't feel at all rattled by his insults or intimidated by his presence. In fact, I felt relatively immune to anything he could say or do, which was not an unpleasant feeling.

"I wander around the town now and again, just to make a change of scenery."

"Are you safe, Father?"

"What do you mean?"

"Well, I don't know what sort of things you people get up to, do I? I've no idea what tricks you could pull off while the balance of your mind is disturbed, have I? For all I know you could be a serious threat to society, and not the harmless little non-entity you pretend to be, couldn't you?"

He sat back smirking, and I realized just how much I disliked him. How did he become like this? I felt guilty, guilty for loathing him and guilty for being partly responsible - as I assume I am - for making him like this, however inadvertently.

"Oh well, I can't hang around here all day making idle chit-chat."

"Are you going home?" I asked, knowing he would consider any questioning of his actions to be meddlesome.

"Well, I may, and I may not. I may even take a look around town. Perhaps I'll warn a few people there are some creepy weirdoes to be found in their midst now and again, sniffing at their crotches, looking up their skirts and fiddling with their kiddies' willies and botties. Perhaps I should make some sort of public service announcement from the town square - assuming it has a town square - that they need to be on their guard against the inmates of the local funny farm. After all, we can't have the good folk of Chingford being threatened by unhinged, marauding foreigners who keep having supernatural visions, can we now?"

He left, swaggering, leaving me to enjoy the fact he was no longer there to taunt me, but also to wonder what mischief he was capable of when left to his own devices.

§

"I want to talk about the visions again," said Dr. MacAndrews, and as I went on to recount what happened in the dream, and the scene with the crowd and the scaffold that had broken me, the image of the first vision I'd quite forgotten about sprung to my mind.

"What's wrong?" she asked, and I realized I'd stopped speaking and was sitting with my mouth open. It wasn't anything in that vision of a strange room that was, in itself, at all worrying or threatening. What shocked and disturbed me was it now seemed to be innately linked with the other two, and when I discovered the connection it would possibly reveal another murky area of my subconscious with the potential to terrorize me.

I told her about the room, which she asked me to describe as clearly as possible, and as I let my mind's eye wander over that strange and disconcerting place, I became convinced I had been there and something had happened there that I didn't want to know about.

"What do you think it means?" I asked.

"The mind has many methods of communicating with us. It uses metaphors in very bizarre ways at times, and what you saw may have been that. But don't assume it's important. Our subconscious doesn't always prioritize very effectively or even at all, and something that may seem portentous could really be extremely trivial. If you don't remember the room, the most likely explanation is either it doesn't exist or you saw it on TV or somewhere in a fictional setting, but your mind may be using it to try and communicate something to you by means of images you can relate to."

That was probably the longest sentence Dr. MacAndrews had spoken to me, and it was certainly the only time she had given me any sort of explanation of what I was going through. But I thought she was wrong in this case to underplay its significance, and the room I had seen was a very real and significant part of my life, and one that didn't hold any pleasant memories.

When the session finished, I went out into the grounds and sat alone on the remotest bench I could find. I'd noticed that nowhere in the hospital - indoors or out - was really secluded, and I presumed one could be observed openly or covertly wherever you went, but the seat I chose was quiet enough for me to be able to think without interruption, and that was what I needed.

The day was overcast and muggy. The sky presaged rain or possibly a thunderstorm, and the impression the weather was about to break was matched by the feeling I had that something momentous was waiting to shatter in my mind.

It was as though the therapy was working inside my head, and I was more likely to discover the cause of my malaise than Dr. MacAndrews. She may have been facilitating the process, but I would be the one to make the revelation, although the unraveling process wasn't one I was controlling in any way. Perhaps this is the method psychiatrists normally use. I don't know. But I was very aware something was going on in my mind - I could almost feel it happening, ticking and whirring towards its conclusion - and I suspected the outcome may be cathartic, but it wouldn't be enjoyable.

I was starting to believe the guilty feelings I was experiencing and what my vision and dream had revealed to me were related to something more tangible than parental inadequacy. I began to rummage around in the areas Dr. MacAndrews had been delving into, my childhood, adolescence, and any other parts of my life that may have been hiding murky secrets I had repressed.

Then I went on to other phases of my life, the predictable years at the onset of middle age, and any other periods I'd glossed over as being too ordinary to be hiding anything traumatic. But wherever I looked I found nothing but that which my conscious mind had always been fully aware and tightly in control of.

I assumed anything my mind knew about would teach me nothing, as my conscious brain was keeping the reason for my disturbed state from me. It was a rebellious exhibition by my subconscious trying to tell me I had something unpalatable to confront, and I supposed my therapy sessions were aimed at getting my subconscious to pop up to the surface and explain to me and the doctor what it was trying to say, but in terms more understandable and specific than the frightening, elliptical imagery it had used so far.

I focused my thinking on the room from the first vision, straining to see if it was a place I had been to, seen on the television, in a film, or in a magazine; or whether it was simply an invention of my mind, meaningful or not. I must have sat there for almost two hours, not thinking so much as letting my mind wander where it would, hoping it would stray into territory where I might learn something. But it didn't, and I went in to dinner feeling exhausted and afraid of my brain and the powerful influence it was having over me, excluding me from what it was up to as though I was a stranger to my own head.

§

I knew something was wrong the moment I saw Cynthia. You can't live with a person for 20 years and not be able to relate at least a little of what's showing on their face to what's going on behind it, even if you're a computer scientist who spends most of his life trying to understand machines as a way of avoiding having to deal with people.

"What's wrong?" I asked.

"Oh. Is it that obvious?"

"Yes. Tell me."

"No, it's nothing. You just concentrate on getting better. It's trivial."

"No it isn't. You don't get upset without reason, but when you do it's invariably something important." I said, and I was aware of the bond between us that had strengthened as our family started to fall apart. I don't think we had ever been closer, and although neither of us was the type to make outward declarations of love, I believe we both knew the years had cemented a link between us that we could never have dreamt of as we sat listening to Leonard Cohen's droning songs depressing the hell out of us at university all those years ago.

"I might have known you'd guess something is wrong. The children never seem to be aware of my mental state, or perhaps they're just not interested in it. I came prepared to make something up, like an incident at the shelter. But I can't talk to anyone about this, except you, and it's probably nothing anyway."

I waited for her to collect her thoughts, thinking how ironic it is to hear our progeny described as 'children', with the innocence the word implies, when they seem more deft at handling modern life and its evils than the adults in the family. We thought Henry Miller was risqué – our progeny would probably classify him as being as tame as Jane Austen.

"I had to go into Leo's room the other day. There was this noise coming from there. It turned out he'd left his computer on and it was making this weird beeping sound every 30 seconds or so, and it was starting to drive me crazy.

"I tried to ignore it at first, but I found myself waiting for it, and after a while I wasn't able to concentrate on anything else. I couldn't even listen to the radio without waiting for that damn beep. I didn't mean to look at anything in his room. I just intended to go in, find out what was causing the noise, stop it and come out."

She paused to sigh. Her forehead was creased in a frown, one that was almost permanently etched into her face. I wondered how the world saw her. She had never been madly attractive, but she must have made one or two heads turn in her day, although she was unlikely to do so now, not looking as careworn as she did. She didn't go on for a while. She swayed her head from side to side, with her eyes welded shut, as though she was reliving the incident, hoping, perhaps, for some new explanation or insight.

"Something caught my eye on the table next to the computer.

Do you remember he had a scrapbook when he was young he kept newspaper clippings in? Mainly ones to do with soccer?"

"Yes." I remembered it. It had a number of sporting images printed on the cover – footballers, athletes, racing cars, cricketers and so forth. I didn't know it still existed, and was surprised to hear it did. I would have expected Leo to have expunged long ago any evidence of a naïve and ordinary childhood, one that was not in agreement with the vicious and cynical adolescent he now was.

"I opened it. I suppose I thought I might find something in it showing me there was still some part of him I could relate to. Stupid. As if ..." She paused and shook her head again, her eyes cast down.

"It was horrible. It's full of cuttings about those murders, and he, at least I assume it was Leo, has scrawled all sorts of bloodthirsty drawings and obscene jottings over them. Most of it was newspaper cuttings, but there was also a photograph that looked like it was taken after the woman was killed. Goodness knows where he got that from."

She paused again and her eyes, which were already red, began to fill with tears that drizzled slowly down her cheeks.

"It was so macabre, sick, but ..."

"But what?"

She said something, but her voice was thick and I couldn't hear what it was. She didn't seem about to say any more, but then she went on, stumbling over her words as I watched the blood drain from her face.

"The first page was blank apart from a title printed on it. It said 'Daddy's Dastardly Deeds' in big red letters."

I stared at her for what may have been minutes, trying to absorb what she'd said and understand it, and the feeling it was something hugely momentous and terrifying strangled my words.

"I don't ... I can't. What does it mean?" I asked.

"How do I know?" she blurted out. "Do you know?"

I didn't know what to say. The obvious answer was "No, I don't", but I didn't say it because something was telling me I did know, but I was unable to confront the intimations out of fear they would metamorphosize into facts.

We sat for a while, saying nothing. She presumably having nothing more to add, and me not daring to open my mouth, terrified of what would come out of it. Eventually I felt I had to speak, because the silence was becoming so painful.

"Does he think I killed those women?" My voice quavered as I spoke and the last word hardly came out at all.

"I just don't know," she said, averting her eyes. "I don't know what to think. I was hoping. Oh, I don't know what I was hoping. I just ... Oh God. What's going on?" She didn't seem to be talking to me, but rather appealing to some higher power, divine or not, to present her with a convenient answer.

"Cynthia, you don't think ..."

"What?"

"You don't think Leo had anything to do with those murders do you?"

She looked at me blankly. I took a shuddering breath and said "You don't think ... you don't think I had anything to do with them, do you?" I wasn't asking for an affirmation of her support for me, but rather I wanted to know if it was conceivable I was involved with the murders in some way I was too scared to confront.

☐☐☐

Shoot Out

"Cheeseman just called."

"How nice," said Devons, "what did he want?"

Spencer was in his office, talking to Devons on the phone. He was trying to keep out of her presence as much as possible, because he was aware of the gathering attraction she was exerting over him, an attraction he felt she was doing nothing to dampen. But now even her voice was beginning to have an unsettling effect on him.

"He's tracked down his prime suspect for the Walthamstow murder, Henry Losely."

"Oh, wonderful, and I suppose he's just called to tell us we can send the case files for the other murders over to him, because he's solved them all single-handed and he'd like to put the paperwork to bed before he nips over to Colchester and gets his promotion to Assistant Chief Constable."

"Not quite as neat as that, but it should satisfy his love of the dramatic - the bloke's holed himself up in some council house in Leyton with a sawn-off shotgun, and he's threatening to blow his head off if we don't leave him alone and catch the man who really murdered his girlfriend."

"What would it take to get him to blast a few rounds at Cheeseman before he does himself in?"

§

Half an hour later, they were in Spencer's car driving to Leyton.

"The TV cameras and the press are already there," Spencer told her. "Roscoe got there about a quarter of an hour ago and he tells me Cheeseman was ready to storm the place and haul the man out Rambo-style."

"Well," she said, "you can tell Roscoe from me that if he was instrumental in dissuading him from that piece of suicidal lunacy, he'll be back pounding the beat before he can say 'Sorry Ma'am.' There's nothing I'd like more than to see Cheeseman's brains splattered over a pavement somewhere. Did you know he'd contacted the Commissioner's office and asked that we should be told to keep out of his hair, because we were 'hindering the investigation'?"

"I heard."

"Well, I'm happy to say the Commissioner told him to go take a flying fuck, although, being a man of breeding, not quite in those words." She turned to him, smiled and winked, which caused a hollow space to open up in the pit of his stomach. It was as though they were a couple going out on an illicit date, not two senior police officers about to attend an armed siege.

§

It was a typical council house on a typical council house estate. Everything was run-down and crying out for repair, everything needed a coat of paint, every pavement needed sweeping and every car needed a valid tax disc. Even the air seemed to be in need of treatment - it should have been sucked away and replaced with something fresher, which wasn't so redolent of hopelessness and filth.

Walls sprouted satellite dishes like their counterparts in richer areas sprouted burglar alarms. Scruffy dogs wandered around at will, as did young children, their eyes cold and cynical like those of angry adults. Any instructions shouted to them by the assembled police officers were either ignored or met with streams of abuse, and not abuse that was delivered slyly or mischievously, but hurled at the officers with vitriol and contempt.

Loud rap music was coming from somewhere, and even louder heavy metal music from somewhere else. A group of youths was huddled under the bonnet of an old but immaculate Jaguar, studiously ignoring the events being played out nearby.

It must have been a major undertaking to clear the area around the house in which Henry Losely was holding himself hostage. Things like this, and worse, probably happened regularly around here, and it would have been difficult to get the inhabitants to take any new drama seriously enough to disturb their humdrum routines.

"I've got bullet-proof vests," Spencer said as they pulled up.

"No thanks, they weren't designed for women, not women with my shape, anyway. The only people interested in killing me will be Cheeseman and the journalists."

Spencer continued sitting in the car for a few seconds after she got out. He took two deep breaths. He needed one large drink.

Observing the gathering of uniforms and rifles, he was struck by the futility of this sort of event. Hoping for nothing of note to happen was the sensible thing to do, and chronically uninspiring. It was like attending a motor sports event, never being willing to admit it, but secretly wanting to see some life and death action to set the pulse racing, and what better to do that than a spectacular crash or an explosion of violence?

Spencer knew a number of his colleagues welcomed bloody outcomes to sieges and shoot-outs, as long as the hurt was confined to the guilty parties. In this way they could be sure of getting some excitement and also, as far as some were concerned, it was the best way to mete out the appropriate type of justice to brutish criminals, who were considered to be better dead than in prison and costing money, or out on probation and preparing to offend again.

Although Spencer was too much of a realist to believe in tidy outcomes where only the bad men die, he sometimes understood this point of view. But in the case of Henry Losely, they needed to take him unharmed, because if there was any chance he was not only responsible for the latest murder but also for one or more of the others, then they wanted a live body to interrogate and not a dead one to conveniently blame or endlessly speculate upon. Devons was making everyone aware of this as Spencer arrived at the cluster of officers.

"We're going to follow standard procedure to the letter. He's got no hostages, the immediate area has been evacuated and made safe, we have all our people in position and the emergency services are ready to go in as needed, so we can just sit this out for as long as it takes. We'll try and talk him out, but there will be no intimidation, is that understood?"

"Excuse me, Ma'am," said Cheeseman, "but I was of the impression this was our case."

"It is," she said, moving her face to within a foot of his. "I'm just reminding you of the importance we attach to taking this man alive, for the sake of a number of investigations we're pursuing. And if anyone were to provoke a situation that might hinder that goal, I want them to be aware that their bollocks will be hung round their neck and their pension will be a dim and distant memory. I'm sure your Chief Constable would concur, aren't you, Detective Inspector Cheeseman?"

Cheeseman sucked his teeth and shook his head, then turned and walked away, muttering something to himself of which only the occasional obscenity was barely audible.

The gunman had phoned his demands into a local radio station that morning, spending an hour shouting, crying, cursing, ranting and rambling to the talk-show host, who had cast himself in the role of mediator and potential saver of lives. Nobody had heard from him since.

They knew that Losely was in the house, that he was alone, and that he had at least one shotgun. They could see him wandering around, seemingly unconcerned that he was in the sights of two police marksmen. Early attempts to encourage him to give himself up - by an unsympathetic Cheeseman with a bull-horn at full volume - had resulted in nothing more than a few random insults being hurled out of an upstairs window, and they had not tried to communicate since.

Having made her position plain, Devons knew she had to take a back seat and let the Essex team run the operation, but she didn't easily adapt to a passive role, so after half an hour of inaction, she invited Spencer to join her in the car for coffee from a thermos flask.

"I hope to God he comes out soon," she said, "otherwise Cheeseman'll be abseiling down the side of the house with a ten inch bayonet between his teeth. What do you think, Spence?"

Nobody had called him "Spence" in years, but Devons had adopted it for the times they were alone. As he turned to face Devons, looking past her through the window, he could see a face leering at them from a nearby squad car, and the expression on the face, which was unknown to Spencer, implied the owner was finding something amusing in what he was seeing.

"I'm sure he's not our man," he said, trying to ignore the anonymous observer. "From what I've heard, this bloke is dim, emotional and unbalanced – the real murderer's none of those things. As to whether he did the last killing, God alone knows, but if he did, then he made it look like the others. My bet is he hasn't killed anyone, and he'll wander out in an hour or two, get pumped full of lithium with a warning to behave himself in future. He's probably just an average, bi-polar misfit."

A car pulled up and a woman hurled herself out of the back seat and teetered towards the house, looking as if she would crash face-first onto the pot-holed tarmac at any moment. A WPC stopped her before she'd got a few yards, at which point she started sobbing and screaming.

"Jesus," said Devons, "that must be the sister. If that hysterical bitch is supposed to calm him down and encourage him to come out smiling, then we've got a bloody long wait ahead of us."

The woman was dressed in an anorak and a skirt so short it looked at first glance as though she was only wearing the anorak. She had been brought from her home in Stoke Newington, where she was known to the local police as the recipient of a number of convictions for shoplifting, receiving stolen property and other petty crime since she was a teenager. She was thought to be an occasional prostitute, although the police had never prosecuted her as such. Her hair, which had been constructed into a formidable edifice on top of her head, was fast succumbing to the continuous rain and beginning to collapse over her face like an ice-sculpture under hot lights. She was stumbling on 4-inch stilettos and her heavy make-up was suffering a similar fate to her hair under the onslaught of water from both the sky and her streaming eyes.

"If I'd been asked to describe his sister without ever having seen her, that," said Devons, gesticulating off-handedly with her thumb, "would be it."

"She must have spent a lot of time getting ready for the cameras. Pity about the rain, she looks as though someone has poured a bucket of river mud over her head."

"I think she'd look like that even without the rain. But I'm sure the press will make sure she gets her 15 minutes of fame, bedraggled or not. Then she can go and drown her sorrows tonight in Tia Maria, or Southern Comfort and lemonade, or whatever it is the masses take solace in these days," said Devons, showing no inclination to get out of the car. But then she suddenly roused herself and within a few seconds was gone, leaving her curious odor behind and wafting it into Spencer's face as the car door slammed shut.

He watched her march across to the woman, who was with Cheeseman and his boss, a Chief Superintendent Spencer hadn't seen before, but whom, to judge from his nervous demeanor, Devons would eat alive if he didn't do things as she thought they should be done. Spencer stayed where he was, reflecting to no useful purpose on the strange mixture of emotions he was experiencing.

The power of Devons, he thought, seemed to stem from her assurance. Even when she was being flippant and conversational, there was an air of confidence about her that one seldom encounters. Not only was she feisty and ballsy, but unlike some of that ilk she showed no signs there were any chinks in her armor, and she was always completely convinced of the validity of her opinions, even if they were patently wrong. One could call it intransigence, obstinacy, insensitivity, or even stupidity on occasions, but there was no doubt it was impressive to see someone so sure of themselves they appeared to be standing on three legs, and not swaying unsurely on the unstable two most of us are blessed with.

Several minutes later, Cheeseman yielded the bull-horn to the sister and guided her to a row of squad vehicles, which she could stand behind and address the house and its single occupant.

"Ello. Jesus Christ is this bloody fing workin? Ello Enry. It's me. Can e ear me? You sure? Ello Enry. It's Christine. Are yer listening? Gimme some sign yer listening an I'm not talkin to meself."

"I can bloody ear yer. Waddya want?" Losely appeared at an upstairs window holding the gun butt in his right hand and the barrel in his left, showing no sign of using it but flaunting it to anybody who needed confirmation he was armed.

"What yer doing in there? Why don't yer put that gun down and come out ere?"

"Like I told the bloke this morning, I ain't coming out till the fuckin police tell me I ain't a suspect, and they're gonna find the fucker what killed Jane, and not keep finking I fuckin done it."

Cheeseman, who was standing beside the sister, mumbled something to her.

"They don't fink yer did it, they just wanna talk to yer."

"Like fuck they fuckin do. Do they fink I'm bleedin stupid? I know they've bin looking for me, telling everyone I done it. Well I fucking didn't do it, and I'll blow me bleeding ead off before they stick this one on me, an I'll shoot any fucker who tries to stop me an all."

"Why don't yer let me come in an talk abart it? I'll come on me own."

Cheeseman took her arm and spoke to her, but she shook him off.

"Yer can't stop me talking to im," she said, addressing Cheeseman through the bull-horn at point-blank range. Spencer saw Cheeseman wince, step backwards and growl something. "Oh, sorry," she said, still talking through the bull-horn "I was forgettin." Devons, who was standing a few yards away, turned to face Spencer, a schoolgirlish grin lighting up her face.

"I ain't got nuffing to say to nobody, I just want the police to do what I say. Why the fuck are they after me? I loved er. Why the fucking ell would I wanna kill er?" His voice rose in pitch as he spoke. Although the scene was farcical and the protagonists pathetic, Spencer wondered if the outcome might not be dramatic and tragic. He got out of the car and walked towards Devons, who was staring at the ground and shaking her head. Spencer assumed she was laughing to herself, but when she looked up there was just an expression of exasperation on her face.

"How do people end up with lives like that?" she said.

"Genetics, nurture, environment, peer pressure, lack of opportunity, drugs, booze, poor parenting, bad education, anger, pure chance. Who knows? They've probably got no more idea than we have. And who's to say he wasn't in love with the whore? There are stranger love stories than that in the world. They've made operas out of some of them."

"You're a sympathetic character, aren't you, Spence?" she said, and as was usual with her, he couldn't tell whether it implied respect or derision.

"Just realistic. The more people you see the more you realize we're all in the same boat, but some are traveling first class and others are up to their necks in water, hanging onto the side just trying to stay alive."

"And where are you?"

"Sometimes I think I'm sitting on a beach watching it all happen. Coppers don't participate in people's lives, they walk into them and walk out again, trying not to get sucked in and drowned themselves."

The conversation between brother and sister was going on as before. Nothing new was being said, but the fact they were talking was a positive sign and implied the gunman would give himself up. Spencer found the sister's amplified voice so annoying, however, that had it been him with the gun, he would probably have blown her head off rather than put up with any more of the inane dialogue.

Devons appeared to be reflecting on what Spencer had said, but instead of replying she turned around and marched to the sister, who had the bull-horn still pressed to her lips, even though she wasn't speaking. Devons pulled the bull-horn from the surprised woman and started addressing the gunman.

"Henry, my name is Chief Superintendent Sally Devons. I can assure you we're presuming nothing, and there is absolutely no likelihood of our charging you with something you didn't do. But we really need to be able to talk to you so that we can eliminate you from our enquiries, and as soon as we've done that, we'll leave you in peace. We really want to track down Jane's killer, and as you knew her you may be able to help us, so we really need to have a chat with you. Now I'd like you to unload the gun, throw it through the window and come out of the house, then we can tidy this matter up and you can go home and forget about it, and we can get on with our investigation and find the real culprit. I'm sure you'll agree with what I'm suggesting, but we can't go looking for Jane's killer while we're tied up here, can we? So just take out the shells, throw the gun out of the window and come out and have a talk with me."

"Are you police?"

"Yes, I'm a police officer."

"Then why are you fuckin trying to pin this on me?"

"Henry, really, we're not, and I'm sorry if you've got that impression. But you knew Jane and we always have to talk to the friends and relatives of anyone who meets with a violent death. It's just standard procedure in cases like this, but we can't eliminate you until we've talked to you."

"Eliminate me?"

"Eliminate you from our enquiries, so that you can tell us anything you know."

"Like what?"

"Well, you might have some idea who did this, for example."

"I ain't."

"But you can probably tell us who Jane's friends were, who she mixed with, then we can go and contact those people and see if they have any useful information. That's what police work is about, Henry, following leads until we come up with something useful, and you're just one loose end at the moment that we need to tie up ... I mean sort out, and then you can get on with your life."

"I loved er. Why would I kill er?"

"Henry, I have no earthly reason to believe you killed her. You have nothing to fear from us. We just want to talk."

"Why should I fuckin believe yer?"

"Nobody has to believe anybody Henry, but the world would be a pretty awful place if they didn't, wouldn't it? You want us to believe you, so it's only fair you believe me in return. I guarantee you'll get a fair crack of the whip, I promise you that Henry."

The sister made a grab for the bull-horn, saying "Ere, lemme talk to im, e don't trust yer." But Devons said "No. Wait and see what he's got to say."

"Yer promised, yer fuckin promised, didn't yer?" he shouted, sounding more like a little boy negotiating with his mother.

'Yes Henry, I promised, and I'll stand by that promise, and so will every other police officer out here, I guarantee it."

"Yer fucking better ad," he shouted, and then repeated himself, more quietly, as if reflecting on it. Nothing was heard for a while, and then Spencer's heart stopped as a shotgun blast rang out, followed a few seconds later by another. Everyone ducked. Devons - who had every right to think the shots were directed at her - had the presence of mind to drag the sister down with her, and the two of them were crouched behind a patrol car, the sister screaming hysterically.

"What the fuck is e doing? What the fuck is the stupid bastard shooting at me for? I'm trying ter fucking elp im. Fuckin lunatic!"

Spencer could see the house, and as he watched he saw the shotgun come flying through a pane of glass in one of the downstairs windows and land in the overgrown and litter-strewn mess that constituted the garden. Seconds later, the front door flew open and the man walked out with his hands in the air. He was swaggering as he walked down the garden path, but before he arrived at the broken front gate four policemen jumped on him and slammed him to the ground. Spencer winced as he saw Henry disappear under a mass of well-filled police uniforms – he would have done better to have a horse fall on him. A half strangulated cry puffed from Henry as the impact with the concrete of the garden path knocked the wind out of him.

"What they fuckin doing to im?" the sister shouted. Devons grabbed her before she could run to her brother, and entrusted her to a nearby WPC. Devons walked over to the man, who was now being hauled to his feet, his hands cuffed behind his back.

"Yer fuckin said yer wanted ter talk. What are these cunts doing to me?" he gasped, still not able to get his breath.

"Just precautions Henry, we need to make sure you're not armed. Now they'll take you to a place where we can talk, and if it all turns out okay, as I'm sure it will, you'll be cleared of anything to do with Jane's death."

"Yer fuckin promised, remember?"

But Devons had already turned her back on him and was striding towards the car.

Despite Cheeseman's efforts to show otherwise, it was proven within 24 hours of the siege ending that Henry Losely had never killed anyone. Weller attended his interrogation and reported "It was bloody hard to see how he could tell one end of the shotgun from another, let alone use it to shoot anyone, including himself."

□□□

It's a Family Affair

They continued to work through the names on the optician's list, and from the thousand or so they had processed so far they had labeled eight as being worthy of further consideration, although the selection criteria for picking suspects were based more on coppers' instincts than anything scientific.

Two days later, Spencer was diverted from the case by a curious and depressing crime that occurred in an immigrant family in the Brick Lane area. He was called out late one night to a flat occupied by an Indian man, Vijay Natarayan, his wife, mother-in-law, three children, a male cousin called Ravi, and a number of other people whose relationship to the Natarayans was never clearly resolved and irrelevant to the case anyway. Twelve people occupied a space that would be cramped with six, and Spencer found it impossible to work out the logistics of how they managed to live there in anything other than complete chaos.

The facts were hard to determine, but the outcome was tragic and obvious - one of the children had been stabbed to death. Spencer was on the scene within an hour of the fatal wound being inflicted. But it was at least another two hours before anyone was calm enough to talk about the events cogently, and although nobody seemed to be willfully trying to hide anything or escape justice, it was late the next day before Spencer felt he had the definitive version of events.

Vijay and his immediate family arrived in England legally five years ago. His mother-in-law and cousin Ravi followed a year later, ostensibly to visit their relatives, but they stayed on illegally and almost certainly had no intention of returning to India. The two men and the other adults who shared the flat worked in local shops, restaurants, filling stations and garment factories, earning enough money to support themselves in England and send cash back to a network of relatives in India.

The long-term plan of the Natarayans and cousin Ravi was to open a grocery shop, then a restaurant, then a newsagents, then more retail outlets in an ever expanding commercial empire to which they saw no reasonable limit. But at the rate their savings were growing - given the significant calls being made on them by the many Natarayans back on the subcontinent - it was inconceivable that any part of their plans would come to fruition any time soon, and this imposed a severe strain on the morale of the two men and the morals of one of them.

Unable to focus his enthusiasm on the business empire that was starting to look like a foolish dream, cousin Ravi - a handsome man with curly, jet-black hair and a notable handlebar moustache - turned his attentions to Mrs. Natarayan; although given his somewhat caddish looks, Spencer thought such a man wouldn't need too many excuses to let his eye rove, especially to a woman whose doe eyes, pouting mouth and pert breasts had registered with Spencer from his first sight. Vijay said he had suspected nothing, but how the two managed to have a clandestine affair in the meager square footage of the cramped flat was a mystery to Spencer.

Earlier that day, Vijay had returned unexpectedly from work due to a sudden attack of diarrhea (English food had not lost its ability to cause him such problems with unwelcome frequency). He found Ravi and his wife going at it in earnest, as Vijay graphically and tearfully described it, on the floor of the bedroom, while the children played in the adjacent room.

Vijay simply lost control of his senses. He ran to the kitchen, grabbed a knife, and then hurtled screaming back to the room where his wife and cousin were trying to collect their composure and their clothing. Being blinded by anger, instead of attacking either of the fornicators, he simply stabbed at the first figure that moved into his deranged line of vision, which turned out to be his 5-year-old daughter.

And that was it. Nothing but a tragedy brought on by constrained living conditions, poverty, disappointment and, of course, human chemistry and uncontainable lust. Spencer had no reason to believe Vijay was a criminal who needed to be locked up, and was sure he was driven to his terrible act by circumstances that were unlikely ever to repeat themselves. Vijay was going to suffer more than enough for what he'd done, and to impose any other punishment on him seemed, to Spencer at least, unnecessary and gratuitous. But the judgment was for the court to decide, and having processed the people and the paperwork, Spencer stood aside to let the awful events drag on into a depressing future he didn't even want to think about.

The whole incident careened through Spencer's life in 24 hours, and normally that would have been the end of it, but he was left with a strange feeling of incompleteness which almost amounted to hopelessness. The case disturbed and depressed him much more than he would have expected. There was something so pointless about the whole thing. He felt he wanted to spend more time with the family and try and help them get over what had happened, then at least he may have been able to convince himself his own role wasn't simply meddlesome, vindictive and bureaucratic.

It was deeply ironic that the man who would suffer most in the trials to be played out for the rest of his life in his own mind, Vijay, was the only one whom the criminal justice system would think of punishing, whereas the key protagonist, Ravi, with the active cooperation of Vijay's wife, wouldn't be convicted of anything by any court in the land. It was just a matter of tidying up a tragic bit of human misfortune that would repeat itself in other places and with other players from time to time for as long as humans inhabit the Universe.

In contrast to the case of Vijay Natarayan et al, the multiple murderer he was pursuing was intriguing, glamorous and intellectually demanding - a fact he found embarrassing and degrading to admit.

"Is that," he asked himself, "why I stay in this job? To be stimulated by what I come across, to be intrigued by it and even turned on by it. Have I totally lost the idea I want to help people and improve the world, no matter how slightly and ephemerally?"

Vijay's accidental act of murder left Spencer feeling like a doctor who tries to treat people for an infectious disease that has no cure - all he manages to do is catch the disease himself.

He had said as much in a conversation with Roscoe in the cafeteria, but immediately realized that Roscoe, of all people, was the least likely to know what the hell he was talking about. To Roscoe, police work was just work, something he did with reasonable proficiency to earn a decent living, and for which he had something of a natural talent and affinity. Spencer hadn't ever bothered to wonder why Roscoe became a policeman, and he knew if he did ask, Roscoe would reply as though he'd asked why he'd put on socks that morning – it was just what he did, and whereas unthinkingly doing it was okay, questioning why he did it would be considered distinctly odd. But Spencer was in a mood that was both brooding and careless, and although he knew it wouldn't lead anywhere, he wanted to talk, even if the audience was as disinterested as Roscoe.

"At times I think we ought to have some mechanism for shelving cases if we know that no good can come of pursuing them."

"What's that?"

"There's no possible good going to come out of putting that man, Natarayan, in prison," said Spencer. "We're just going to tie up the criminal justice process, extract some form of inappropriate punishment, screw up a few lives, and cost the taxpayer a load of money."

Roscoe looked blankly at him. But it was a suspicious blankness, as though he suspected Spencer was saying something seditious, but coming from a senior officer with a good reputation, he couldn't be sure.

Spencer continued, unabashed by Roscoe's baffled expression. "A wise man would say the crime inflicted its own punishment, so why take it any further? But no, we have to go through hoops and prolong the suffering, just because."

"But he killed his daughter."

"He didn't mean to."

"No, he meant to kill his wife, or the bloke, and if he'd succeeded he would have been a murderer, not a grieving father."

"Yes, I know that, but fate took a hand, and there's no punishment we can impose that will compare to the one he's already suffering, so why bother?" But as he spoke he stopped believing it himself. Or rather he saw the danger in believing it and letting others see he believed it.

□□□

No Escape Goat

Spencer returned to his office. That afternoon, Devons, who he hadn't seen or spoken to for a couple of days, called a meeting to review progress. Progress. The very word made Spencer feel uncomfortable and bogus. There hadn't been any. The team had worked hard, talked a lot, theorized endlessly and, when there was nothing else to do, just moaned, argued, ate pizza, drank coffee, smoked cigarettes (or, in Spencer's case, agonized about refusing them), joked, chatted and tried to live their lives as normally as was possible, pretending it was "just a job".

To her credit, Devons' attitude gave no hint they weren't getting anywhere. She looked enthusiastic and businesslike, and to see her it was almost possible to believe they would identify their killer by the end of the meeting, apprehend him and get a conviction.

"What's the status on the optician?" she said, turning to Weller.

"We've checked out anyone non-Chinese on the list who seemed worth checking out. It only amounted to about a dozen with records of any sort, and by the time we'd got down to the last one we were looking at some bloke who got into a fight at a football match in the '60s and who's now a Rabbi in Bethnal Green."

"So, what next?"

"We can either start looking at the other non-Chinese males on the list or we ..."

"How many?"

"Eight hundred and seventy two between the ages of 15 and 65. We could have it done in a week with current resources."

"I say do it. Spencer, what do you think?"

"We may as well. It's not as if we've got anything else to work with. We could try more house-to-house around all the murder sites if we get really desperate. We've done reenactments and they did us no good at all. There's nothing else left to try. I suggest we put everyone here to work on the optician's list and work through it as fast as we can. It's getting to be about time for him to have another go."

"Precisely what I was thinking," she said. "The Home Office is making my life a misery at the moment. The Government is expecting to take some stick in the local elections next month for not delivering on their promise of 'safer streets'. Another murder and the Minister will probably be down here himself to run things. You'd think this was the only crime in the country to see the way they're reacting. There have been 23 unsolved murders while our man has been doing his five, but I bet no bloody Fleet Street editor could name one of them. In the last meeting I had with Home Office, they told me they were considering asking the FBI for help in tightening up on the profiling." Her tone left no doubt as to how much value she attached to assistance from across the Atlantic.

"Is there anything else we could be doing?" she said. "Come on, think, anything. I don't care how mad it sounds, just let yourselves go and give me ideas."

There was a long silence which Spencer eventually broke.

"I'm not aware of anything. We've spent hundreds of hours talking to the local prostitutes, madams and pimps. It's not in their interests to hold anything back – just the opposite, this is bad for business – but we've come up with nothing. You're just going to have to step up visible policing and hope we can scare him off or catch him in the act."

"Assuming he comes back to our patch."

"If he doesn't, we're off the hook," said Roscoe.

"No," said Devons, quietly but with barely suppressed impatience. "How can we be off the hook when we've got five unsolved and connected murders on the books here, plus two in Essex that Bennet and his people are making sure we take the credit for, and short of the perpetrator walking into the nick and owning up, not even the remotest chance of catching him? This case is not over just because he stops or because he goes somewhere else and practices his strangling and slashing. It's over when we've caught him and the bastard's securely behind bars for the rest of his wretched, joyless and celibate life."

She was right, of course, but Spencer wasn't completely dismissive of Roscoe's patently tactless comment. If the murderer stopped and never started again, did it really matter whether they caught him or not? If policing is about protecting the community, and their efforts scared the killer off, hadn't they really succeeded, after a fashion?

§

"We've got it down to just over 400, 407 to be exact," said Weller. "That's non-Chinese males between 15 and 65 with addresses in the Greater London area, As far as we can tell there's nobody on the list who's moved within the past two months, so finding someone who's relocated to Chingford and getting a quick result doesn't seem to be a possibility. But we won't know that for sure until we start banging on doors."

"Okay," said Devons, "that's a manageable number. Let's get after them, but for Christ's sake be careful. If our man's on that list, then one clumsy move and he'll be off and running, and he's clever enough that once he's given us the slip we'll never even get a sniff of him again."

Weller didn't need to be told this. But it was true that they would have to be careful, although Spencer suspected that rather than run, the killer would probably commit suicide if cornered. With no further chance of pursuing his bloody obsession, and every chance of spending the rest of his life behind bars, being victimized by other prisoners who would see his fame as a magnet and a provocation, he would probably conclude he had nothing left to live for, given his perverse idea of what constituted a life fulfilled.

The team would pose as tele-marketing researchers checking out TV viewing habits, a subject that most people want to respond to in order to extol their favorite programs and trash the rest. By engaging in conversation with whoever answered the phone, they would try to ascertain if the men were still living in the city. In those cases where they got no reply, or an answering machine, or an unhelpful response then they would resort to other sources of information, such as driving license data and electoral rolls, which although not as up to date, would be enough to rule out those who definitely were no longer in the area. Of course, it was possible the murderer was no longer living in London, and he was commuting to the capital to pursue his obscene hobby. But the weight of evidence relating to other serial killers whose habits had been analyzed indicated that if a killer performed his carnage in one location, he probably lived within 30 miles of that location (50 miles in the USA, "due to the cheaper petrol", as Roscoe had suggested).

"How quickly can you do it?" Devons asked.

"Two days. There'll be a lot of gaps and we'll have to work mainly at nights to find the people at home. If we can cut it down to 150 or so - that'll be suspects and people we couldn't get to - then we can blitz them in two nights of door-banging, which won't give the story a chance to circulate and our man to slope off."

"When can you start?"

"Day after tomorrow. We've got the resources, we just need to work out the approach and brief the team. We'll start with the oldest men on the list, then reconvene briefly and refine the approach, then do the rest. That way we're least likely to screw up when we're working on the most probable suspects, that's white males between 18 and 40-years-old.

It seemed to Spencer that they were talking as if this laborious activity was going to yield a killer, but they all knew that to pin their hopes on 28 square inches of fabric that in all probability had no connection whatsoever to the felon, was an unrealistic display of optimism, borne out of an all too realistic desperation.

"And if our magical piece of cloth doesn't lead us anywhere," said Devons, with sudden irritation, "then we just sit back and wait for him to kill someone else. Great! If it leads to something that damn optician's rag will be more valuable than the holy grail."

When Weller had gone and Devons and Spencer were alone she vented more frustration.

"The Home Office have got these killings chalked up to me. In lieu of having a killer, they've decided to create another victim, a political one. On the surface I get cheesy declarations of support and votes of confidence, but the Minister's made it blatantly obvious that I'm the sacrificial lamb he'll gladly and publicly slaughter if the PM decides the government's losing the Law and Order debate."

"And it was ever thus," he told her. "That's what politics is about. Always make sure you've got an escape route and a warm-bodied sacrifice for the drooling media."

"This could be the end of my career. You know that, don't you?" she said.

"That's a bit dramatic, isn't it? If they canned every C.S. who failed to catch a murderer, then your species would be outnumbered by tap-dancing-yeti."

"I mean an end to my career advancement," she said, impatiently. "I have no intention of remaining a bloody Chief Superintendent for the rest of my life." She spat out the words, as though being a Chief Superintendent was a lowly and menial role that nobody would be happy with, let alone covet. It made Spencer feel inadequate. He would never make C.S. and had never realistically expected to, yet here was a young woman who treated it like an annoying and valueless stepping stone on the path to greater things. But he couldn't really think of any examples to disprove her theory. It was better for a senior police officer to be invisible rather than be associated with failure, however unjustified. That was how the public liked their servants – effective but unseen, like sewers dealing clandestinely with society's unspeakable, stinking detritus.

"You could have made me the sacrificial lamb," Spencer said. "You still can. Assuming I have adequate rank to qualify."

She didn't answer at first, but seemed to be coolly appraising his suggestion, asking herself if that was an option. "Are you offering?" she asked eventually.

"To be honest, the way I feel right now, about this case and a couple of other things that have happened recently, it would be half way to being a mercy killing,"

"Do you feel as if you should be the scapegoat, Spence?"

"No, not really, but since when has that mattered? By definition a scapegoat is a convenient person to blame, not the right one."

"Thanks for the offer Spence, really, thanks, but you failed the audition."

Something in her tone didn't convince him. "But I've been considered for the role already?"

"Yes," she replied, without a pause, "and not by me."

"Not by you?"

"Not once."

"Thank you. I mean thank you for the implied compliment, not for the decision necessarily."

Devons brooded for a moment, then breathed deeply and, pulling herself back into the present, she started to speak quickly.

"I have to go to Liverpool next week for a two-day conference on 'High Profile Policing'. Ha bloody ha. I should be delivering it, not listening to it. I can take one other officer and I want it to be you."

She stopped speaking as abruptly as she had started, and fixed him intently with her gaze. Her eyes betrayed nothing, but Spencer felt an almost physical shock rip through his body, starting in the pit of his stomach and culminating in the dizzying of his head. He had no reason to believe the trip would consist of anything more than an inconvenient journey to a tedious and irrelevant event in a bland setting, but intuition told him he was destined for more, much more and he found himself experiencing a feeling somewhere between adolescent anticipation and mortal dread.

Reflections of Guilt

When Cynthia left, I went to sit in the grounds. I knew I should be feeling desperately upset and confused, but, for some reason which, looking back, I still find largely unaccountable, I was calm. Eerily calm, I suppose one would say. But at the time I was so glad to experience some measure of peace that the inappropriateness of my reaction didn't occur to me. The only way I can account for my coolness - which was far more than I had the right to expect - is that my scientific mind, having put up with my breakdown to a point, was now unwilling to tolerate any further disturbance and it took hold of my errant subconscious, told it to sit in its place quietly while the conscious set about trying to come up with a logical explanation for what I had gone through, and of which I was obviously destined to endure more, much more.

But my stable demeanor in no way detracted from the fact I knew I had unthinkable possibilities to confront, of which the most chilling was that I was involved in the murder of a number of women whilst my mind was in some sort of dysfunctional, abhorrent state. As I muttered this possibility under my breath, trying to use words to make real something too bizarre to comprehend as a mere thought, it was as much as I could do to stop myself laughing out loud. The whole thing was simply absurd, and all I had by way of intimation that I was in any way connected with the killings were the inexplicable visions I had been having, the extreme feelings of guilt that accompanied them, and Leo's macabre and luridly entitled scrap book.

I got up and started walking around the gardens, adjusting my route continually to ensure I kept as far away from others as possible. I don't know how long or how far I walked, it must have been close to three hours. I remember being overcome by successive waves of intense anxiety and then complete detachment. But strong and resolute amidst the wreckage of my life stood my indomitable belief in science and its eternal companion, logic, shining like beacons and offering the inevitability of a rational, though inevitably complex and potentially shocking explanation of what was happening. I regained my faith in what had always been the central component of my life, and it provided me with just enough confidence and stability to survive a course of events I'm sure I could not have survived otherwise.

It was as though I was standing outside myself, able to review terrible possibilities as if looking at someone else, someone with whom I had no physical or emotional connection and for whom I bore no particular empathy. The body I saw as I looked at my reflection in the windows I walked past was that of a stranger; a body for which I was able to feel no responsibility or guilt; an actor performing the script of an evil and perverse play, which the real me was simply observing like an interested audience. Was I hiding from reality? Yes, of course I was, in the same way that a man who determines the physics behind a bomb denies responsibility for the people it kills and the widows and orphans it leaves behind.

At the end of the day I ate every scrap of the dinner placed in front of me, took my medication as directed, and slept almost 12 hours of deep, apparently dreamless sleep. I woke up adjusted to the possibility I could be a murderer, inasmuch as a 'normal' person can ever adjust to such a suspicion. Now I had to find out if I had killed, why and how I had done it, and, most importantly, if I was going to do it again.

I was puzzled by Leo's role. He was a recurring component in so much of what was happening to me that I felt sure he must be in some way actively involved, and not just as a scrapbook-keeping observer but rather as some sort of malicious and manipulative catalyst. If I was involved with the murders, which I still didn't know for a fact, how did he become aware of it? Had I wandered off in a deranged state, only to be followed by Leo who witnessed what happened? Even that sounded too passive. My gut was shouting that Leo had something to do with causing me to do what I did, rather than simply recording what I had done. I had no evidence to support this, but then I had no reason to believe any of the half-facts being presented to me, so intuition was as reliable as anything else I had to work with for the time being.

The only pieces of 'evidence' I could point to were my hallucinations, the guilt feelings they engendered, and Leo's scrapbook. The hallucinations could be due to something else entirely, such as the guilt of bad parenting I had earlier ascribed them to, but the scrapbook was altogether different. The scrapbook supported my intuition that the hallucinations were connected with something very strong and very repugnant to my conscious mind, and when Cynthia told me about it and what it implied in its twisted, grisly title, my reaction had felt more like the shock of discovery than one of false accusation.

I tried to analyze the hallucinations in detail, but it was only the first that offered anything substantial, and that was in the shape of the mysterious room which appeared to me as I was running diagnostic tests on a troublesome computer.

The second and third episodes were more like allegorical dreams, dreams that simply codified and referenced the acts and the harrowing guilt that would engulf a normally law-abiding citizen who had killed. I presumed the room was associated with one of the victims; possibly it was one of the murder sites. The women were prostitutes, and the room had more than a little of the look of a bordello – I say that without ever having been to a brothel, but that's certainly how I imagined one would look.

The obvious thing to do was confront Leo, but merely to think of that option was to reject it. I could imagine his supercilious reaction, and I'm sure he wouldn't tell me anything until he had played with me for a while. If he wasn't extracting some benefit or pleasure from my situation he wouldn't be monitoring and recording the events, so he was hardly likely to help me put an end to them. Also, I didn't want him to know I was aware of his role, active or passive, until I had some definitive measure of my own part, and an idea of his reason for being involved.

I identified four potential avenues of investigation: the scrap book, the reports of the crimes, the image from the first hallucination, and the contents of my own mind. The first two were purely physical and, as a consequence, the ones with which I felt the most comfortable. The third was a matter of comparing my mental image of the room with any information I could garner regarding the crime scenes, to see if there was a match. The fourth was the most difficult and the most imposing, because it involved looking into my mind to try and resolve if it was possible I could be killing women and, if so, why. But it was too frightening a trail to follow even though it had the advantage of being convenient since the object of scrutiny was always sitting atop my shoulders.

I could get information about the murders from the Internet, but I was too frightened of being swallowed up in the computer again, so I wandered into town intending to scour the library for newspaper articles. The newspaper section looked as though a stampede of puppies had been through it. After half an hour of trying to put things in order (with the occasional supervision of a librarian who thought I was doing her a huge favor) I saw there were many gaps.

"I'm afraid," said the librarian, "some of our customers prefer to read the newspapers at home. Only they fail to remember they should buy one themselves if that's the case, and not take ours."

"Fail to remember or choose to forget," I said, feeling immediately comfortable with her. The fact she wasn't a nurse or a doctor made her friendliness more valuable, because I assumed it to be natural rather than a professional requirement.

But as we continued to chat I started to feel uneasy. Here was a woman, a stranger, patently not a prostitute, but how could I be sure she was safe from me? If I was capable of slipping into fugue states and - if Leo's indication was to be believed - committing unspeakable acts, then I should keep away from people, for their sakes as well as mine. It was as if the comparative isolation in which I'd lived my life through immersion in my work was going to be a necessity rather than a choice from now on. I became deeply unhappy and confused, and I only felt slightly better when the librarian went to attend to customers and I could get back to sorting mechanically through the papers to divert my mind from more troublesome thoughts. I was just glad she hadn't asked me what I was looking for.

Eventually I managed to assemble a stack of papers that covered all the murders, some local, some national. By the time I'd done this my hands were black with newsprint. I went to the restroom to wash it off, feeling like Lady Macbeth trying to wash the blood of Duncan off her hands.

I felt sick as I read. I'd never paid much attention to detailed reports of crimes in the past, let alone murders as they are treated in the gutter press, and it was an unwelcome novelty for me to be scrutinizing sensationalized accounts of the so-called 'Criss-Cross Murders.' It probably would have been disconcerting even if I had no reason to think I had anything to do with them, but knowing I might made it many times worse.

The first murder, the only one committed indoors, may have related to my hallucination of the room, although there were no photographs of the crime scene in any newspaper that I could cross-check with my nightmare. Only two of the dailies even mentioned it, and then with only a few column inches – one murder of a prostitute in a big city doesn't make news, I suppose.

But as the number of killings mounted, the frenzy took hold, and the accounts in the national press soon overwhelmed those in the local press, in terms of both coverage and hysteria. The tabloids took the angle of "Jack the Ripper," who had terrorized whores in an almost identical area in the previous century. I paused to wonder if I had shown any particular interest in the Ripper's murders, an interest my subconscious could have hidden and then somehow triggered into action, but I wasn't aware of any.

By the fifth murder it seemed the police were being vilified as much as the killer. There was constant allusion to a Chief Superintendent Sally Devons, whom more than one journalist had cast in the role of an ice-maiden who didn't really care if a few prostitutes were taken off the streets by a self-appointed executioner.

As I read, I felt myself being sucked into the stories, but I can't say there was any flash of insight that told me either I was involved or I wasn't. I felt guilty as I read, but only with that sense of collective guilt I'd previously felt when hearing about shocking acts in the past, as though being a human makes one somehow responsible for what other members of our species do.

After almost three hours in the library I replaced the newspapers, smiled at the librarian, and left. As I walked back to the hospital for dinner and another night of blank, medicated sleep, I knew somehow I had to get my hands on Leo's macabre scrap book and bring this terrible episode in my life to some sort of conclusion, no matter how painful that conclusion might be.

□□□

Breaking the Code

Spencer couldn't participate in the door-to-door – he and Weller were confined to the operations room overseeing the exercise. But both would much rather be out on the streets than coordinating the activity, interrupted occasionally by a stalking and irascible Devons.

"Why doesn't she just damn well leave us alone?" Weller asked after one of her unhelpful and agitated late evening visits to the operations room.

"We want to be out there doing the interviews but we're stuck in here," Spencer replied, "and she wants to be down here running the show but she's stuck in her office. The hierarchy dictates that we fret down here and she frets up there. The irony is that the poor sods out banging on doors would gladly swap with either of us, or rather be at home with their feet up on a dirty night like this."

It had started to rain shortly after the teams had first gone out, and when they came back for the meeting to compare notes and refine the process before moving on to the more likely suspects, they were all soaked. Most had the foresight to bring one or more changes of clothes, but not all had been so prescient.

"Good," said a bone dry Devons, "if it's pissing down with rain they're more likely to find the targets at home." Which was true, but the weather also put the officers in bad moods, so they were less likely to do a thorough job and more inclined to rush through their individual lists quickly so that they could get out of the non-stop rain.

Although the first day threw up no positive suspects, it had gone well. A sizeable proportion of the men on the list had been located and seen, on the pretext that they were being asked for their opinions on a "new series of TV programs designed specifically for men." First reports showed the survey hadn't raised suspicions, and had enabled them to get a conversation going.

The psychologist who had assisted at the briefing had given them a checklist of features to look for in the men they spoke to, features more likely to point to potential suspects, such as those who appeared to be introverted or uncommunicative, living alone or with one other person in a home marked by extreme neatness.

He observed it was often easier to describe how to exclude suspects rather than include them.

"If an open, cheerful, friendly, chatty individual comes to the door, dressed in bright colors, holding a baby perhaps, or with children playing around his feet, or with a smiling wife in the background, then he's highly unlikely to be the man we're looking for. Our killer has locked his heart in a cage, together with his emotions, and he only lets his feelings out when he kills, so the more he does it, the more important his killing becomes to him. His greatest threat isn't us, it's his conscience, because if he looks objectively at what he's doing he'll be as outraged as the rest of us, and his self-disgust will probably lead him to end his life. The killer is set apart emotionally, and that separation isn't likely to be something he can turn on and off, so anyone behaving openly and warmly or showing any trace of a feminine side can probably be ruled out, unless the world's thrown up another Bundy. The TV angle of the survey is a particularly fertile one, because the killer is more likely to be regular viewer, an obsessive viewer even, watching 30 or more hours a week and living in an unreal world where killing is common and emotional repercussions limited or non-existent.

"These are markers to look out for. I don't want to give you too clear a picture of what the standard profile points to, as this man may turn all that on its head and you might miss him if he fails to conform to the image I've created in your minds. So if all else fails, follow your instincts. It's better we don't exclude any possible suspects at this stage, even if it means the next phase is more laborious as a consequence."

As he listened, Spencer felt achingly disappointed. He realized how much he wanted the whole thing to be over, at almost any cost, and the thought of a laborious 'next phase' made him feel tired to his bones, tired enough to want to go sick and hide under the bed covers for days and days, emerging to a sunny dawn and a different profession, one imbued with less hopelessness than he increasingly confronted in his current one. He would like to get a conviction, but he guessed he would also be happy if they just called the whole thing off, admitted failure and drew a line under it. He couldn't shrug off the feeling the present exercise should lead somewhere, given the huge amount of effort they were putting into it, but his deeper intuition told him it was a well-intentioned waste of time.

What a novelty, he thought it would be, if policemen could stand up at press conferences and say "Well, we're just giving up on this one. Better luck next time." His profession seemed rare in that admissions of defeat were never acceptable. The public felt their taxes had bought them the right to be protected and revenged, and that right was never abrogated. A doctor could fail to save a life – every life fails to be saved at some point – and businessmen can win some deals and lose others and still point to a profit. But policemen are never allowed to consider the prospect of failing to solve a crime until the felon is identified and removed from society. Locking up two rapists didn't win them enough points to absolve them from catching a child molester. Of course, they often did give up, and every policing decision was a compromise of some sort. By putting extra officers on duty at a football match on a Saturday afternoon, it was inevitable that more than the average number of bags would be snatched from shoppers on the High Street. But defeats and inadequacies were never allowed to be publicized, in the hope that silence would be more comfortable for the general public than honesty, which, he knew, was true in most parts of life, even in our dealings with ourselves.

§

"Spencer," said Devons, "I want to take another look at the marks on the bodies again. Get the clearest set of prints they can possibly make of the mortuary photos of the victims backs."

They'd tried it before, many times, even in their dreams. Tried to work out if there was some sort of message in the gouged noughts and crosses. They'd lined them up, one string of grisly markings after the next, shuffled them around, inverted them, reversed them and put them through every combination of positions imaginable. But no pattern had emerged, let alone any meaning.

"She fucking well must be desperate," said Roscoe, confronting the thought of another marathon session locked up with his colleagues and a set of photographs the team had stared at for weeks.

"Now," said Devons, as bright and fresh as the Head Girl at the start of a new school year when she, Spencer, Weller and Roscoe were assembled, a set of prints pinned on the wall in front of them. "I want to see some creative thinking."

Spencer swallowed hard, Weller sighed quietly, and Roscoe groaned audibly.

"Yes Roscoe, even you," Devons told him. "Try and get that stodgy brain of yours to think of something other than your next tea break. Get over to the whiteboard and start writing down what these marks could mean. Spencer, Weller, call out ideas he can put on the board. I want to see fifty things those damned scratches could stand for. Go!"

They'd listed thirty items, everything from Biblical quotations (Weller) to page references to the Karma Sutra (Roscoe), before Weller stood up and walked over to the wall where the prints were pinned.

"What if the scratches stood for something else? What if the 'X' stands for a '1', then you've got ones and zeroes." The room fell silent whilst they digested this interpretation.

"So what?" said Devons, sounding interested but unclear where this was going.

"Computer code," said Weller. "You know, the way the computers store letters and numbers."

"ASCII," Spencer added, feeling a slight thrill, a thrill he'd almost forgotten he could feel while doing detective work, the thrill of discovery.

"Yeah, that's it," said Weller, "ASCII."

It took them almost four hours and the help of two people from the computer department to decipher the code and make something meaningful out of it. Some of the scratched sequences turned out to run from top to bottom of the victim's back, some from bottom to top. Several scratches were partially obscured by other mutilations, but eventually they came up with the only message that made any sense "DADDY'S."

Seven bodies, seven symbols, six letters and an apostrophe. They'd struggled with the apostrophe, but when they'd got it they'd cheered in unison like schoolchildren who'd just solved a puzzle the teacher had defied them to unscramble. Then they added the "S" from the final corpse and sat looking at the message in silence. "DADDY'S."

"So fucking what?" said Devons, angrily slamming her pen on the table. The silence returned as the others turned to stare at her, waiting for her next words as the pen slowly rolled to the edge of the table and fell to the floor. The euphoria they had felt at cracking the code was slowly replaced with the understanding that it could well be of no tangible value in finding the killer.

"It tells us something," said Spencer. "I may be the only person in the country left to be convinced of it, but it tells us that it's one killer, or a group of killers working together. No copycat could have got the scratches right and in sequence, unless it was a one in a billion coincidence."

"Given the luck we're having, I wouldn't even bloody well rule that out," said Devons.

"It's a complete word," said Roscoe. "If he'd stopped at the apostrophe we'd know there was more coming. Maybe he's finished."

"Or maybe he's starting a book," said Devons, "and he's publishing it on scrubber skin."

Mind over Matter

As Bates lifted the sandwich to his mouth, a dollop of mayonnaise flopped on to his lap. He looked down at it and continued to look at it for some moments, being involuntarily reminded of the two and a half weeks that had passed since he'd had sex. He wiped the mayonnaise off with his finger and licked it clean, then he took out his handkerchief and rubbed at the stained patch on his trousers. But the act of vigorous rubbing put him even more strongly in mind of masturbation than the gob of mayonnaise had, so he looked out of the car windows on all sides to ensure he wasn't being observed by anyone who might have the same thought.

It was still raining, but less heavily than earlier, and with only 15 names left on his list he was starting to think about the end of the exercise. Based on what had happened so far, three or four of the remaining calls wouldn't find anyone in at all. Three or four more would be answered, but the suspects themselves would be out, and he'd just have to try and strike up a conversation with whoever answered the door. Which left seven or eight interviews, so he reckoned he'd be finished in under three hours, have reported back by ten, and be at home sitting in front of the television by 11. But the thought of being back at home was only an appealing one until he remembered how much being at home on his own reminded him of his enforced celibacy.

It was another week and a half before his girlfriend would get back from visiting her sister in Florida, and it would be par for the course if she came back at the start of one of her periods - a coincidence he was beginning to have suspicions about. Why did her menstruation seem to coincide so precisely with the time of the month when his needs were the greatest? It hadn't been like that at the start of their relationship, but the longer they knew each other, the more it seemed to him that events conspired magically to put obstacles in the way of their love making. He was beginning to believe this could no longer be attributed to either statistics, biology or the fact that he was subjectively biased to think he wasn't getting enough sex.

He yawned and looked out of the window again. He saw his life stretching in front of him, frustration piling upon frustration - work, women, money - nothing turning out as he wanted it to. He loved his girlfriend, in a way, and he knew regularity and urgency of sex tended to dwindle as relationships wore on, but in the case of this relationship the rate of dwindle had been remarkable, and was made all the more remarkable by the fact she never stopped dropping hints they should get married. He wondered if there wasn't a connection, and if he gave her some sort of commitment she might let him have his way with her a bit more. But he wasn't convinced it was in her nature to give him the amount of sex he needed, and being an honorable person, sort of, he didn't want to make protestations of love just to get her to open her legs more often.

He thought of a joke someone had told him. Scientists have found a substance that renders women sexually inactive - it's called wedding cake. He'd laughed, but hadn't found it funny; in fact he found it deeply unsettling. Bates suspected he was slowly finding out what men through the centuries had painfully discovered and been forced to come to terms with; that men and women are different in sexual appetites as in just about every other department. Even their armpits smelt different. He sighed, and thinking the act of sighing might lead to yet further depression, he pushed open the car door and hauled himself to his feet on the wet Islington pavement.

Brazenose Street was just around the corner. He didn't want to park too close, but as he started peering at the numbers on the doors and gateposts he was annoyed to see he had come in from the wrong end and had to count down from 224 to his target of number 52. He thought of going back to the car and trying to find a closer parking place, but he hadn't been to the gym for a week – just seeing lithe females there caused pain in his loins - so he could do with the exercise.

The area was much different to the Islington he remembered from his childhood. He'd come through the district on the way to a Spurs game with his Dad and Uncle Ray about 15 years ago. Although his recollection of it was only hazy, he did get enough of an impression to record it as being shabby, and nothing like the gentrified street he was now walking down. With freshly painted front doors, BMWs parked in the road, and a distinct absence of the smell of poverty - which he equated with a heady mixed aroma of cheap fabric conditioner, cigarette smoke and dog shit - Brazenose Street had come up in the world.

He'd remembered Uncle Ray saying something like "Islington, home of the laboring masses." Not anymore. Ray would have been about 19 at the time, just started at University and acting the enlightened socialist – a phase which lasted for about six months, at which point he met a girl he described as a "raving nymphomaniac", and who seemed to be very effective in refocusing his interests in areas other than second-hand Marxism.

At the time, Bates didn't know what "nymphomaniac" meant and he had to go and look it up in a dictionary, which led to one of the most exciting discoveries of his life – that such creatures existed - and subsequently to one of the greatest disappointments - that he never got to hook up with any.

The critical, worldwide supply-shortage of available nymphomaniacs was just the first in a line of many disappointments that had permeated his existence and would probably continue to do so until the day he died, laid in his coffin with a half-erect penis and half-fulfilled dreams.

Bates continued counting down the numbers - 86, 84, 82. He supposed he could find himself living somewhere like this 20 years from now. That would make him 45, and if he was still on the force he could be, what, a Detective Inspector by then? Possibly. He didn't see himself as anything more than that, and at times he wondered if he'd even make it to Sergeant. But in the only piece of career advice his father had ever given him, he stressed the inevitability of promotion if "you stay in the same place, keep your nose clean and don't turn out to be a complete dork", which, as far as he was aware, he'd managed to avoid so far, albeit narrowly on more than one occasion.

56, 54, and ... missing number, but the one after it was 50, so this one must be 52. The first thing he noticed was the racket coming from somewhere inside. As he stood at the front door he felt as if his bones were rattling in time to the deep thump of an angry and insistent rhythm. It wasn't the sort of place to be occupied by a heavy metal band, it was too tidy for that, but the music was of a variety and intensity that Bates didn't associate with the demur middle classes and well-maintained paintwork. He rang the bell. Nothing. He could just about hear it ring over the music, so he knew it was working, but he assumed the residents were having their ear drums completely dominated by the decibels from The Aryan Hate Band or whoever it was playing, leaving no room for a feeble tinkle of a doorbell. He rang again and knocked too. He didn't want to hang about, and didn't feel able to put it down as a "not at home" when it was clear somebody was at home, so to hurry things along he knocked hard, hard enough to hurt his knuckles. The volume of the music didn't seem to alter, but through the frosted glass in the door he saw a shape move down the hall towards him.

In certain circumstances, and at certain stages of his life, what Bates saw before him would have given him intense pleasure, but in his current frustrated state it disturbed him more than he could bear.

The vision was pretty, young, long black hair falling over her face, no more than 16, maybe less. But what affected him with an almost physical pain was that she was wearing a black micro skirt, a red blouse falling open to reveal the edge of a black bra, which appeared to contain two small but firm breasts, and she was eyeing him with a pouting, provocative expression that made him want to turn and run before he was overcome with a lust he wouldn't be able to control. He heard his mind mutter "Oh my God" as he struggled to regain his composure. Moments like this revealed the world and his role in it transparently. Life was so often a matter of not knowing what to do, and trying to hit upon the best course of action.

Right now, however, he knew precisely what he wanted to do, but, unfortunately, he knew if he did it, it would probably be the end of his career and might even involve a long custodial sentence.

The girl could have been about the same age as his cousin Cindy – a petite teenager he still saw as a little girl, to whom playing with dolls was still more appealing than playing with boys, parts of boys, and boys' emotions. But this girl's expression left no doubt about what game she was interested in playing, and it was causing the physical reaction that had started in his penis to grow into an excruciating ache, which was quickly taking over his whole body and mind. To make matters worse (not that they could have got much worse, short of his trousers popping open of their own accord to reveal the extent of his agitation), the girl now proceeded to lean back against the wall of the hallway, and bend one leg so that she could plant the sole of her bare foot on the wall, a pose in which so much of her thigh came into view that Bates actually thought he might faint or lose possession of his senses in some other way.

He realized he hadn't said anything, and in so doing he also realized his mouth was propped open. He swallowed quickly, thinking he might be about to start dribbling, but his mouth was dry and the act of swallowing caused him to utter a rusty croak.

"Good evening," he said. It came out better than he had expected. The girl said nothing, but simply eyed him up and down for a few seconds that seemed like an eternity.

He was about to go on when she drawled out a casual "Hi." and shifted her position slightly. He swallowed again. An image of Lauren Bacall in an old Humphrey Bogart film sprung to his mind, but it then sprung out again leaving his mind completely blank, as if completely sucked clean of any ability to think sensibly.

"Is Mr. ..." He'd forgotten the name. He looked at his hand and was surprised to find it clutching a clipboard. He was so disorientated he'd completely lost track of what he was doing and why he was doing it. He brought the clipboard up to his face, much closer than it needed to be for him to read it. For a moment he couldn't work out how to find the name he was looking for, but then he noticed the check beside the name "Dorrell", and saw the name immediately beneath it was "Henderson". He swallowed again, but there was no saliva left in his mouth and he heard a grunt as his esophageal muscles groaned again at having nothing to work on. The dryness of his throat was in distinct contrast to the sticky dampness he could feel spreading through his underpants.

"Is Mr. Henderson in?"

"What?" she said, after another exaggerated pause. Her eyes hadn't left him since she'd answered the door. He became aware again of the music thumping away in the background.

"Is Mr. Henderson at home?" It was an effort to get his dry mouth to generate sufficient volume, but the combined frustrations of not being able to speak fluently, of not being able to think like a grown man in the presence of a young girl, and the overwhelming frustration of not being able to suggest what he would like to suggest, made him suddenly angry - angry enough to overcome his gaucheness.

"Could you turn the music down a bit, perhaps?" He was surprised he'd said it. This was her house and for all she knew he was a salesman or some other bloody nuisance caller who had no right to disturb her evening, let alone dictate at what volume she should play her music. But he was wound up enough not to care. He had disgraced himself by his reaction to this suburban Lolita, and he would probably embarrass himself further by the time she slammed the door on his back, or even his front, so he really had nothing to lose.

"No," she said.

"Oh," he said, and he assumed that would be the decidedly unsatisfactory end to their negotiation on the subject of the appropriate decibel level against which to conduct a conversation. But she continued.

"It's my brother. You can ask him to turn it down, but he won't do anything, and depending on how you ask him and how he's feeling, you may wish you hadn't mentioned it." Her voice was a young girl's voice, but the drawl added years and worldliness to it.

"Okay, never mind," he said, repressing the thought he was a policeman, a policeman on duty, an authority figure, one who had the right to a bit of respect and compliance with his wishes. You're a nerdy market researcher he told himself. Act humble. His penis inopportunely readjusted its position to make itself more comfortable and, he was sure, more obvious. The bloody thing had a mind of its own, and at this moment was determined to make him, and probably the girl too, aware of its presence and state of grossly inflated anticipation. She may not be able to read my mind, he thought but sure as hell she can read the shifting creases and bulges in my trousers.

"So, is he in then, your, er, father? Mr. Henderson?" The girl was probably thinking he was a half-wit. How could a grown man, a copper, an adult with an attractive, doting girlfriend and an occasionally active sex life, be intimidated by a stripling of a girl, who took her poses and poutings from re-runs of Baywatch and old copies of Playboy, probably discarded by the same brother who was disrupting their conversation with something that now sounded like a Nazi marching song inciting the pure-bred populace to do nasty things to anyone not of their persuasion or ethnicity.

Again a pause. Again a drawled answer. "No, he's away" The pauses and the slow responses made him wonder if she was all there, and he couldn't stop himself from thinking if she wasn't all there it might be easy to screw her and get away with it.

"Oh, okay. We're doing a survey you see, on television viewing habits of adult males. Will he be in tomorrow?" he heard himself asking, his voice reverting to normal.

"No, he's in Chingford for a while."

"Oh, okay. Shame, I mean … well …"

"But I may be interested."

"What?" Bates said, seeing and feeling a blinding light flash inside his head.

"I like watching adult males. So do I qualify for a going over?"

Her eyes were boring through him, and there was no doubt about it this time, he was definitely going to faint, run, or grab her.

But at that moment a door at the end of the hallway moved, and as Bates looked towards it he saw emerging something that turned out to be a paw, followed by a large dog that bounded towards him, tail wagging in an outpouring of delight at the sight of a new person to investigate. He wasn't good at identifying dogs, but he thought this one might be a Doberman, and although it didn't seem to have any malicious intent, it would probably have been better if it had, because what it chose to do out of friendliness was to launch its muzzle at Bates' crotch, which, he later deduced as he reflected on his evening, was probably sending out enough smells and hormonal markers to attract all the bitches in the borough.

The high velocity collision between the dog's nose and Bates' uncomfortably enlarged organ brought matters to a rapid conclusion. The pain and shock caused him to step back, nearly falling off the doorstep as he did, and in correcting his balance he found himself backing half way down the garden path, at which point retreat seemed not only prudent but practical and half completed anyway.

"Okay, never mind," he called, "some other time."

The last image he had of the Henderson household was of the girl hanging on to the dog's collar. The two of them being about the same size, it was hard for her to restrain the excited beast, but Bates made it to the front gate and was soon striding down the street, feeling an uncomfortable mixture of humiliation, relief and dampness.

He'd walked over 100 yards before he saw he was heading in the wrong direction, but he had no intention of walking back again, in case his own weak will or the Siren's call dragged him towards number 52. He would go round the block and take the opportunity of using the additional exercise to regain his composure and deflate his ardor.

But then he stopped dead in his tracks. "Chingford," he said, out loud, and then "Chingford" again, under his breath, and by the time he got back to his car and had picked up the radio handset with his shaking hand, he had recited the magic mantra a hundred times, "Chingford, Chingford, bloody fucking Chingford!"

Bate and Link

"We've heard from a highly excited D.C. Bates," Roscoe told Weller.

"Norman?"

"Eh?"

"Norman Bates was it? Asking if we've found his mother yet? And if not, could we suggest any good motels locally? Prefers ensuite facilities." said Weller, getting into his stride.

Roscoe had a habit of releasing information piecemeal, requiring the recipient to constantly prompt him for the next part, as though constructing a jig-saw from pieces that were only taken from the box one at a time, and not always in the right order. Weller had found it amusing when they first worked together, but once the novelty wore off, which took less than a week, he found it annoying. Knowing he had to control his annoyance if he wanted to have an agreeable working relationship with Roscoe, whom he liked, he developed the technique of placing witticisms, flights of fancy, or even just the first thing that came into his head in the gaps Roscoe laid in front of him.

"He called from Islington." Pause.

"Funny, I though he lived in the U.S.A."

Weller realized Roscoe probably hadn't seen Psycho, the Hitchcock movie, so his joke was wasted. Roscoe didn't always seem to understand Weller was poking fun at him, or even that he was joking at all, and this was one of those times. Weller didn't think any the less of Roscoe for this, nor for the prolonged pauses he interjected between some of his sentences, which to begin with Weller had interpreted as a possible sign of simpleness on his colleague's part. He now knew Roscoe wasn't simple, a bit slow at times perhaps, and not much of a profound thinker, but he wasn't daft. Weller guessed the pauses stemmed partly from the fact he liked reassurance he was being listened to, which is why he waited for prompts to lead him on. Weller often wondered whether his colleagues were listening to what he said himself, so it was understandable Roscoe should feel the same and have developed a mechanism to continually test them.

Spencer dealt with the silences by saying nothing, just waiting for him to continue. Devons would say something like "For God's sake get on with it man!" which had little effect on Roscoe's manner of delivery and made Devons even more impatient, but they seldom spoke, so it hadn't done him any harm as far as Weller knew, although it would probably hold him back from promotion. Not that Roscoe ever showed any sign of wanting to be promoted.

"He was interviewing a girl in a house in Islington, suspect name of Henderson, and according to the daughter he spoke to, the father is temporarily in Chingford," said Roscoe in one of the longest uninterrupted sentences Weller had ever heard him speak.

"How long has he been there?"

"Don't know."

"Is he due back?"

"Don't know."

"Do we know any more about Mr. Henderson, other than he's in Chingford?"

"No."

Weller paused for a moment.

"Okay, let's give Norman the benefit of the doubt and assume he didn't press her for fear of making her suspicious."

"Who?"

"Norman Bates."

"Do you know him?"

"No, but I knew his mother." Weller realized he had gone too far, and should explain, but he was unusually tired and couldn't be bothered, which also explained why at first he couldn't get too excited about the Henderson/Chingford link. But as he thought about it he realized it was probably their best lead so far, and as his enthusiasm started to grow his tiredness started to recede. It was a promising coincidence, if nothing else.

"When will Bates be back?"

"About an hour and a half. I told him to finish his list and come straight to me when he got here."

"Good. I'll tell Spence."

When told, Spencer who was also tired, but not unusually in his case, reacted in the opposite way to Weller, in that his first reaction was excitement, which then went on to be tempered with skepticism. But he tried to maintain the excited aspect for public consumption, particularly since Weller was now fully convinced they were on to something.

"It doesn't sound as though we're going to get any more out of Bates," Spencer said, "so we should think about how we're going to fill in the gaps on Henderson without putting the cat amongst the pigeons. We should drag up anything we can on the bloke before we close in on him, and check with the optician to make sure we've got the right man – for all we know something may have got lost in the translation from Mandarin Chinese to PC Plod English."

"Looks promising though, doesn't it?"

"Yes. It's the best news since we found the cloth."

"Yes!" said Weller, adding an uncharacteristically boyish gesture, clenching his fists and shaking them in the air like a footballer celebrating the scoring of a goal. Spencer felt mildly embarrassed at what he took to be his colleague's rather contrived show of enthusiasm.

"But remember the profile. A man living in a family is not a likely suspect. Our chap is more likely to be on his own or in a loveless, childless marriage. Having a daughter and living in a comfortable house in Islington bucks the trend, so don't get too carried away."

Spencer knew saying this would have little effect on Weller, who was one of those coppers who think psychologists have as much use in solving crimes as clairvoyants. Roscoe, strangely for a man with such down to earth opinions in most areas, shared this distrust of psychologists but had an unshakeable faith in clairvoyants, based exclusively on the success of some tea-leaf reader, who told him when he was 19 how his life would work out. Roscoe had told

Spencer about this pivotal moment in his past some time ago, causing Spencer to wonder how a man convinced by a cluster of vague allusions and 'one size fits all' predictions could make a reasonably good detective – it was a question he still hadn't resolved.

"Will you tell Devons?" asked Weller.

"I'll tell her, but not until after we've seen Bates. If she knows beforehand she'll want to be in on the meeting, and the way she's acting at the moment she'll scare the living daylights out of him."

"So why should he be any different to the rest of us?" Weller asked.

"No reason, I just think if he's got anything interesting to add he's more likely to do it without a fire breathing Amazon scorching his backside. He probably thinks he's won a promotion through getting lucky on this one. Let him live with that delusion for a day or two, then he can come down to earth gently, rather than having Devons burst his balloon."

☐☐☐

According to Plan

"Tell us about it," Spencer said, trying to come across as affable and avuncular. He knew Bates would be excited, possibly even over-awed by finding himself at the center of a serial murder investigation, and what had turned out to be the most publicized investigation in the city for a long time.

"It was the daughter I saw, sir. The son was in the house too but I didn't get to see him, I just heard his music."

"The wife wasn't there?"

"I didn't see her and the daughter didn't mention her. I don't even know if there is a wife, actually. I didn't think I could probe into that, being a market researcher and all that."

Bates had been practicing this interrogation for the past two hours, and he knew he would have to account for gathering so little information. He could hardly say he was distracted by his libido and really didn't know anything apart from the words Henderson and Chingford – he just hoped that was enough.

"What sort of house was it?"

"Nice, comfortable, well looked after, good area. Definitely middle class. Range Rovers and Mercs in the street, but I didn't see a car outside their house."

"And the daughter didn't say what her father was doing in Chingford?"

"No sir, and I didn't ask because, well ..."

"Yes, I know, don't worry about that. The main thing is you got the information we need and you didn't put your foot in it. You didn't put your foot in it, did you?"

"No sir, I couldn't have been there more than a couple of minutes" - even though it had felt like an excruciating lifetime under the gaze of the pubescent prick teaser.

"Nothing else?"

"No sir. Oh, well, there was a dog, but ... well, it was just a dog." Saying it reminded him of the pain and the embarrassment and the pain of the embarrassment.

"Okay, go home and put your feet up."

"Thank you, sir. Is that all then?"

"Yes."

Bates got up. He was a little unsteady on his feet, and he had a feeling of incompleteness, of dangling in space, as if there was some unfinished business. He hadn't really known what to expect, but he didn't think it would be quite as low key as it had turned out.

"Oh, Bates."

"Yes, sir?"

"Good job."

"Thank you, sir, well, I didn't really do anything wonderful, did I?" he said, immediately regretting his modesty.

"You must have done something right to get the Chingford connection out of it, and you may just have helped solve a murder case. That's no small thing, no matter how much of an accident it was. Police work takes sweat, brains and luck, and if you can only have one, pick luck."

"Yes, sir, thank you, sir." As he walked to his car he thought that if he'd been confident and matter-of-fact he may not have got anything out of the girl, and perhaps his discomfort in front of her had somehow exercised the magic that had caused her to utter the word "Chingford", which, in the circumstances, was potentially more valuable than 'Abracadabra', or 'Rumplestiltskin', or 'Open Sesame' in finding this particular treasure. Perhaps, he thought, testosterone in a pressurized container stimulates the brain to do exceptional things if it can't find any other outlet.

§

When Spencer told Devons, she said nothing. She nodded slowly and continued deliberately nodding for some moments.

"Okay," she said at last, "and what do you plan to do next?" She surprised him in the way she spoke. There was no condescension in her voice, no implication she would only be interested in views inasmuch as they could be compared to and modified to suit her own. Although Spencer thought she treated him as well as anyone, he had never, before now, managed to feel she would defer to his experience and wisdom and watch as a supportive observer. As a consequence, her question took him by surprise.

"Well," he said. It was just past midnight and he'd only got four hours sleep before getting up at six that morning. He had to coax his tired brain into activity. "We'll run all the background checks on him we can. We've already got someone watching the house, so we'll know if he goes back there and we can tail him or nail him after that. If the checks don't enable us to track down precisely where he is in Chingford, we'll have to pay an official call, but I'd rather not do that if we can avoid it.

"If he's our man, the family almost certainly doesn't know about his little hobby, but even if we don't tell them why we want to see him, their first reaction may be to warn him off. I don't think we can play the market research game again, so our next approach to the family will have to be overt, and I'd like to delay that for as long as possible. Also, if he's not our man, I see no reason to shake down his loved ones unnecessarily."

"And what if there's another murder tonight? How will the press react when they find out we had identified a strong suspect, but didn't manage to reel him in before some other poor innocent scrubber got her neck tied in a knot?"

Spencer felt stupid. He hadn't really considered it likely that Henderson was their man – it would be just too lucky – so he hadn't thought through the improbable but possible scenario Devons painted. But his overwhelming reaction was anger. She had lulled him into a false sense of security by soliciting his views, by seeming to leave the case in his hands, but now she had pointed out an elementary blunder that would embarrass a rookie with two months on the force. By now he was wide awake. He could feel his heart beating as it pumped adrenaline through his system.

"If we think there's a good chance of that ..." he said, "if we think there's *any* chance of that, then we have to go in with all guns blazing and get the family to tell us where he is so we can round him up."

"And what's wrong with that?" she asked.

Spencer thought he could detect a smile playing on her lips, but he had no way of telling if it was one of malice or of comradely amusement.

"It blows everything into the open."

"So?" She added no more and he didn't reply.

They just looked at each other. After a substantial pause she continued, which made him feel he'd scored a small victory by out-staring her – a feeling, which immediately made him feel puerile.

"If we've got a serial murderer running around out there we can't identify, what harm does it do to feel a collar, even if it's the wrong one? And if you're tempted to say 'we might embarrass an innocent party', don't bother."

"Suppose the family say they don't know where he is. What would we do? Arrest them all? Put the whole family under 24x7 surveillance and set up a phone tap immediately? Intercept all email? Extend surveillance to all third parties the family deals with in case one of them acts as messenger? We could be trailing half of London within a few days," said Spencer.

"So what if they did warn him? At least it would stop him killing tonight, and his running would demonstrate we've got the right man," she said

"Not necessarily. It could mean he's got something to hide, but maybe he just fiddled his taxes or didn't pay his TV license. If it's a toss-up between getting him tonight at the risk of losing him, and waiting until tomorrow night and risking another murder, I would say we wait. If you think there's a real chance of him killing again tonight, then let's go in, but that has to be your decision, because it wouldn't be mine."

"Is this a mutiny, Spence?" she said, her expression now

definitely a smile, but not quite a friendly one.

"No. If you tell me to raid the house I'll be there before you are." He doubted that, but it sounded vaguely impressive, not that he felt at all impressed by his role in this provocative and discomforting conversation. "I obey orders"

"Do you?" she said. Her remark took him by surprise. Her smile was now sly, conspiratorial, laden with some meaning, but he didn't know what meaning.

"Yes, always. Almost always."

"Okay," she said after a long pause. "We'll do it your way. Now go home and get some sleep. You look awful."

"I ..."

"But be back here at eight."

"I'll be ..."

"And if you're wrong about this. It'll be you standing in front of the television cameras explaining what went wrong ..."

"I can handle ..."

"... because I'll be sitting at home with my feet up. Unemployed and unemployable."

Spencer left, feeling as he had done when, as a young detective, an antagonistic but respected superior, his reluctant and irascible mentor, Detective Inspector Lambton, had laboriously pointed out something thoughtless Spencer had done or said, and was intent on driving the point home with an excruciating degree of humiliation. It was as though his brain had been sucked out through his ears and replaced with barely set, flavorless jelly, all future hopes of independent, sensible thought banished to a position of complete impossibility.

☐ ☐ ☐

Masking Reality

"You can't trust anyone," said Bill Eckert, my fellow patient and self-appointed sage. "You can't never trust nobody." He paused with an astonished look on his face, but I couldn't tell if he was surprised by the statement or the unusually bad grammar he had used in making it.

"What do you mean?" I said, worried. A week ago I would have put this sort of authoritative announcement down to Bill Eckert being Bill Eckert, but after what I'd been through it seemed an ominous statement to be making to me, of all people.

"Nobody is what they seem"

Even more ominous. Did he know something? I was being paranoid. "I don't understand," I said.

"Take me, for example. How do you know I'm not a doctor, or a social security spy put in here to unmask frauds and winkle out malingerers? You don't, do you? I could be boring old Bill Eckert, or I could be some sort of plant, you know, a snitch, a grass, a fifth columnist."

"Are you?"

"Well, I'd hardly be likely to tell you if I was … or were …" Again the puzzled expression, as though he was having a bad grammar day and couldn't quite work out why. A number of the patients in the hospital had the habit of looking confused by their own words, as if someone else was saying them and their brains were baffled by what was coming out of their mouths.

"Why would you not be what you seem?" I said, hoping the same was true of myself. If I didn't remember killing anyone, the most logical inference was that I hadn't, and by worrying myself into a state of nervous collapse I was simply pandering to the sick tastes of my malevolent son.

"Are any of us what we appear to be?" he said, as though I was a half-wit for thinking anyone would be. "Don't we all put on a mask," he went on, "and live our lives behind it? Is anyone really what they appear?"

"We may put on masks, but perhaps the face under the mask isn't radically different from the face on the mask."

He replied with silence, his face tightening longways, then tightening across his cheeks, as though he were donning a succession of masks to show me what he thought of me. Then he yelled something I couldn't make out, shook his fists at the sky, got up and strode away, all in the space of a few seconds. Seeing him in this bizarre mood gave me some selfish comfort. It was a variety of schadenfreude that enabled me to take a little relief in my sanity, compared to his apparent lack of it.

§

Cynthia came to see me that afternoon. Was it just my impression, or was she being guarded? Was she wondering if it was feasible I was capable of what Leo was implying? It was impossible for me to tell, and there was nothing I could do about anyone else's reactions until I discovered the truth for myself.

"I need to see Leo's scrap book."

"Why? I certainly wish I hadn't seen it."

"I've got to find out why he's saying those things about me."

"What things? He doesn't actually say anything, just records events and adds some bizarre phrases."

"The title and the contents say all that's necessary. He's making out I killed those women."

"I'm not going to bring it to you."

"No, I didn't expect you to. I can come to the house and see it. If I leave here right after breakfast I can get home in an hour or so. That leaves me plenty of time to look through it and still be back here for lunch, so I wouldn't be missed. But I need your help."

"How?"

"You can phone me when he's out, and his room is not locked, and check to see if the scrap book's still there. The girls will have to be out too – they'd be surprised to see me and might tell Leo I'd been in his room."

"We're scared of him, aren't we?"

It surprised me she needed to ask. I'd been scared of him for at least two years, and for the past few months I'd been close to terrified. Now I was beginning to see him as some sort of vindictive force out to ruin me, or at least ruin my mind, which was all that really mattered to me.

"Yes, of course we are. But I've no idea why he hates us. Me, that is, why he hates me to the extent he's doing what he's doing."

"But if ..."

"What?" I said, although I knew what she was going to say.

"What if you ... what if you are doing these things? Then he's ... he's protecting you, isn't he? By not telling anyone else, I mean"

"Do you think I want to be protected if I'm ... if I'm a mur ..." I stopped and gulped air before continuing, "... if I'm a murderer? And I don't think he has my interests at heart anyway."

"But what if you are doing it?" she said, tears trickling down her cheeks.

"Then I want to be locked up and treated, and not released until I'm cured, and if I can't be cured, not completely cured, I never want to be let out into society again. In fact ..."

"What?"

"In fact if I can't be cured I want to die."

She looked shocked. "You don't mean that." We stared at each other in silence before she added "Do you?"

"Would you want to live with a murderer? A callous murderer of women? You don't need to answer. You don't, and nor do I. Death is the only way I can get away from myself if I can't be completely cured. I have no other option. Do I?"

§

I was okay until I got to the underground station. Then the nature of my task hit me, augmented by the frightening sight of the largest group of people I'd seen in one place since my last hallucination had summoned up a hostile, bloodthirsty crowd. I didn't want to see the damned scrap book, and the possibility that Leo could come home whilst I was looking at it made the prospect of the exercise seem even more unpleasant. But I had to find out what was happening and why it was happening, and this seemed the only promising avenue, short of turning myself into the police and asking them to prove to me I was or wasn't a murderer.

Our house has a secluded alleyway running behind it, and out of fear of bumping into any of the neighbors I went round that way rather than going to the front door. Cynthia let me in. I'd planned to say something casual to make light of the enterprise, but I could barely speak when I saw her. I wanted to hug her, but I was worried she might recoil, given the person that I might be, so I just squeezed her arm gently instead. I was thinking about her last visit to the hospital and what I had said, and meant. She was probably thinking if I found out I was a killer over the next minutes or hours, I wouldn't be seeing her for some time, may never live with her again, and might even take my own life – a range of possibilities I still considered more likely than not. I hoped she felt sad at the thought our relationship could be about to end, I know I did. Being alone with her in the house under a cloak of secrecy reminded me of the start of our relationship when we were intimate strangers, and I realized most of our marriage had been conducted on the same impersonal terms, until now, ironically.

I stopped outside Leo's door. Cynthia was behind me.

"He's out?" I asked, stupidly, as if she would now say "Oh no, he came back a while ago. I forgot to say."

She nodded

"And the scrap book's there?" I asked, and although she might have said "Why don't you just open the bloody door and find out?" she didn't, and just said "Yes". It was as though I was about to try to defuse a bomb and was looking to confirm all the necessary facts before putting my life in jeopardy - the analogy of tangling with an explosive device occurred to me then, and it remains just as poignantly with me now.

When I opened the door I realized how much I had been dreading this moment, how much I disliked and distrusted Leo and everything to do with him, including his room. It was years since I had been in there. I looked around. I had prepared myself to be shocked by the journal, but I had omitted to bear in mind how shocking the room itself would be. It was as though part of our home had been converted into a squatter's hovel, a shabby slum within a neat semi-detached. It wasn't completely filthy as far as I could see (although it was laughable to think Leo would clean it), but it seemed to have been arranged in purposeful disorder. Clothes, books, CDs, mud-caked boots, magazines, empty bottles and cans were all over the place. There were posters on the walls with Leo's added graffiti, all of it stark, crude and accusatory. Phrases like "Hard White Power!" and "Red hot cock!" screamed out in spattered red paint. One of the posters, more than softly pornographic, had "Eat my crusty dick" printed in bright blue - by my son I presume - across the top. There was a stale, inorganic smell in the air, as though he repaired engines in there, but there was no sign of purposeful activity, mechanical or otherwise. It was simply a place of aggressive relaxation, tarred by the lingering presence of a deviant personality who was the child of the two wretched adults who now quavered on its threshold.

"It's over there, on the floor." Cynthia pointed to a corner of the room. She'd turned the light on when we came in because the curtains were, as always, drawn. She had often said it was a relief Leo wanted to shield his room from inquisitive eyes, because we would have been ashamed of anyone looking in. I picked up the book and carried it to a desk strewn with used tissues and screwed up balls of paper.

"Are you going to look at it in here?"

"Well, yes, I may as well." I was thinking I didn't want its harmful and hurtful contents to be displayed anywhere other than this squalid room, as though it would pollute any environment it was opened in.

"You can leave me here. I'll be alright," I said. She hesitated, but then turned to go.

"I'll leave the door ajar, and I'll keep a … well, I'll keep a lookout, I suppose," she said, embarrassed, no doubt, by the need for subterfuge in our own home, with respect to our own son.

I looked at the cover, from which it was impossible to know it wasn't the container of an enthusiastic schoolboy's sports cuttings. I felt sad, as though the young Leo was there somewhere, and I might be able to rediscover him, which is probably the feeling Cynthia had experienced and which had persuaded her to open the book in the first place. I opened it, and a shudder ran down my spine.

You Suspect Who?

Dr Spencer was downstairs making tea when she heard her husband moving about upstairs. She assumed he was just getting up to use the bathroom, awoken by his aging bladder. She couldn't begin to count the number of patients who complained to her about this, both the men themselves and the women who were having their sleep interrupted by their partner's need to urinate. But in many cases there was no solution, save saying "don't drink too much" to the husbands, and "sleep in another bed, or another room" to the wives. But when she heard the shower running she realized he was getting up, and when he joined her 20 minutes later she was annoyed.

"This is too much. You're trying to exist on about four hours sleep every night. You'll suffer and you'll not do your job properly."

"And if I'm not at the station by eight I'll not have a job to do at all."

"That's absurd. They're not going to fire a man of your experience, just because he can't skip about like a spring lamb." She paused, resigned to the futility of her words, but hoping they might sink in as sensible advice at some point, though probably not today, given the stormy look on her husband's face. "It's very important, I suppose?"

"Yes. We think we've got a solid suspect. Well, some of us think that."

"But not you?"

"You know me. It's not over until the fat lady's behind bars and singing her life story to the tabloids. They probably think I'm the most negative man on the force."

"You probably are, but suspicion isn't such a bad thing. It's closer to reality than wide-eyed optimism."

"Yes, well I agree with that, of course, but to the modern eye my attitude is considered symptomatic of imminent retirement and a sleepy existence in a chocolate box cottage in Sussex."

"Which might not be such a bad thing," she said, raising her eyebrows, "for both of us."

"I wouldn't argue with that, and as I feel today I might just be persuaded to give my right arm for it."

"Oh, don't do that. Cottage gardens take a lot of tending, chocolate box versions or not. You'll need all of your limbs to maintain it."

They were silent for a while as she poured him tea and made him toast, and he tried to get the sleep out of his brain and think about the case.

"So, can you tell me about it?" she asked.

"The door to door threw up a man in Islington who is temporarily in Chingford. All of this is based on the words of a young girl and an excitable junior detective, but if you put that together with the optician's cloth, we may be on to something. Mind you, knowing our luck on this case it's probably the wrong Henderson, and the right Henderson is a dead Buddhist monk."

"Unlikely name for a Budd ..." she said, stopping in mid-sentence, holding a piece of toast in one hand and a honey-laden knife in the other.

"What?" he said, thinking she'd probably heard someone coming to the front door.

"You said Henderson, Islington, Chingford. Phillip Henderson?"

"Yes. How do you know?" She said nothing, so he carried on, now wide awake. "The optician's records are bad, and partly in Chinese. They were working on checking him out when I left last night, or this morning rather. We should know everything there is to know about him by the time I get back to the station, inside leg measurement and all, hence the early start, hence the interruption of my beauty sleep, and hence a head like a bag of soggy rags."

Still she said nothing.

"Does this silence have anything to do with the Hippocratic Oath?"

"I have a patient of that name, from Islington, who's been resident at a psychiatric hospital in Chingford for a while. I'm not going to say any more, but if you don't come up with anything, you'd better call me. I won't disclose any confidential information, but I may at least be able to tell you where to find him."

"Tell me now," he said, his heart beating faster than he thought it could beat at that time of the morning and at this stage of his career.

"No, try and find out yourselves first and keep me out of it. But just call if you don't get anywhere."

"Just one thing," he said. "Do you think he could be our man, based on what you know of him?"

"Never in a million years. But then I thought Margaret Thatcher would be good for the National Health Service."

Spencer didn't know if he loved his wife very deeply, although he had no doubt about how much he enjoyed talking to her and being with her. But of late he had scarcely been able to think about their relationship without the image of Sally Devons coming to his mind's eye. Where his wife brought him companionship and intellectual stimulation, Devons' hovering, assertive presence was associated with something darker and more troubling, but physically provocative for those very reasons. As he watched his wife get into her car and drive off, he thought of the time he would be spending away from home with Devons at the conference, and he had no idea how to even start untangling his confused emotions.

§

By the time he got to the police station it was almost eight thirty, and Spencer found himself becoming angry at the time Devons had arbitrarily set for his appearance.

There were enough experienced men on the team overnight to do everything necessary, including Roscoe, who despite the reservations Spencer and others might have about him in general, had proved to have a notable talent for fast and efficient background research.

When Spencer arrived, Devons was nowhere to be seen and when he found out she wasn't there yet he became even angrier, as though the deadline had been petulant and just to establish her authority. He knew he was being neurotic, but he was tired and was confronting what would probably be a long day, and even when he was told Devons had been there until four in the morning, he still felt annoyed and resentful of the almost continuous presence she had established in his mind, whether he was in her company or not.

"Okay," he said to Weller, who had been there for half an hour and had caught up on how things stood. Spencer could have got the information straight from Roscoe, but he was in no mind to labor over extracting the details piece by piece, and just wanted a sharp summary of the facts. "What do we know?"

"Phillip Richard Henderson. Married to Cynthia Margaret Henderson. Three children, two girls and a boy, all living at home. Nothing on the parents and one of the girls. The boy has a bit of a record, nothing serious, probably just adolescent high jinks, but he did set about some bloke who broke into their house with a baseball bat and did quite a lot of damage to him. The wife, Cynthia, works at a battered women's shelter, and a husband tracked his human punch-bag down to their place. The son saw him off. The husband didn't press charges, but the local police told the son, Leo, to take it easy in future."

Spencer yawned. "Sorry," he said in reply to Weller's slightly offended expression, "I'm just tired." Tired of all this, he thought, tired of barging into people's lives and trying to put a recalcitrant and ungrateful world to rights. But the name was a match for the one his wife had come up with, so tracking the man down could be easy. He opened his eyes wider, hoping it might make him look enthusiastic, but even if this ratcheted up his eagerness by a factor of ten he thought he would still look catatonic.

"Did you say one of the girls has form?"

"Not form exactly. Special Branch track extremist's web sites on the internet. You know, white supremacists, anarchists, militant tree-huggers, Animal Liberation Front, Colonel Ghadhaffi's Fan Club, 57 varieties of nutter, most of them harmless, weekend radicals, but some not-so-harmless, full-time loonies. The girl's been known to visit a few of them and get into online chat rooms with other fruitcakes of a similarly distorted disposition. Probably just a phase, she's only 15, but she's not doing herself any favors if she wants to be chairperson of the local Tory Party one of these days."

"Which sites does she go to?"

"Drugs, bomb making. Christ, when I was that age girls obsessed about Peter Frampton's underpants and what was inside of them, not the bloody Symbionese Liberation Army. Why, do you think it means anything?"

"Could be the father using the girl's identity. No porn or anything sexual?"

"Not that Special Branch knows about, but they only follow subversive stuff. They might track child porn, but if they looked at every porn site on the internet they'd do nothing else, and probably turn in to a bunch of perverts in the process, not that some of them already aren't."

Spencer smiled perfunctorily in acknowledgement of the joke at the expense of Special Branch. "Any more?"

"Really not a whole lot. We haven't worked out what he's doing in Chingford yet, or where he's staying. He works in a government computer department, so we'll be visiting them when they open for business."

"Is that it?"

"Yup. Mr. Nobody. Doesn't give us much to go on, does it?"

"Certainly not enough to keep Devons happy."

"So, do we visit the missus and tell her she's not looking after her hubby properly, and he nips out and slices up the occasional hooker when the mood takes him?"

"Not yet. I've got a phone call to make first."

§

Spencer's wife wasn't pleased.

"Damn. I should never have said anything."

"Hippocrates probably didn't have a serial killer on the loose when he drew up his code of conduct."

"You're underestimating all the ramifications of what doctor-patient confidentiality means."

"And it looks like I'm also overestimating my powers to influence you, but I'm not asking for information on his illness or what's passed between him and you, just his location."

"Okay", she said, and gave him the name of the Chingford hospital.

"Of course, you could have checked the hospitals in Chingford yourselves and not bothered me."

"That's right, but I'm getting lazy in my old age," and he thought, with not a little shame and deceitfulness, I want to impress Devons.

Life Captured

As I read through Leo's book, I began to feel disassociated from the activity, as if my mind had been replaced with somebody else's. The pictures, mainly just newspaper cuttings, most of which I'd already seen in the library, were a meticulous catalogue of the murders. To begin with, it wasn't the content that was disturbing as much as the clinical nature of the way the information was laid out, and, even more ghastly, the way parts of the newspaper reports had been highlighted. Individual words, some innocuous, had been singled out and, given the context, cast in a newly macabre light. Words and phrases like 'slashed', 'naked', 'multiple stab wounds', 'frenzied', 'buttocks' and 'bloody underwear' had been stained with gaudy orange or lemon marker ink.

The feeling it wasn't me in the room leafing through that disgusting record of events was bizarre and troubling. At worst, I thought, it could be explained by the fact that a separate, repressed part of my personality was involved in the murders, and that part of me was struggling to come to the fore and not quite succeeding or, conversely, struggling not to be exposed to my conscious mind and not quite succeeding in that either.

But as dreadful as the press cuttings were, the most shocking item was the one Cynthia had mentioned when she first told me about the book: the photograph of one victim taken, I presume, at the crime scene. Its presence implied Leo had been there soon after one of the women had been killed, either that or he had somehow managed to get hold of a police photograph, but given the amateurish nature of the picture I assumed the former. Which meant what? That he has followed me, watched me at my satanic work and photographed my handicraft of brutality and defilement once the coast was clear? I put my head in my hands and sat for some moments in total despair.

Cynthia knocked on the door. I nearly jumped out of my skin, both at the surprise of the interruption and the subsequent thought she might be warning me of the return of Leo or one of the girls.

"It's alright," she said. "I just wondered if you wanted a cup of tea?"

The question was so banal, given what was going through my mind, that I laughed, although I don't think I fooled either of us into believing there was any trace of humor in my laughter or my predicament.

"Do you know what happened to that old Polaroid camera of mine?" I asked her when she returned with the tea.

"No, I haven't seen it for ages. Why?"

"This photograph. If Leo took it, he couldn't have got it processed at a shop, and it looks like a Polaroid."

"Oh, I see. Yes, he may have it." She paused and looked around the room. "In which case it's probably in here."

We looked at each other, but I don't think either of us was attracted by the prospect of searching Leo's room, not knowing what else we might discover – I know I didn't want to do it.

"So," she said, "what do you make of it?" She nodded towards the scrap book.

I shook my head. "I don't know. It's horrible, and the implication is that I ... that I did it. That I killed those women. And I can't prove to myself, to you or to anyone else that I didn't. I've no conscious reason to think I'm in any way involved. But ..."

"But what?"

"But for my visions and the guilty feeling, and for this bloody thing." I flicked the pages, arriving at the improvised title page I had skipped over on first opening the book, not because it was uninteresting, but because its accusation was too unspeakable. 'Daddy's Dastardly Deeds'. I held it up to her. "He thinks I'm responsible, and there's something buried deep inside me that stops me saying I'm not. If I'm having blackouts and living some sort of heinous double-life as a modern day Jekyll and Hide, well he knows more about it than I do."

"What will you do next?"

I breathed deeply and tried to think, but thinking didn't really get me anywhere, I knew what I had to do, and pretending I had a choice was just a way of avoiding the inevitable.

"I can either go to the police and ask them to investigate me," I paused. She reflected my dismissive tone by shaking her head. "Or I can confront Leo. Theoretically there's a third option, which is to do nothing, but I couldn't live with that. So I know what I have to do."

"Do you think he'll tell you anything?"

No, I didn't, but I thought I would learn something from the manner of his response, and apart from going to the authorities with one of the most bizarre stories they would probably ever hear, and ruining my life even if it was a pure fiction, there was no alternative.

§

Until 15 minutes before I left the house, I felt I was no wiser than I had been when I'd entered it. The scrap book had contained much as I had expected and seen before at the library in newspapers, and nothing gave me any insight into my own involvement, not even the Polaroid picture. There was no physical evidence as to who the killer was, just a disorganized pile of inference. I was resolved to come back and see Leo.

But then, as I closed the book and carried it back to the corner of the room, a photograph slipped out from the back part of the book, a part I had assumed contained just blank pages. I picked the photograph up and sank into a chair, sitting on a pile of rubbish and dirty clothes in the process, too shaken by what I was looking at to care what I sat on. Anyone else seeing the picture wouldn't have been shocked by it at all. I remembered the setting in which it was taken. It would have been about six or seven years ago, when Leo was twelve or so. It was Christmas, and the whole family had been playing board games after lunch – Ludo, Monopoly, Snakes and Ladders, that sort of thing. Then, with a lot of the day to go and nothing particular to do (we didn't have a VCR at the time and the television was airing its normal maudlin Christmas drivel, which none of us has ever had an appetite for), we'd started to improvise and tried playing one of the mind reading games in which Leo and

I had sometimes demonstrated an unusual ability to communicate, and which seemed to entertain the rest of the family.

I don't remember much about the game, or whether it had been a success or a failure or even just amusing. I remember Cynthia taking the photograph, but subsequently had forgotten completely about it, and I had no recollection of seeing the result, until now. I had turned away from Leo and was facing the camera. In the photograph I could see my face and his, behind me, but instead of looking at the camera he was looking at me, and the expression on his face was one that combined intense concentration with chilling malice. As I had picked the photograph up from the floor, I had noticed some words on the back. I hadn't really attended to them at first, being more interested in the photograph itself, but now without turning the picture over, I knew what they would say. We had used a catch phrase when we were playing "Thought Transference" as we pompously called it. With mock solemnity we would chant "Your mind is my mind, your body is my body, your will is my will, your soul is my soul." It was a family joke, but as I turned the photograph over to see those very words inscribed on the reverse, I knew the joke and the subterfuge were over.

As I sat on the tube going back to Chingford, I began to cry, and barely a day has passed since then when I haven't cried.

I couldn't face going back to the hospital. I needed to be alone. The mere thought of lunch made me retch, and the proximity of other patients was almost enough to make me retch again. I got off the Underground train, not knowing where I was. I wandered around. Time was meaningless, so I've no idea how long I walked through the streets of central London, or where I went, but I eventually found myself standing in front of Euston station. I needed more time on my own, but I felt threatened by the city and the people dashing about it, so I forced myself to walk smartly into the railway terminus and bought a ticket for the first destination I saw on the departures board, Birmingham.

□□□

Hide and Seek

"Bit of a cock up, really," said Weller. He and Spencer were on their way to Islington.

"A bit more than a bit. Not that there's much chance we missed anything as a result of it, but it was an elementary blunder."

"How did Devons take it?"

"God knows. I made my excuses and left before the shit hit the fan, or the sergeant's brains hit the wall, to use a better analogy."

On taking over surveillance of the Henderson house at noon, the relief team was surprised to find the back entrance to the property wasn't being observed.

"What back entrance?" said Sergeant Tullow, who had been responsible for setting up the surveillance. "The local coppers said there was front access only."

But his failing was he hadn't checked and double checked, and no excuse would absolve him. At that precise moment Devons was probably mapping out the uninspiring future he could expect to have in the Metropolitan Police Force.

"I can't imagine he's sneaked back there and away again," said Spencer, "but Devons won't be seeing it like that." Spencer had sympathy for Tullow, because he knew he could find himself the focus of her rage unless luck started to turn positively in his direction for the balance of the day.

When they had visited the hospital, Henderson was nowhere to be found. The hospital staff said this was perfectly normal, that he often went off for walks, or wandered into town to look around, and would doubtless be back at lunchtime. But their ease was in no way matched by the feelings of the officers, who assumed there was as much of a chance of not seeing him at lunchtime as there was of finding him munching his way through the steak and kidney pudding being prepared in the hospital kitchen at that moment.

The call on Henderson's employers had been similarly unproductive. All they could tell the officers was he was off sick with some sort of nervous disorder, and nobody knew specifically what the problem was, or where or how it was being treated.

"He's dedicated to his work," said his manager. "A model employee. Keeps himself to himself and does his job extremely well. He's a bit of a legend, actually. Knows more about computer operating systems than most of the rest of us put together. Can be a bit temperamental at times …"

"Temperamental?"

"Oh, nothing to be concerned about, just intellectually self-opinionated, like several of the people here."

"Opinionated about what?"

"Oh, programming languages. He really thinks Algol 68C was an exceptional language and it was vastly underrated in comparison with Modula-2 and Pascal. There have been a few heated arguments in the cafeteria about the merits of various structured programming languages, and personally I would say that with C++ and Visual Basic and Java it's about time we …"

"I was thinking more along the lines of political or sexual opinions. That sort of thing."

"Oh no, nothing like that. He's a real boffin, a nerd, a propeller head. Loves computers, loves them."

§

Spencer knew if they couldn't track him down, Devons would be ranting and raving at the decision, Spencer's decision, not to converge on the house the previous night, because it was possible they may have been able to snare him if they'd acted quickly. There was no reason for this to be true, but he knew she was more likely to express irrational anger than empathetic understanding. Now, compounded by Tullow's sloppiness in surveillance planning, Devons might be thinking her team was incapable of even elementary competence, and if she had cause to demonstrate that opinion, Spencer would rather not be in earshot or throwing range.

"If he's not at the house," said Weller, as they waited for traffic lights to change, "and he doesn't turn up at the hospital for lunch, then he must know we're on to him, and so he could well be the bloke we're after. That's a major improvement on where we were this time yesterday, isn't it?"

"If those are intended as words of comfort, they're not working on me. It may prove he's a bloke somebody is after for something, but that doesn't mean he's our killer, so we can't just slam the book shut on the matter and piss off down the pub to celebrate another job well done, at last."

"She can't blame you."

"She can," said Spencer, looking out of the window, "and she will. She thinks this case is the iceberg with the potential to wreck her career, and woe betide the poor sod who steers the ship into it. The only consolation for me is she may sate her appetite on Tullow's testicles before she starts gnawing on mine."

"You must be hoping this is a wild goose chase."

"No, I want to catch the bugger, and if my professional pride takes a bashing on the way, that's just a casualty of war as far as the greater good is concerned. As long as it doesn't affect my pension I can put it down to experience. I still think I made the right decision at the time, the only problem is that sacrificial lambs don't usually get a chance to bleat their case – you can't plead through a throat that's dripping blood all over the carpet."

The two men sat in silence. A silence only broken by Spencer asking Weller to drive faster.

§

"Mrs. Henderson?"

"Yes."

"I'm detective chief inspector Spencer and this is detective sergeant Weller. Do you think we could come in and ask you a few questions?"

Spencer wondered how many times he had used this or a similar introduction over the years. Many hundreds certainly, possibly many thousands. The reaction to the statement varied, from the verbally abusive and the physically hostile, to fears, tears, fainting and even spontaneous flight, but for most part it was met with the vacant, frightened, deer-in-headlights stare confronting him now. It didn't mean anything. Anyone getting a surprise visit from the police was bound to be shaken by the prospect of either arrest or tragic news. But it never ceased to depress Spencer to see how shocking a few stock words could be, even on those to whom they offered no threat or upset. United in guilt and grief, he thought, just by being human.

Spencer was reminded of the temptation to read signs that weren't there. Like why hadn't she asked them what it was about, or why had she just shown them in without looking more closely at the identification they had both perfunctorily waved at her?

They sat down in a comfortable lounge. The two men said nothing, but the woman didn't say anything either, so Spencer accepted he wasn't going to have a "We were waiting for you to come" statement presented to him on a plate.

"Your husband, Mrs. Henderson, he's Phillip Henderson?"

"Yes."

Shouldn't she now look confused or worried? Shouldn't she be saying "What's happened? Is he alright?" Instead she said nothing. Her face was strangely blank.

"He's not here at the moment, so I understand?"

"No," she said, and didn't appear to be about to say any more, but then she seemed to pull herself together. A light came into her eyes where previously there had been dull vacancy. Without knowing the woman, Spencer couldn't be sure the way she was reacting wasn't her normal state, but his feeling was she was in mild shock. "No," she went on. "He's in hospital."

"In West Park Hospital, in Chingford."

"Yes, how did you know? What's happening?"

Better late than never, he thought.

"I don't want to alarm you unduly, Mrs. Henderson. As far as we're aware, nothing's happened to your husband, but when we visited the hospital this morning he wasn't there, and we'd like to ask him a few questions. It's just part of an enquiry we're engaged in at the moment. Nothing for you to worry about." Either that, he thought, or the most devastating thing that's happened to you or ever will happen to you.

"What's this about?"

Perhaps she was overcoming the blind panic stage and was starting to get logical. This could be tricky if she's become cautious enough to be guarded, and no longer frightened enough to be careless.

"I'd rather not go into details, Mrs. Henderson. We think your husband might have some information we could be interested in."

"Has he ... is he a ... suspect or something?"

"Oh I don't think so, but his name has come up in relation to a case we're investigating and we'd like, well ... to eliminate him from our inquiries, so to speak."

"Oh," was all she said.

"What's the problem with your husband? Nothing serious, I hope?"

"Oh no, not at all. Well, I suppose it's quite serious, but not ... well it's ... sort of ... exhaustion, you could call it."

"West Park is a psychiatric hospital," said Weller, half way between a statement and a question.

"Oh ...well ... yes, yes it is. Yes," she replied, then added "Oh!" Both men looked expectantly at her. "Would you like a cup of tea ... or something ...?"

"No, no thank you," said Weller, with a slight laugh. He looked at Spencer, who was similarly surprised at the incongruity of her offer, but not amused like his colleague.

"No, me neither, thank you. Mrs. Henderson, it would help us a great deal if you could tell us something about your husband's illness, and how he is at the moment. I'd rather not have to explain why. As I said, this is just routine background work, and if we can clear it all up here and now, so much the better."

"Well, look, do you think you could tell me what this is about? I think I'd rather be told, if you don't mind."

Spencer sucked his teeth. "Yes, if you insist, but it may alarm you."

"I'd rather know. I can't imagine my husband is knowingly involved ... I mean, is involved in anything illegal, knowingly or otherwise, but I'd rather know what we're talking about."

"Of course, I can tell you more, but I'd ask you to treat this conversation in confidence, if you don't mind." He watched her as he spoke, and she nodded, once, slowly.

"As you probably know, Mrs. Henderson, there have been a number of murders of prostitutes in the London area lately. First in the East End, but now in some of the suburbs more to the east."

He thought he noticed her eyes widen slightly as he spoke, but nothing dramatic. Come on Spencer, he said to himself, this is a red herring. How would the average suburban housewife react to having the murder squad walk into her front room one day and start asking questions implying that her loving, cardigan-wearing husband might be a homicidal maniac and pervert?

"We may have discovered some evidence linking your husband to one of the crime scenes. He might have been there shortly before or after one of the killings, perhaps, and he may be able to help us."

"Oh, I see."

"Most police work is pretty tedious stuff, Mrs. Henderson, just tidying up loose ends." But if she was smart, and he guessed she was, then she would be wondering why two senior detectives were following up on petty evidence, when a junior uniformed officer would normally be allocated to a task as routine as Spencer was describing.

"So?" he said.

"Yes?"

"I was asking about your husband's health."

"What's that got to do with a piece of evidence?"

"Well," said Spencer, "I have to tell you that as well as seeing if he's got any information for us, the fact your husband may have been in the vicinity of the murder means we have to account for his presence there, and as he's not around to ask, then at least it's useful to know a bit about him."

"He's been having some hallucinations, that's all. The doctor thinks it's just fatigue, stress, pressure of work, that sort of thing, and he'll be over it in a week or so. It's nothing, really, nothing."

"Has he had any problems like this in the past?" asked Weller.

"No, no he hasn't. It's nothing, really. The hospital is very open, he can wander around. He's perfectly ... well ... perfectly safe, if that's what you're thinking. They don't lock him up or anything like that. They don't think he's a risk... to himself I mean, and certainly not to anyone else"

They both looked at her. She turned her face towards the carpet and coughed, then looked up, her eyes watery.

"Is that all?"

"Does your husband call home often?"

"Sometimes. I try to go and see him every other day, so we don't need to talk on the phone too much, and he'll be back home soon, I'm sure. Next week perhaps."

They chatted a bit more, but it was getting them nowhere. She said she had no idea where he might be, and she assumed, like the people at the hospital, he would be back there for lunch. They left, noticing one of the surveillance vehicles as they drove down the street.

"Um," said Weller.

"Just what I was thinking."

"There's something there."

"Yes," said Spencer, "I think you could be right, but is it multiple murder or some other tacky little family secret?"

"He could be in the house. He may have slipped in the back before we got it covered. She was definitely edgy about something."

"I don't mind if he's in there. He won't get out without us knowing about it, and unless he tunnels under Tullow's team we'll nab him eventually. But if he doesn't show up at the hospital for lunch, the balloon's going to go up."

"Don't worry, it'll come down again."

"That's alright for you to say. It won't be your balls in the basket. What time is it?"

"Two, just gone."

Spencer called the station to get the search warrant process started and to see if Henderson had returned as expected.

"No guv, no sign, the hospital are starting to get worried, but not as worried as us," Roscoe told him, and as he said it, Spencer realized it was the answer he was expecting. This case was simply going to go wrong at every conceivable turn.

"Bastard," he said, not referring to anyone in particular, himself included.

§

"Bastard!" growled Devons, through gritted teeth, and with more anger than Spencer had been able to muster. "How the hell does he know we're on to him? He's been a good little boy, doodling off into town day after day, always back to eat up all his lunch, but as soon as we're on to him he gets some sort of premonition and fucks off out of the known universe. Damn!" she said, thumping the desk with her fist. A small fist, Spencer noticed, but a hard and unremitting one that sported an obviously expensive diamond ring on an insignificant finger, demonstrating wealth, not commitment, except to herself.

"At least we know, he's our man," she said, but then looked at Spencer who didn't dare state the obvious. "Alright Spencer," she added "it doesn't prove he's the killer, but don't be reasonable with me at the moment, I'm not in the bloody mood."

"We're watching the house and we're watching the hospital, all the entrances," he said. "The hospital's small, we can easily track whoever comes and goes. We've got a photograph of Henderson from his employer, so the surveillance teams will know him when they see him."

"What about the phone? I suppose his home phone isn't tapped, so when his wife calls and tells him the game's up, we won't know about it."

"Weller's getting that in place now," he said, "it should be running within the hour, and we'll search the house this afternoon."

"Why bother? He knows now. Spence, this is a real fuck up, a right royal fuck up, and you're partly to blame."

Nice of her to say that, he thought. He'd assumed that he was wholly to blame. He didn't feel like arguing, but nor did he feel like bearing the brunt of the criticism.

"Unless we've sprung a leak, he can't have known we were on to him, maybe he still doesn't."

"He could have guessed. Perhaps the daughter saw through our market researcher hokum, perhaps he spotted the surveillance van, perhaps someone here has a big mouth they opened in the wrong places. The fact of the matter is we should have turned the house over last night and put an immediate phone tap in place. At least then we'd know we'd reacted as fast as we could ..."

"Over reacted and definitely scared him off for sure."

"What could be more effective than the way he's scared off now? We've lost the bugger, our best lead, our only lead apart from that suicidal nutcase of Cheeseman's over in Leyton, and we've let him slip away," said Devons.

"We don't know that we've scared him off."

She looked at him as though he didn't deserve an answer, and she didn't give him one.

"Get the wife in here," she said at last. "Let's put the frighteners on her. I want her to be so scared she'll tell us everything we need to know about her husband, and a lot we don't need to know. The pussyfooting is over. If I'm wrong, then I shall personally apologize to the Hendersons, and," she added as an afterthought, "to you. But until I know I'm wrong, we're going to stir things up."

Yes, he thought, let's wreck a few more lives, why don't we? Not because it makes any sense, but because we're too paranoid to wait things out and would rather run around like a bunch of headless chickens for a day or two. We're not saving lives here, we're trying to save reputations, ours, and no bystander is safe from our ass-covering wrath. Spencer disliked himself for keeping quiet, for not fighting his corner, but his dislike of himself paled beside his growing dislike of the job, and the trampling coarseness it involved.

If Henderson was the killer, and if he fitted the stereotype of the genre, they would see no more of him until his body turned up on a desolate river bank, or swinging by the neck from the light fitting in a cheap hotel in some dreary provincial city. But even as she had been ranting and raving, Spencer thought he saw the smile playing around Devons' mouth that he'd noticed before, and he found himself more interested in that than he was in the location of Phillip Henderson.

☐ ☐ ☐

Hard Day's Night

Sometimes she felt just fine about what she did. It was normally in proportion to how much she'd drunk, smoked, snorted or pumped into herself during the course of the day, but it wasn't always that simple to relate the cause and effect, and for some reason, today, while it was too early for her to have ingested anything, she felt good.

Remorse usually visited her in the early mornings, telling her that being a whore was destroying her self-esteem just as surely as the drugs and the booze were destroying her body. Often, around four in the morning, as she lay tossing and turning, out of sleeping pills and unable to turn off her racing brain, she would see the full extent of the hopelessness of her situation and the chilling void her life had become. At such times she might decide there was just nothing in the world that interested her, and certainly not the onerous act of merely living. But the remorseful times were, thankfully, becoming less frequent, and her brain seemed to be more willing to leave her alone and let her get on with the business of blanking out unpleasant thoughts. In fact, she was getting pretty good at blanking out all thoughts, and morality being more thinking about than feeling, she was hardly judging herself at all anymore.

Getting up was the hardest part of the day. Going to bed was bad enough, not knowing if she would sleep, and fearing if she did manage to drop off some freaky nightmare would invade her rest and catapult her back, sweaty and shivering, into a terrified, whimpering wakefulness. But getting out of bed was an altogether more intimidating challenge. Getting out of bed to face another day, to earn enough money to fuel her habits, habits which were now as much a part of her as breathing, and more of a part of her than eating, which didn't interest her at all anymore. Eating was like shitting or pissing, another necessary evil, and given the choice she'd rather shit and piss, because they were free and didn't divert money from the drinks, pills and powders she was more interested in consuming.

Sometimes, having decided that she had to get up, she would defy the judgment and pull the stinking covers back over her head, telling herself she could stay there forever, stay there until the pain ended, until nobody bothered her any more, until there was no craving left to satisfy, no man left to be fucked by, no reason at all not to stay there for eternity, to stay buried in the musty bed until vile reality retreated into the distance and left her in peace. But so far she always had got up, eventually, and today would be no different.

In the intimate confines of her bed she looked at her body, as if scrutinizing a third party. She was thin. She wondered why men were willing to give her money to have sex. She put no passion into the act, complemented their frantic gruntings and groanings with no sounds of her own, encouraging or otherwise. She made herself into a bland semen collector, nothing more, and yet some came back time after time, obsessing over the plump breasts and protruding nipples on the otherwise emaciated frame.

Wouldn't an inflatable doll be just as good, and cheaper? Why did they need a human when the human in question was such an obviously unenthusiastic participant? Wasn't it humiliating for them? She laughed to herself. What the fuck did humiliation matter? Nobody could be more abased and lacking pride than she was herself.

She shared the cramped, decrepit flat with Lizzie, who didn't do quite as much of anything as Michelle, and so looked to be in better shape. She did all the same things Michelle did, including some prostitution, just less of them. Lizzie was sitting in the kitchen, flipping through *Cosmo,* a cup of coffee in one hand and a cigarette dangling from her mouth. Lizzie smoked more than Michelle, but that was far less damaging than Michelle's excesses, so she had the aura of someone stable who was going to be around a relatively long time, whereas Michelle would be surprised if she and most of her close acquaintances would live past 35, or want to.

"What time is it?" Michelle asked, her voice thick and trembling.

"Half three. You're up early." It was late, even by Michelle's standards of getting up. She was normally out of bed by two. Maybe that explained why she felt okay – she'd managed to catch up on sleep, even if it had left her groggy.

"We need some money," said Lizzie, without looking up from the magazine.

"Why?"

"Rent. We didn't pay last month and what we owe for this month is two weeks overdue. I knew it was a mistake to rent from a woman. With a man there's a good chance he'll take payment in kind now and again. There's a chance with a woman too, I suppose, but not much of one, and none with that tight-assed bitch Kenyon."

"I gave you some money a while ago, didn't I?" said Michelle, with little conviction. Time was becoming an elusive and meaningless commodity in her life, and she had no idea if she had last diverted money from drugs to rent a week ago or a year ago.

"Not lately. I'd pay it myself if I could, but I'm broke."

"I'll put in a full night tonight and give you some money tomorrow. How much do we need?"

"We need a thousand, but a couple of hundred will keep her off our backs for a week or two. I'll get you something to eat."

Lizzie never asked Michelle if she wanted food because she knew she would say no, so she just made it anyway. Michelle provided most of their income. She was attractive enough to be able to make good money, and she was driven enough by her need for stimulants that she spent a lot of time working. Lizzie's skill was in getting enough cash out of her to keep the household together before it all went to drug dealers.

Neither of them questioned their roles. Lizzie would work the streets too now and again, but generally she kept the flat going while Michelle's labors paid the bills. It was an unspoken arrangement which had worked out for three years, so neither of them thought to change it or question it. Their joint lifestyle enabled Michelle to enjoy her habits and Lizzie to enjoy her idleness.

Michelle wasn't keen on the idea of food, and although she felt okay after she'd eaten the bacon sandwich that was put before her, she felt much better after Lizzie had left the flat and she had vomited the undigested mass of meat, fat and bread into the toilet. She hadn't done it intentionally, but she was glad she'd purged her stomach and had prepared her system for the first heady fix of the day.

The next few hours passed in a blur, as they increasingly tended to do. She was aware of Lizzie coming back and her seeming to be annoyed about something, and of a visit from Scrouch. Scrouch was one of her pushers. He called himself the "Traveling Greengrocer" but instead of delivering mundane British vegetables he traded in the products of altogether more exotic plants. "The only vegetables I deal with are me customers," he had said, many times.

On this visit, Scrouch had traded heroin for sex, which was just as well because that was all Michelle had to trade. She didn't remember the sex, apart from the occasional flashback to Scrouch's contorted face the first time, and the crazed yelps he emitted from behind her the second time, but she remembered him handing over the packet of powder before he left, and he even threw in a tab of ecstasy as a goodwill gesture. "And my Will's feeling pretty good at the moment, if not a bit over-used," he had said as he handed it to her.

The next thing she knew it was ten o'clock, and Lizzie – who had replaced the coffee with gin, *Cosmo* with *Playboy*, and *Marlboro* with a joint - was telling her to get out and get busy.

Seduced by the Lead

The atmosphere in the operations room that evening was a mixture of excitement and frustration, additionally laced with the ever-present dose of boredom which the repetitive labor of investigative work invariably induces. Some of the team were inspired by the fact a flimsy lead seemed to have led them straight to the murderer. Others were dismayed that their quarry, no sooner identified, seemed to have got wind of his discovery and disappeared from the face of the earth. Others were so busy trying to track down the absent man through endless, useless phone calls that they just wished their shift was over and they could piss off home.

Roscoe was leaning back in his chair, chewing at the end of a pencil and staring vacantly into the distance. Weller was reciting disinterestedly into the telephone. Spencer was, for a second time, reading through the reports of the other 'possibles', of which there were only six and all of them 'highly bloody unlikelies' in his and everyone else's opinion. Of the three detectives, Spencer thought it probable that the blatantly idle Roscoe was the most gainfully employed.

Weller hung up the phone. "Nothing, nada, niente, null, nihil, nowt."

"Are we going to go public?" asked Roscoe.

"Devons is thinking about it," Spencer replied. "She'd like to, but if we start putting his face on the TV and it turns out he's the wrong man, then we'll look like we're panicking and he'll probably sue us for a hundred million quid."

"Well, we've checked all the friends, relatives and associates the wife gave us, and none of them is owning up to anything. Isn't it a bit of a coincidence that the son's nowhere to be seen?" asked Weller.

"Not according to the wife," said Roscoe. "He comes and goes as he likes. Midnight and past is her best bet for him getting home. We'll know when he does."

"You two may as well go," said Spencer "there's nothing more to be done tonight." And precious little to be done tomorrow, he thought. It was now a matter of waiting for a break or the discovery of Henderson, or Henderson's body. Tomorrow would be time enough to root around in the history of Phillip Henderson and his family, but tonight seemed like a good time to pause for breath and hope the fugitive walked into a police station somewhere or ended his life without upsetting anyone or frightening animals in the process.

Devons buzzed him.

"Spencer, I'm leaving," she paused. Her statement had been so curt and the pause so long he wondered momentarily if she was telling him she was resigning.

"Do you want a drink?" It was the last thing in the world he wanted, but he felt unable to refuse, and, as always, was fascinated by her wish to socialize with him and nobody else.

"Sure," he said.

"I don't want to sit in a bar. Why don't you come to my place?" He couldn't repress a feeling that could be trepidation, but which may have been excitement, and he was aware of a slight tremor in his voice as he asked her for directions.

§

Devons got home just before Spencer arrived and was still sorting through her mail when she opened the door. He hadn't known what to expect but was, nevertheless, surprised by what he saw. The apartment was stylish, not modern, but it had an air about it that exuded taste and expense. White leather sofas, dark mahogany floors, colorful abstract art on grey walls and a strange wooden sculpture, made it appear bold and almost strident. It was, he thought, more the sort of place you would expect to find a man living in, but probably an effeminate man, the robustness tempered with soft edges. It was not the type of place you could walk into without comment. In a word, it was impressive.

"Don't blame or compliment me," she said. "You should praise the interior designer if you like it, and ridicule me for paying her bill if you don't."

The statement sounded practiced, as if she'd read the bemusement on other faces in the past and had perfected her glib answer to it.

"I like it," he said. "But then what I know about interior design could be written on the back of a postage stamp, so you can hardly take that as valuable praise."

"Don't apologize. I'm an ignoramus when it comes to this sort of stuff myself, but it turned out to my liking, and most people seem to think the same, although for the amount I paid I deserve some bloody spectacular bragging rights. Sit down or have a look around. I'll get us a drink."

He wandered around the lounge for a while and then went into the kitchen where she was pulling the cork on a bottle of claret.

"Take those into the lounge," she said, pointing to two bowls, one of olives and the other of croutons. "I'll bring the wine."

"So, Spence," she said when they were sitting down, "what happens next?" Her face gave no clue as to what she was asking about, and again he thought he saw a smile playing on her lips. He answered as if she were asking about the case, although he wasn't at all sure she was. She'd taken off her jacket and a closely fitting white blouse had made her breasts prominent, more prominent than they ever appeared in the office, and without the jacket her shapely hips were on display. Perhaps it was the environment, but he'd never appreciated her femininity as much as he did now, and he was enjoying it.

"We wait. If Henderson is our man, then I expect the next we'll see of him will be his corpse. This has been his first excursion into crime as far as we know, and he won't relish the thought of what comes next. The fact he's disappeared means he knows he can't go home. He's probably dead already."

"So he won't kill again?"

"Not on our patch. I suppose he could reinvent himself somewhere else and start off again, but it's unlikely. Serial criminals tend to be organized, they have to be if they're successful, and they wouldn't be serial if they weren't successful, but being organized makes them predictable, creatures of habit. Knowing we're on to him has turned his universe upside down. He won't like that. He's a psychopath, so he's inherently unstable. This situation will be driving him nuts."

"If he's our man."

"Precisely," Spencer answered

"You still don't think he is?"

"I think he probably is, and his running has made it even more likely, but no, I'm not certain, and none of us can be, and if he jumps in a river and doesn't leave a suicide note, we'll never know, and that will be his ultimate victory. Killed 7, Caught 0."

"You really do think about this work, don't you?"

"Think about it, brood about it, love it, hate it. Yes, all of those, and all at the same time." Except the loving part, he thought, which was now almost entirely absent from his work experience.

"And which are you doing most of at the moment?"

"Hating it." His honesty surprised him, but he said it without thinking. Now it was too late to unsay it, and he didn't feel as if he wanted to anyway, but she didn't show any surprise at his remark, she just said "Why?" as she took an olive from the bowl, popped it in her mouth and licked her fingers clean.

"It's a necessary job, a vital job, but it's fundamentally a dissatisfying one and it just seeps into your life if you let it."

"And you've let it?"

"Yes. I've lived and breathed it for so many years it's become a part of me. I used to think a lot about the work itself, but only as much as was necessary to catch the next villain. I didn't question what effect it was having on me. Now I just feel like a traffic warden – somebody has to do it, and I'm glad they do, but it doesn't have to be me anymore."

"Is this a resignation speech?"

"I don't think so, but it might not be too far off."

"And who's going to round up the scum of the earth if Spencer's not around to do it?"

"You, Weller, Roscoe. The ones who like the job still, or are ambitious, or can just do it without thinking about it, as long as it pays the mortgage and doesn't shorten their lives more than it should."

"I'd miss you, Spence," she said leaning over and filling his glass. He couldn't help but pay attention to the full curves of her body as she moved, and he knew she knew he was watching her. "I trust you more than anyone in the division. I really hope you don't pack it in." Now her eyes were locked onto his, and he didn't think she would ever let them go.

What was it about this woman that so beguiled him? It wasn't her looks, which were ordinary, and although her figure was pleasing, she did little to make it appear so, and seemed to positively play down the femininity of her shape by holding herself formally and moving abruptly, almost angrily.

But there was something like risk he felt when in her presence. Something unpredictable about her that, compounded with her position of power, made her dangerous, and being with her now, he was being sucked further into the overwhelming gravitational pull that surrounded her and influenced those who fell within her orbit.

And she knows it, he thought. She knows she has the power to intimidate, and she loves it, feeds on it. The magnetism to manipulate and control. She's dominating my emotions as much as she governs my working life. But thinking this didn't absolve him of her influence, if anything it enslaved him. It was as if a doctor had diagnosed a puzzling illness "The good news is we know what the problem is. The bad news is you'll be dead in six months."

§

She stood, bottle of wine in hand, and came and sank down next to him on the sofa, her eyes still fixed on his. If there had been any doubt about her agenda for this evening, there was none now.

"I hope you won't interpret this as sexual harassment," she said, the same barely detectable smile from earlier that day, and from the night before when she had been goading him about making the right decision, was now once more on her face, now clearly a smile, but still not obviously one of tenderness.

She put out her hand and placed it firmly on his stomach, still looking into his eyes. He felt useless, unable to contradict anything she might say or do. He felt stupid, idiotically immature, as though he was a teenager being introduced to sex for the first time by an experienced woman; not a middle aged detective being seduced by a woman 15 years his junior.

Why, he wanted to say, why me, why are you doing this to me? And why do I feel like this? But he had no conviction his thoughts were his own, and he felt whatever he said would sound inappropriate and ridiculous. She had him in the palm of her hand, the palm that was massaging his stomach, and it wasn't a matter of wanting or being able to break free of her influence, he was incapable of making any decision she didn't make for him.

She picked up his hand and pulled on it, rising to her feet and leading him into the bedroom, a more feminine room than he had expected, and he was glad of that – it didn't make him feel stronger or any more masculine, but rather that his weakness was slightly more forgivable. He was simply treading the path of many before him, other men with other women in other rooms in other situations, different situations, but the same in the long run.

She began to kiss him, and although he responded, it was always she who led, and as they began to shed clothes, it was as though she was undressing both of them. Then she stopped, and reached across to the bedside table. She opened the drawer and took something out. He expected it to be a condom, but it wasn't, and it was some moments before he registered what it was. He felt himself go numb as she looped a cord around her neck and handed the ends to him, before dragging him down on top of her. He felt his mind and his body and his personality disappear within hers.

□□□

Hand to Knife Control

Oh, it's good to be out and about, looking for some fun. It's been a few weeks since the last one, and it's about time I was enjoying myself again. The only problem is this area isn't as well known to me, and I feel more conspicuous than I did in the East End. But, never mind. Everything has worked out well so far, and I've no reason to think it won't be hunky-dory this time as well. I feel a buzz. A buzz like no other. I suppose it's the magnitude of the event and the ... well, the finality of it. Nothing like it. I can't imagine living without it. I wouldn't want to live without it.

I see her on the street, but it's not time yet. She's a whore alright, no doubt about that, and a drugged up one as well by the look of her. Staggering on her stilettos, glassy eyes, her head moving around slowly and loosely, as though it's attached to her body by a rubber collar rather than a neck. Skinny, but big tits, if they're real.

She looks a bit like that silly bitch Cynthia brought back to the house, the one who had some half-brained Neanderthal come to try and snatch her back. Attractive, in a tarty sort of way, and that's the only way for tarts to be attractive. Maybe I should experiment, do it differently this time, change my *modus operandi*. That would confuse everyone, wouldn't it? No, stick with what you know best. Be consistent. Yes, I'll do the same. Carve the next letter. A space. I'd like it to be her. If she's still around when I'm ready, it'll be her. Yes. I feel good already. She's perfect. I feel a tickle of excitement in my stomach, not my prick, my stomach. I feel like it's Christmas Eve, and I'm a kid about to open some fabulous presents. Rip open the wrapping and dive inside.

But not yet. I'll take a look around. See how the land lies. Mix with the filth and the low life a bit and see what they're up to. I wonder if they're scared? I wonder if the whores know they're in danger? I suppose they always think they're in a bit of danger from being caught by the police or molested by some psychopath. But I wonder if the killings have put the shits up the scumbag population of the British Isles; have made every hard working scrubber and pimp think their career, income and life is about to go down the toilet?

There's still plenty of them doing business, and they still will be doing business long after I've ... well, I don't want to think about that. There's too much fun to be had to think about ... Yes, focus on the possible. Focus on tonight. Focus on what these hands can do, these modest hands that can change lives.

I go and have a drink. Double vodka. Ice and a piece of lemon, which I chew on to get some bitterness. I blend into the crowd. I play a slot machine. I put money in the music machine. The Who, 'Don't get fooled again'. Ha. Bloody well get fooled again you dumb bastards! I have another drink, but I won't have any more. I don't need booze to get my kicks, not tonight.

I can't stop thinking about the girl. She doesn't know anything about what I'm thinking, and that makes my pleasure even more sublime. I control her future more than she does, and she doesn't even know me and I don't know anything about her. She thinks she has a future, but I know she doesn't, not beyond tonight. I will even control what she feels, what thoughts go through her head in those last concentrated moments. My will is going to completely dictate the destiny of another human. It's a mingling of the spirits greater than any sort of sex act can attain. It's the ultimate shared experience, but I'll be controlling it, totally. My mind will be her mind; her soul will be my soul. It's a sort of intellectual cannibalism really, and I laugh at the thought and take another sip of my drink, toasting my good luck at having found something in life I find so fulfilling, so excruciatingly fulfilling.

I go back to where I saw her, but she's not there. I feel anger, but force myself to calm down. She'll be back. She's a whore. She'll be off turning a trick somewhere, sucking some blokes dripping dick in a nearby alley, but she'll be back, and if everything is right, I'll be her next customer, her last customer for the night, her last customer for every night.

§

"Good evening, Madam. What's your name?"

"Michelle, what's yours?"

"Rumplestiltskin. Are you doing business?"

She looks at me through dope-addled eyes. I can almost see my words being processed in her screwed up, junkie brain trying to make sense of what I'm saying. For a moment I think of giving up on her, it'll be too easy, she probably won't even know what I'm doing, I might as well snuff out a rag doll. But she's sexy looking. Short, tight skirt, good legs, not much ass but nice juicy boobs, young, cute face, bit pasty, but cute.

"Oh, yeah, yeah, sure, what do you want?"

"What do you do?"

"Anything, everything," she says, as though she was a plumber or a car mechanic, then "for a price," as she remembers she's in it to make money, I assume.

"Blow job then," I say, looking around to make sure there's still nobody about.

"Fifty quid."

"Okay, your alleyway or mine?"

"What?"

"Never mind. Where are we going?"

There's a building site round the corner I've had a look at. I'll see what she suggests first – she may be more comfortable if it's a place she's used to – but if it looks risky I'll get her to go to the building site. The state she's in I doubt if she knows where the fuck she is anyway, but she's not going to make any mistakes about the money. She asks me for it and counts it out deliberately as she starts walking "… ten, twenty, thirty …" She stuffs it in her bag and I catch sight of a big wad of notes. Stupid bitch to be walking around with that lot. Can't she find somewhere to put it between tricks? Oh well, I'll help myself when I'm done with her, a bit of extra cash always comes in handy.

Oh yes, nice dark alley. Perfect, better than my building site.

This is too easy, almost not worth doing. No, don't say that. You're getting cocky. She could still scream or a copper could decide to walk up here for a quiet piss, or she could turn out to be a copper herself; no, not likely, she's definitely a druggie, but don't get careless. One slip and the whole fucking house of cards can come tumbling down, and I wouldn't want that, would I?

I feel in my pocket for the tools - cord and knife. The cord came off a kite we used to fly, bright blue it is, some really strong nylon material now stained in places with whore blood. The knife was a modeling knife. We used to cut up balsa wood with it to make model airplanes. There's even some patches of dried glue still on the handle, but tonight it's going to cut up some tarty, fucking whore, not that she'll know anything about it, not by that time.

"Okay darling," I say "get busy," and I pull my cock out and wait for her to go down on it. She drops on her knees and starts gobbling.

"Hey, ain't you gonna use a condom?" Jesus, I don't want the dopey slag's mouth touching me, and by the look of her she could have all sorts of diseases – I can almost see needle marks on her arms from three feet away in the dark. And I sure don't wanna leave any DNA in her cakehole.

"Oh, yeah, if you like," she says, "wait a minute," and she starts rummaging around in her handbag.

I spot a packet of Marlboro, the wad of cash, some pill bottles, and eventually she pulls out a condom. I'm running the cord through my fingers in my pocket as she gets herself together, and when she puts the condom on and starts sucking I pull out the cord and in one movement loop it round her neck and quickly pull tight so she can't scream. Too bloody easy. I've got the thing round her neck and she's still got my cock in her mouth! Then she jerks back. As she does I go to step around her so I can finish her off from behind, maintaining the tension in the cord all the time.

But then I trip over the silly cow's fucking handbag and fall half behind her and half on top of her. I try to keep hold of the cord but it's got wet somehow, and the nylon slips through my fingers. She's gasping for breath and starting to make a noise. In a couple of seconds she'll have filled up her lungs and will be able to scream blue murder. I don't want that to happen, so I throw myself on top of her and grab her round the neck. She manages to pull away and get out a half-hearted cry, so I ram her down into the ground and grab for her throat again.

A couple of minutes later it's all over. I feel annoyed I had to wrestle her on the ground, but now it's done I sit looking at her body and it's just like the others. Better if anything, because I did it with my bare hands this time. I get the knife out and do my stuff with it. I tidy up, take the money and go.

I take care leaving the alley, making sure there's nobody around, and then I walk away feeling as though I'm floating on air. I'm starving hungry, so when I'm well out of the area I buy a burger and eat it out in the street, washing it down with Coke. It could be caviar and champagne, it tastes that good. It's just before midnight when I get back, and as I'm opening the front door I look down at my hand, and it's as though time stops, as though it's somebody else's hand.

I stare at my hand on the door knob, and I see it as it was when I was strangling her. I didn't wipe the prints off her neck. Everything else but not her fucking neck. I never thought of it because I'd never needed to before. I'd always used the cord. I don't know if they can take prints off of skin. But the fuckers seem able to do anything these days.

Don't worry, I tell myself. They took my prints when I whacked that bloke with the baseball bat, but they won't check every pair of prints they've ever taken against anything they manage to get off her neck, will they? Course they fucking won't. They can't do that, can they? Bravado triumphs for a couple of seconds, then I feel the burger in my stomach, and before I know it I'm dumping my guts into one of Cynthia's fucking flower beds.

□□□

Character Flaw Spectacle

"Say that again, but slower and in words of one syllable, and not many of them," said Weller, talking to Roscoe. Weller was in the operations room and Roscoe was calling from his car.

"I came out here to check with the optician. You know, Spence said we should."

That was one great thing about Roscoe, he followed orders to the letter, even if they were more throw-away suggestions than orders, and even if they'd been given to someone else, days before. He would have been wonderful in the First World War, thought Weller, very wonderful but also very dead, first out of the trenches on every charge, whether it was his duty to or not. But he still wouldn't accelerate his delivery.

"And?"

"I checked on the name, Henderson, and the address."

"Yes, Roscoe, and?"

"It's not P."

"What isn't pee?"

"The initial."

"What?" said Weller.

 "It's the characters."

"What characters?"

"The Chinese characters."

"You know what I'm going to say next, don't you Roscoe? What bloody Chinese characters?"

"The person who maintains the optician's customer list is Chinese. English isn't her native tongue and she sometimes gets letters mixed up because they don't relate to the characters in the Chinese alphabet."

"Keep going," said Weller. When Roscoe had started talking about 'Chinese characters' he'd assumed he was meaning people. Now he felt stupid, and even more annoyed at Roscoe for making him feel stupid.

"The glasses weren't prescribed for a P. Henderson," said Roscoe. He was silent, but Weller welcomed the silence as the facts seeped into his brain and coagulated into a jumble of thoughts.

"Oh Jesus. Oh, bugger me, no. Does that mean we're barking up the wrong tree?" The image of Spencer sprung to his mind, and he felt annoyance towards his colleague, unreasonable but extreme annoyance. Did this mean that Spencer's caution about this not being the right man was justified? Was the old fucker right again?

"Yes. Wrong man."

"Oh God. Why didn't we check on that before?" said Weller, realizing this was the one man he had no right to say it to, the only one who had proceeded with the necessary check. "Devons will be abso-fucking-lutely delighted."

"She may be," said Roscoe, and something in his voice told Weller the conversation had another point.

"What do you mean?"

"They were prescribed for an L. Henderson."

"So?"

"Same address."

"What, you ..."

"The son, his name's Leo, remember?"

§

Spencer walked into the operations room as Weller was hanging up the telephone. They set off to the car park immediately, en route to the Henderson house, but as they left the building, Spencer heard a woman's voice yelling his name. He froze on the spot. It was Devons, shouting from the doorway. What on earth was she doing? Was this connected with last night? He couldn't rid himself of the idea it was, but he knew it was ludicrous. Why should she be drawing attention to what had happened? But her shouts reminded him sharply of the cries she had made the night before as they performed her version of love making.

The two men walked back to where she was standing. Spencer

was convinced a scene of some sort was going to follow, and when he saw the anger on Devons' face he almost recoiled physically.

"Where are you off to?" she said, impatiently, and not sounding as if she wanted to know the answer.

"To the Henderson house, Roscoe has turned up some…."

"There's been another murder. Chingford area again. First reports put it down to our man. Whore in an alley, strangled, slashed."

Spencer felt faint, and looking at his two colleagues he found it hard to believe they weren't feeling the same, not that he could imagine Devons swooning, whatever the reason. Weller gave her the news of Roscoe's discovery, and Spencer thought Devons was actually going to laugh.

"What a bloody fiasco," she said, looking from man to man as if they were complete imbeciles not to have found this out before, as if the investigation was a game to which she knew the answer and couldn't understand why the two of them hadn't figured it out yet. "Go and find the little bastard," she said, turning on her heel and marching away.

☐☐☐

Travelling Head to Head

I knew it was him when I saw the photograph in the album, the one of Leo and me that Christmas some years ago. I wondered if he had been able to get inside my mind somehow and make me kill on his behalf, but I knew that it wasn't me, and that his thoughts and his guilt were what I'd been experiencing and suffering in his stead. 'The sins of the fathers shall be visited on the children', but in this case it's the other way round. I felt his guilt and his shame. I presume he felt none of it, and to judge by the title of the scrap book, "Daddy's Dastardly Deeds," he blamed me anyway.

"Well, I'm your son, aren't I?" I could almost hear him saying. "Formed out of your genetic material and body parts, and those of my dear mother. You made me, you own me, so you must accept what I do, mustn't you? You made my brain and, having made it, you formed it as you nurtured me, so what you are, I became. Don't try to wash your hands off me, because I'm you."

And I did feel guilty. Not because I had done anything wrong, but because the unspeakable mutation that was my son, was my son. It was an accident that such a deviant personality should be born to anyone, let alone a couple like Cynthia and me, but we were the cause of the accident, and although nobody would openly blame us, they would bear us the grudge of responsibility none the less.

I spent hours walking around Birmingham, letting these thoughts soak in. I don't know where I went, and apart from some random images of New Street Station, a shopping precinct, a street that seemed to consist of nothing but Indian restaurants, and a number of down and outs asking me for money, I remember nothing about that day apart from what went on inside my head.

At first my mental state was such that I didn't think I would be able to survive. I don't know exactly what I mean by that, because I can't say I seriously considered suicide – at least, when I did consider it, the prospect seemed so unlikely that I rejected it with hardly a moment's hesitation. I suppose I simply didn't see how life could carry on against such a bizarre backdrop of events, and the thought of what would have to happen next made the future even less conscionable.

How could I work, eat, go for a walk, watch the television, do any number of normal things after what had happened? How could I, a quintessentially normal man, think normally and act normally after this? Surely, nothing could be the same again? I could hardly believe the people I walked past didn't see the terrible events written on my face. It was as though I was living the third hallucination in which everyone saw me as being guilty of heinous acts, only now I knew it wasn't a hallucination; it was what I would have to live with for the rest of my life. The shelter of ignorance had been blown away, and I was left exposed to the cold brutality of established fact. I, the scientist, the seeker after truth, had never before found the truth so completely unwelcome

But then, the world trudges on, despite what obstructions we put in its way, trampling over our pleasures and pains without differentiation, obeying only the heartless march of time. The inevitability of getting on with my life eventually set me back on the road to the station and the last train of the day to London.

When I arrived at Euston I felt hungry, which wasn't surprising as I'd not eaten since breakfast, and even then I was too wound up to stomach anything substantial. I bought a burger and ate it sitting on a bench outside the station, washed down with Coca-Cola, and my hunger and thirst were such that they tasted like caviar and champagne.

I couldn't face the thought of being with people so, although it was cold I pulled my coat around me and settled down to stay on the bench for a while. Eventually I moved from a sitting to a lying position, but after a short time I felt sick and quickly rushed into some bushes behind the bench and brought up the hamburger I had so enjoyed. I was sweating, but when I lay down again I felt so tired that I could barely keep my eyes open, and the next thing I knew was when I awoke to the dawning of a dreary grey day.

I determined to go home, tell Cynthia all I knew and call the police.

The thought depressed me and I wanted, more than anything, to be able to admit to the killings myself. More than that, I wanted it to actually be true that I had killed the women. If I was suffering the guilt, then I might as well take society's punishment as well, then at least Leo would have a life ahead of him. But that seemed no more realistic than denying that the macabre series of events had happened.

I waited for rush hour to be over, and then decided to take a bus home. As I boarded, I felt there was no energy left within me, and that some automatic force would have to propel me through the next hours and days, as though the scientist within me was still resolutely pursuing the truth, no matter how painful and destructive.

□□□

Talk About Sins of the Brothers

The phone rang for a long time in the stillness of the house before Charlotte answered it.

"Hello.

…

"Oh, yeah. Hi Rachel."

…

"Yeah. Yeah. Yeah, it's true, no, really."

…

"Yeah, don't I bloody well know it?"

…

"Yeah, I think so, I mean, let's face it, as far as brothers go, he was the worst, really. I thought he'd just been up to some bloody nonsense, probably vandalism or some of that white supremacist shit he's been spouting about lately."

…

"Yeah, well that sort of thing."

…

"Oh, they got here about ten, then …"

…

"Yeah, this morning, then, right after they turned up, Dad walked in the door, just as they were leaving with Leo in handcuffs. Dad looked as though he'd been sleeping under a hedge all night, but he spoke with Mum and one of the policemen for a while and then left with the cops and Leo."

…

"Mum? Well, weird, as if …"

…

"Well, I don't know. She didn't do anything at first. She just sat in the chair like a zombie, I mean … really spaced out, but then she started crying, and then howling, you know, really loud, just awful, embarrassing …"

...

"Yeah, really, almost hysterical. Yuck. I made some tea, just to get out of the way really, you know, but then she calmed down and I sat there with her. She wouldn't tell me anything at first, just saying 'You don't need to know' and 'Oh my God' and so on, but then she started to talk and ended up telling me everything. I mean, God, really, I just didn't believe it. I mean, how could you believe that sort of thing?"

...

"Yeah, exactly. Then I thought about it, and I bloody did believe it. I've believed Leo was a fucking psychopath ever since I knew what the word meant, so it wasn't as much of a surprise as it could have been. But, you know, even then, it's not every day you find out your brother is accused of, well, being a … well"

...

"Yeah, I know, shit, just saying it gives me the creeps."

...

"Oh, I don't know, I suppose so, but in a way I felt kind of, well, proud, no, not proud, no, but … well, special, as if this was something really important and it would change my life. But then as the day went on and I started seeing news reports on the TV and hearing stuff on the radio, I realized it was going to change our lives alright, but not how I wanted them to be changed."

...

"Fuck. Yeah, that's right. And then when they started reporting on that last one, the one last night. Jesus! He was out doing it last night. Can you believe that?"

...

"Fuck.Yeah, exactly."

...

"Yeah, but the doctor had been round by then …"

...

"Yeah, Dr. Spencer, and she gave Mum some pills. She asked if we were alright, and I should have got some pills really, you know (laughs),"

...

"Yeah, exactly, but I felt okay. The dog needed them more than me (laughs) ..."

...

"Really, the dog's been going bloody nuts all day."

...

"Yeah, I suppose so."

...

"No, we didn't call the doctor, she just turned up. It turns out she's married to one of the detectives, so she just came round when she found out ..."

...

"Yeah, really. Bloody lucky she came. If Mum hadn't swallowed those pills I think she would have lost it altogether when we heard about that woman last night."

...

"Oh, shit, yeah, but then it just got worse."

...

"No, really, listen. We got the first phone call this evening, about 6:30 ..."

...

"Yeah, just after the six o'clock news had that thing about him on it. The first one was some woman yelling and screaming. Then another one came about ten minutes later, but this time it was some creep of a bloke wanting to congratulate us!"

...

"Yeah, really, you wouldn't believe it, would you? Fucking sicko. Then we had the press call, loads of them, well, four or five, then more police, a couple more loonies, and just about everyone else you could imagine. Relatives, people we haven't heard from for ages. You'd think we'd won the lottery or something. 'Oh yes Auntie Mary, little Leo's always been a sex-crazed psycho, didn't you know?' (laughs)."

...

"No, it bloody isn't. It's just awful. Bloody Leo. He's even a nuisance when he's not here."

...

"He got in late last night, after ... oh Jesus! I still can't believe it. I just can't, even for Leo, it was ... (sighs). He was still in bed when the police came. If he'd got up earlier someone might have told him the police had been round the day before."

...

"Yeah, but they were looking for Dad then, because he wasn't at the hospital, so maybe there was no connection, anyway, that's what they said. But Leo would have smelt a rat, and it would have given him the chance to get away. He could have run off to join that bunch of Nazi racist scumbags in Wales he's always talking about. They would have hidden him and idolized him. Then Mum said the police were originally looking for Dad over the killings, and not just because he was missing, which is just abso-fuckin-lutely incredible."

...

"No, really, I know it's crazy, but that's what she said, and she wouldn't make that up, would she?"

...

"Right. Of course not. No. The thought that Dad could do anything even slightly illegal is just bloody completely ridiculous, let alone murder. God. No. He was gone for most of the day, but he's back now. He looks about 20 years older than he did when I last saw him, and 40 years older than before he started having his things, those, er, hallucination things or whatever they were. He says he's not going back to the hospital. He says he needs to be here. I saw him hugging Mum earlier. I can't ever remember having seen the two of them hugging before. I couldn't have been more surprised if I'd seen them having a doggie fuck on the kitchen floor (laughs), really, I mean, they don't go in for that sort of thing, do yours?"

…

"No, (laughs) hugging I mean, not doggie fucking, you stupid … (laughs). But they didn't look like they were very happy; it wasn't a passionate hug or anything like that, more like they were hanging onto each other for dear life."

…

"Yeah, alright, look, I've got to go, there's someone at the door."

…

"Yeah, I know, right, sure, okay. Bye."

Images by Alison J. Macmillan

If you like the images in Fathering Sin, you can order calendars, posters and postcard packs from WordisWorth's catalog:

www.Wordisworth.com/catalog/catalog.html

The ebook version of Fathering Sin is in full color. As a purchaser of this print edition, you can get the ebook for free. Just send an email to alison@WordisWorth.com, with the subject heading "Fathering Sin free ebook", and include your name.

About WordisWorth
Where would we be without words?

WordisWorth has all sorts of information: Fact, fiction, business advice, personal coaching, relax and learn management guides, plus writing, design and editing services.

You live a busy life, you want to succeed, but you don't have time to go to lots of different sources to get relevant information and knowledge. If you've suffered conventional learning through dusty textbooks, with dry jargon and complex information designed to make the author look smart, then you might have switched right off and switched on the TV instead or turned to a magazine.

WordisWorth is your TV or magazine. It is designed to entertain you while you absorb its content. It will help and inspire you to get the most out of work and life and be the best you can be. Theory has informed its look and its content. But there's nothing theoretical in WordisWorth. We present a non-academic and jargon-free guide to knowledge and learning.

WordisWorth brings you *edutainment*. There's no need to struggle to learn so that you can get ahead. If you don't enjoy what your reading, it's not worth it. Educate yourself through entertainment.